Watching the Asparagus Grow

Watching
the
Asparagus
Grow

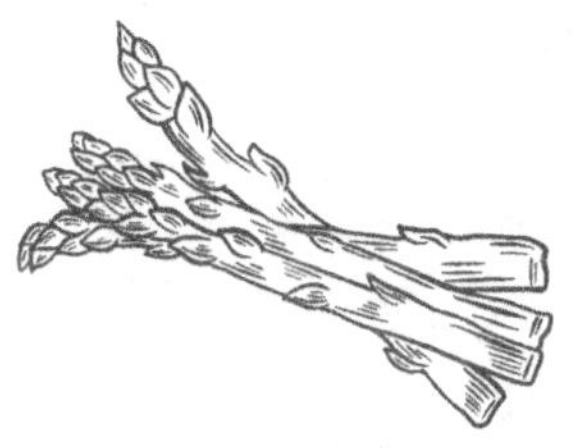

Jeff Wilkins

Dedication

To Opal Alice, another bright ray of consciousness. And, to my life partner Obie. Thank you for coming into my life eleven years ago and for your patience as all of this materialized in the form it is today. I love you.

I wish to thank all my family, friends, and strangers who have played a part in my life and brought me to the point I find myself today. To all the incredible places I have lived and traveled and to my spiritual guides and teachers, who've influenced my growth as a human being. I am forever grateful.

I thank my editor, Jules Hucke, for her input, guidance, and encouragement. In her editorial assessment of my work, she counseled me on the sensitive issue of a modern-day white man publishing a novel from the point of view of a young black girl facing social injustice fifty years ago. In her words, "What may have read as an award-winning concept in 1977 is likely to be seen as offensive today."

To my readers of color, that was never my intent, and I apologize if any of this is taken that way—quite the opposite. Many African Americans are still facing the same struggle for social equality more than 150 years after the end of the Civil War. Wars rage in two different parts of our world, and when one of the most beautiful and lushest parts of our planet, the island of Maui, erupts in flames, I believe the Earth needs some healing.

I hope this book may play a small part in that.

Jeff Wilkins

January 2, 2024

1

IT WAS ONE of those hot and sticky summer nights in Ohio when the sweat seemed to run off your skin in torrents. The young novelist found himself unable to sleep. He quietly left his sleeping wife and went down the winding staircase to the veranda of their stately bed-and-breakfast. Their black lab, Haddie, followed closely.

Night had settled over Cooper's Cove. On this seventeenth of August in 1980, Dave could hear the deafening sound of the male cicada chorus serenading females. Local legend said the first fall frost was only six weeks away when the cicadas began buzzing.

The Lake Erie resort town had been named after Daniel Cooper, an English cask maker who'd settled there in the early 1800s. It was one of those small tourist towns where everyone knew one another, except during the summer months, when the population swelled as thousands of happy tourists flocked to the lake to boat and fish. Curious shoppers milled about Main Street downtown and browsed the boutique and specialty shops. They came together at Panza Winery to laze around, drink, and become inebriated. After one too many bottles of wine, they hopped back on their boats and headed back to where they'd come from.

The drunker ones became seasick and threw up over the side. The next day, they all said it was worth it and could not wait to return.

DAVE RELAXED IN his rocking chair and lit a joint. He stared blankly at the neighbor's house across the street. *My god*, he thought. *What an ugly fucking house.*

The owner neglected it. Compared to the other houses on the street, which had manicured yards, this one was aberrant, much like its owner. In the early seventies, Quentin Tewksbury was a burned-out stoner who'd migrated to Cooper's Cove from Portland, Oregon. It may have been his altered state of mind, but Tewksbury fancied himself an accomplished gardener. Despite that, his flower beds needed weeding, and he maintained a hideous-looking asparagus patch in his front yard that the young author loathed.

Dave often wondered if Tewksbury knew the neighborhood dogs pissed on it during their morning walks. Whenever Tewksbury offered his neighbors free asparagus, they politely refused.

BERTHA MURKOWSKI, QUENTIN'S next-door neighbor, had told everyone, "That man is batshit, looney! I think he permanently fried his mind doing all those drugs out there in Oregon or wherever he came from."

Tewksbury had spent time at an Oregon nude commune and felt comfortable roaming his home sans clothing. One evening around midnight, Bertha was outside watching him through his bedroom window. Tewksbury noticed her gawking, so he stood at his window to offer her a show.

The following morning, Bertha telephoned her good friend Evie Crandall. "That nut was prancing nude up there, gyrating his hips to the music, and his pecker was just ah-flopping up and down. I was so shocked that I dropped my keys and crawled in the dark. Honey, when I found them, I couldn't wait to hightail it out of there."

She forgot to tell Evie it took her fifteen minutes to find them.

DAVE SMILED AND leaned back in the antique rocker. He took another hit off his rapidly disappearing doobie and focused on his writing—or, instead, the lack of it. He seemed to have lost his touch and couldn't' understand why.

In his first book, he'd fascinated his readers with characters they related to and plots that thickened with each chapter. Somehow, that had all changed. He'd lost his zeal to create a page-turning tale that mesmerized readers from the very first chapter, one they could not put down until they were stunned by a surprise ending.

Many times, lately, he'd sat behind his Royal Aristocrat typewriter in his library and attempted to transfer his thoughts into words. But all he ever created were more wadded pieces of paper in his overflowing wastebasket. Writing had once come effortlessly, but Dave now struggled to find inspiration for his subsequent work.

There was also the matter of finances. Dave's New York agent had telephoned and told him the publishers were threatening to sue him for failing to produce the second novel he was contracted to deliver. He was also worried their seasonal inn would not provide adequate income to make it through the winter without the earnings from his writing.

Lately, it seemed the more he tried, the more he failed.

Something feels different this time, he thought. *A secret messenger is trying to send me a signal, but I can't see or hear what that is. I know what I need to do, but I can't find my way. It's as if I'm paralyzed and can't take the next step. What if this book fails? I'll be a failure! Maybe I'm not a writer after all. If I were, I would have finished the book by now!*

He and Haddie made their way back upstairs to his still-sleeping mate. As he lay down, Haddie assumed her usual position at the foot of the bed and intently gazed up at her master with her deeply inquisitive Labrador eyes. She'd sensed something was wrong.

Dave closed his eyes and envisioned the ceiling tiles

floating above him. He floated up into the tiles, became part of them, and drifted off to sleep as thoughts and memories swirled in his head.

IN HIS DREAM, Dave Meyers saw himself as a towheaded five-year-old. He was holding onto the truck bed of his father's 1932 Ford and hugging his yellow Lab puppy. It was the summer of 1960, and they were headed to the family homestead with a load of peaches picked from their orchard that afternoon. Dave had nicknamed the truck the Doodlebug. It hauled peaches in the summer and transported ice fishers in the winter.

Dave and his dad loaded the juicy Redhaven peaches onto the shelves of the fruit stand in front of the family's home. Baskets of fresh, juicy peaches awaited the tourists who'd stop by and make their purchases using the honor system, an old Maxwell House coffee can labeled *Pay here.*

Dave lifted the yellow Lab puppy down from the truck. She was eleven weeks old, and the two had already bonded; the puppy followed him everywhere. He'd named her Sandy. The dog seemed to know she was Dave's protector and insisted on being by his side.

As they walked from the fruit stand to the house, they could hear Percy Faith's "Theme from a Summer Place" coming from the stereophonic hi-fi in the living room. His mother was at the kitchen stove getting dinner ready, humming to the popular tune of that sultry summer.

Frank, in his dirty overalls, turned off the hi-fi and sat at the table. He lit a Chesterfield cigarette and poured a shot of Canadian Club whiskey with a water chaser. He tuned the AM radio to WJR, broadcasting the evening news from Detroit. Frank had been working in the orchard since seven that morning and looked dog tired. It showed on his face as he scowled at his wife. "When's dinner going to be ready, Kathleen? And what are we having?"

Kathleen had been working at the fruit stand all day and seemed just as tired. "I'll have it ready when I have it ready! You're not the only one who works around here, Frank. And for your information, we're having Salisbury steak TV dinners."

Dave's father just grunted and took another swig of his drink.

Kathleen turned to her son. "David Meyers, I'll not tell you again. If that dog eats one more shoe, she's off to the pound!"

The puppy dropped her head to her paws as if she knew she was in trouble.

"I'm just kidding, Sandy. We could never get rid of you." Kathleen cuddled the pup, who had eaten three of their shoes so far.

～

DAVE'S PARENTS HAD met in 1942 when Frank awaited the passenger train at the Terminal Tower in downtown Cleveland. The country was at war, and he had received his draft notice two weeks before.

Kathleen was a Red Cross volunteer, handing out coffee and donuts to the young men going off to fight for their country. Frank's attention had drifted to the attractive girl at the canteen, and he'd gone over. "Hello there. Is there a charge for any of this?"

Kathleen grinned. "No; it's the least we can do for you brave men. Would you like a cup of coffee and a donut?"

"Just a black coffee, please."

She handed him a cup. "Where are you headed?"

"Looks like I'm joining the Navy." He sipped the coffee. "I'm being sent to basic training at the Great Lakes Naval Training Station in Chicago."

There was an instant attraction between the two, and they exchanged addresses. They both promised to write to one another. They kept their promises, and after the war ended, a short courtship led to their marriage.

The couple unsuccessfully tried conceiving a child. Eventually, they gave up hope of ever having a baby. Ten years later, Kathleen learned she was pregnant with Dave. She was overjoyed, but Frank had grown used to living without a child and did not share her enthusiasm.

LISTENING TO HIS parents bickering, Dave sat on the faded yellow linoleum floor. He wished they wouldn't and began playing with his toy Tonka dump truck. He'd gotten it the previous Christmas after spotting it in the window of Carson's Five and Dime downtown.

"Mom, I'm going to ask Santa Claus to bring me that," he'd said. "I promise I'll be extra good next year."

He'd misbehaved a few weeks before Christmas, and his mom had scolded him. "Davie, if you don't stop acting up, young man, all you're getting for Christmas is a lump of coal in your stocking."

Dave knew it had been a slow-picking season that year. There'd been little money for frivolous gifts, and he was in awe when he saw the shiny red truck sitting under the tree on Christmas morning.

The holidays had been a cheerful and festive time at the Meyers home. They threw parties for their neighbors, and Frank welcomed the adults with a hot Ben and Jerry, his Christmas toddy tradition. Kathleen had prepared a turkey dinner, and afterward, they all exchanged Secret Santa gifts and sang along with Mitch Miller.

Dave wished his father's mood could continue into the New Year. After the tree had come down and they'd put away the ornaments, his father was often depressed. Frank tried self-medicating with alcohol, and that seemed to provide a reprieve from his depressive thoughts. When he was sober, as he was most of the time, he was gruff to his wife and son.

But he worked hard to provide for his family.

THAT FALL, DAVE started kindergarten at Cooper's Cove Elementary School. He cried when his mom kissed him goodbye. As the bus pulled away from their house, he saw tears in his mother's eyes. Dave sadly watched as she and his dog faded into the distance. He sat numbly, staring out the window.

The bus driver, Ida Mae, a transplant from Tennessee, noticed him in her rear-view mirror. "What's your name, little boy?"

"Davie," he answered.

"Well, Davie, y'all look mighty sad, but school ain't that bad."

"I hope you're right."

"Hey everybody, listen up!" someone shouted. "There's nothing to be scared about!"

Dave turned around. The youngster who'd said it wore a red checkered shirt with a black bow tie and tan corduroy pants. He'd slicked his black hair with Brylcreem and gave Dave a cocky smile.

Dave moved a row back to sit with him. "Hi, my name's Davie Meyers. That was cool. I'm a little nervous about today."

"I'm Mario Panza, and my big brother Anthony told me the first day is no big deal! He told me not to worry. He said the toughest part would be old lady Rossmore."

THE SCHOOL BUS turned off Shoreline Drive into the school's parking lot. As they all filed off, Ida Mae yelled, "Now when you young-uns get off, don't forget anything and y'all have a wonderful day at school!"

Mario and Dave entered the classroom together. They'd seen their teacher standing guard at the door with her clipboard, checking off students' names as they entered. The petite sixty-two-year-old Miss Heidi Rossmore, her salt-and-pepper hair pulled back in a bun, wore a plain conservative dress. She had a reputation for being rigorous and introduced students by their proper first names, never their nicknames.

When it was Davie's turn, he introduced himself. "Hello. I'm Davie Meyers."

"In this classroom, I shall refer to you as David!" she said.

Mario, in line behind Davie, covered his mouth to keep from laughing at her.

She finished accounting for each child and instructed them to sit on the floor mats before her. "Now, when I am speaking or reading to you, I am not to be interrupted for any reason unless it's essential, in which case you will raise your right hand to be recognized. Does everyone under-stand?"

The children nodded, and she began reading from Dr. Seuss's new book, Green Eggs and Ham. She was about two minutes into the story when Dave felt a gurgling sensation in his stomach.

His nerves were getting the best of him. He had to go number two. He raised his right hand.

Miss Rossmore ignored him.

He clenched his butt cheeks and rocked back and forth, flailing both arms in the air, hoping to catch her attention.

When she finally acknowledged the boy, she asked, "Yes, David, what is it?"

It was too late. Davie had shit in his pants, and the smell was wafting about the classroom.

The horrified Miss Rossmore excused him, and as he got up to leave, he knew the seat of his white jeans would be dark. Some children were laughing. In tears, he ran out of the classroom and into the restroom.

Mario followed him. "Don't worry, buddy; we'll get that nasty witch," he assured Dave.

The next day, Mario brought a pile of fake rubber poop to school and left it on her chair.

When Miss Rossmore went to sit down, she screamed, "All right, which of you did this?"

Of course, no one admitted guilt, and the teacher could prove nothing. But she kept looking at Mario, who stared back at her with a poker face, clearly content he had kept his promise to his new friend.

Davie and Mario sealed their friendship that day and became bosom buddies.

SHORTLY AFTER THAT, Davie's parents appeared before the school board to voice their concern about Miss Rossmore's treatment of their son.

The board was comprised of five men. In the audience sat Heidi's lover, Trish Higgins, eighteen years her junior. The two shared a lake-view ranch near the school. They'd met ten years previously at a women's golf tournament at the Cooper's Cove Country Club. Trish was a self-assured forty-four-year-old with short-cropped brown hair and preferred casual blue jean attire. She worked the second shift at the Roby Tool and Die Company, the town's largest employer. At five foot eight and one hundred sixty pounds, she could deadlift over two hundred pounds and had even competed in a women's weightlifting competition in Chicago.

The school superintendent called the meeting to order. He asked Frank to come before the board and explain why he was here.

"My boy did not deserve what she did to him. He's a good little boy; believe me, if he said he needed to go to the restroom, he did! I thought it was unkind to make him sit there like that. I don't mind saying I don't like her. I had her as my kindergarten teacher when I was the boy's age, and she was the same way with all of us. I think you should fire her!"

The board called Miss Rossmore before them. They asked her to explain what had happened in the classroom.

"I honestly did not see the child trying to get my attention. I never intended to ignore him. But you must understand, as a kindergarten teacher for the past four decades, I've had my share of hand-waving children who want attention on the first day of school. I try to teach them to be patient, especially when I am reading to them. I'm sorry for what happened to David." She looked over at Trish, who smiled at her.

Heidi beamed back, and all five men took notice. Heidi could tell by the expressions on their faces what the patriarchal group was thinking. They excused themselves from the room to discuss the situation, and when they returned, the superintendent addressed the teacher.

"Miss Rossmore, the board has considered what you and Mr. Meyers have told us. While you may not consider your actions that day inappropriate, the board does. The child desperately needed to go to the restroom. The board regretfully requests you retire."

With no regrets, Miss Rossmore submitted her resignation the next day to the biased group of men, some of whom she had taught. *Besides,* she thought, *this gives me more time to enjoy my life with Trish, which I've always wanted to do.*

A RECENT BOWLING Green State University graduate assumed Miss Rossmore's open position. The misinformed kindergartners soon learned a valuable life lesson. They'd all believed that after Miss Rossmore left, someone they considered more likable would replace her.

Much to their dismay, the new grad seemed even stricter. It didn't take long for them to learn it was not okay to talk over one another. Two weeks into the school session, the students had grown accustomed to it and realized grownups sometimes needed to be strict to maintain order.

NOT LONG AFTER Davie's incident, Mario's mom telephoned Kathleen. "Hello, Mrs. Meyers. Mario told us what a nice boy your son Davie is. Would the three of you like to join us for dinner this Saturday?"

"Davie has said the same about Mario. Dinner sounds very nice. Would you like me to bring anything?"

"No, unnecessary. Just yourselves." She gave their address and hung up.

Kathleen told Frank she had accepted Joyce's invitation.

Frank appeared upset. "Why the hell did you do that? You know how I feel about being around strangers."

"We rarely go out, and aren't you the least curious about their winery and vineyard? I think you would be. You're both growers."

Frank seemed to think about it. "Well, it might be a good time. I've always wanted to know more about making wine. I'll guess I'll go."

The Meyers arrived at the Panza home on Saturday, and Mario greeted them. He grabbed Davie away and whisked him to his room to show off his Lionel locomotive train set.

Introductions exchanged and formalities waived, the adults sat in the living room. The boys eavesdropped from the stairs. Mario's dad, Rocco, offered Frank a glass of Italian wine.

Frank said, "Oh, I don't know. I've never had one of them. The only wines I've drunk are from around here. Sweet, you know?"

"I have a new vintage. A nice chardonnay, a crispy mellow oak taste. Would you like to try it?"

Frank hesitantly agreed, and Rocco poured him a glass. He took a sip and smacked his lips. "Hmm...this wine seems bitter."

Rocco smiled. "That's what everyone thought when we moved here. I have a sweet concord as well. Would you prefer that instead?"

"No, oh no. It just tastes different from what I'm used to drinking. But I think I'll stick with it."

After a few minutes, Frank admitted, "It's not bad once you get used to drinking it."

Rocco told the Meyers his story. "My parents owned a large vineyard and winery in the southeast of Sicily. After you Americans liberated us in 1943, I met Joyce. She was a U.S. Army Corp Nurse serving there and had visited our winery. I had learned to speak English while attending the University of Catania, and I was conducting one of our wine-tasting tours, and we fell in love right there on the spot! Right, Joyce?"

Joyce shook her head. "Well, I wouldn't say it was right there on the spot. Initially, I wasn't sure about him, but his sense of comedy drew me to him. I'd never dated an Italian before."

Rocco laughed. "And you found out how great we are, didn't you, Joyce? Anyway, I knew I wanted to marry her, and after the war was over, we finally did in 1946. Dad had died earlier that year and left the winery for me and my mother, Giovanna. Joyce didn't want to stay in Italy and told me about the grape-growing region here. She grew up in Cleveland."

"Joyce! That's where I'm from!" Kathleen said.

"You're kidding. Whereabouts?"

"Well, actually, it was Rocky River, a suburb there." They began sharing their stories while Rocco continued his.

"So anyway, Frank, most of the winery owners here are from Germany and grow the Concord grape variety, which produces sweeter table wines, the ones you are familiar with. This is a perfect region for growing grapes. In the spring, when the lake is still cold, the temperature reduces the risk of frost and prevents them from ripening too soon. During the summer, we have those cool evening breezes. It helps the grapes to ripen evenly. And, in the fall, when the lake's temperature is still warm, it gives us a longer growing season. Over in Sicily, we made dryer wines from Nero d'Avola and Grillo grapes grown in the Mediterranean climate with mild winters. Here, the winters are freezing, and we get a lot of snow.

"We chose Cooper's Cove because of Joyce's Ohio roots. I purchased this home and built the small carriage house behind ours for my mother. We needed to put her someplace else because she and Joyce never got along."

"*What* do you mean, Rocco? Your mother has always hated me. The nasty old witch! Ever since we fell in love, your Sicilian mother has never approved! There's nothing I can do that will ever satisfy her. When I asked her for the family recipes so I could cook some of the food you like, she refused to give them to me! Do you remember what she used to call me? 'That floozy American nurse?' Your mother doesn't think anyone else but her can care for her precious Rocco as she does! Give *me* a break!"

"Joyce, please! Let me finish my story! So, anyway, Frank, no Italian growers were living here. I knew I could succeed and start a new life for us here in America. I planted a modest vineyard my first year and grew the same varieties as everyone else. My father made me work in the vineyards when I was young, so I thought it only proper my sons do the same. I've taught them how to cultivate the soil, prune the vines, and harvest the grapes. They learned the secrets to making the best vino, just like their old man did! In a few years, our winery began producing some of the finest wines in the state."

Frank nodded while enjoying his wine. "You work hard as I do, Rocco. Peach farming isn't much different from growing grapes. My dad had me in the orchard when I was just five, so I make sure Davie is learning what I hope he will do when he grows up."

"Really? Mario and Anthony scream at me for having to spend their summer toiling in the vineyard while all of their school chums fish and swim at Rocky Point."

"Well, I don't know about that. Davie knows better than to talk back. He does what he's told."

Joyce offered everyone another glass of wine. While pouring Frank's, she told him, "Mario told us about Davie's unfortunate experience with Miss Rossmore. I'm sorry that happened."

"She isn't the nicest person I've ever known. And I don't regret taking it to the school board."

Mario and Davie perked up from their hiding spot and entered the room. "Taking what, Dad?" Davie asked. He knew nothing of his father's confrontation with the school board.

"None of your business, boy! And respect your elders. That includes Miss Rossmore."

Dave felt confused and embarrassed, but he knew better than to ask any more questions.

The Panzas seemed uncomfortable with Frank's scolding. Joyce lightened the tension. "I think I just heard the oven timer go off. How does dinner sound, everyone?" She had prepared her mother's meatloaf recipe with a mushroom-brown gravy, scalloped potatoes, and lima beans. "I asked Giovanna to join us for dinner, but she never misses an episode of *Perry Mason*."

Mario left his lima beans untouched. He clearly hated them. Dave knew better; the clean-plate rule applied in his household.

After the ladies finished the dinner dishes, Joyce told everyone, "I've homemade blueberry crumble with vanilla custard if anyone's interested." Everyone was.

When the Meyers returned home, they had full tummies, and all three were grateful for the new friends in their lives.

2

 haven for tourists and locals alike, most always seemed busier on weekends. The vast stretch of sand and limestone pebbles appeared less crowded on the weekdays when the locals preferred to visit. Some seemed bothered by sharing their beach with out-of-town vacationers, so most avoided the shore on those days.

It was a perfect sunny afternoon. Dave and Mario had spent the morning working in the orchard and vineyard. They'd been asking their parents' permission to ride their bikes downtown and swim and finally received the okay.

Davie's mom seemed a little nervous about the kids' first time out on their bikes alone. "Just be careful, you two! No horseplay and be home by dark!"

As the boys rode to the beach, Davie barely kept up with

the faster, more athletic Mario. Davie trailed behind while Sandy tagged alongside.

Soon, they were at Rocky Point. They stopped suddenly when an older kid ran into their paths and dashed toward a graceful weeping willow by the water's edge. Someone had attached a rope to one of the tree's higher limbs. The teenager grabbed the rope as he ran by them and swung out over the water before letting go.

"Who's gonna be first in?" Mario shouted as he sprinted to the lake and stormed in.

Davie cautiously waded in behind. "Mario, are you nuts? There's no way I'm jumping right in. It's freezing in here!"

"No, it's not, Davie. Only when you first get in. That's why I get it over with." Mario pinched his nose and ducked beneath the calm surface. The yellow lab leaped in, and the dog paddled to stay with her pack. The boys horsed around for a few minutes before getting out and toweling off. "You think she knows she's a dog, Davie?"

"No, I don't think so. She sleeps in my bed and shoves me out like it belongs to her. I don't mind, though."

The canine's warm, comforting body against his own made Davie feel safe. Something he hadn't been sure of in his world.

"Come on, Davie! Let's ride downtown!"

Five minutes later, the pals rode past Veterans' Park on Shoreline Avenue. The townspeople had built the park after World War One to honor those who'd served.

The enceinte sat on the waterfront across from the Yacht Club, where shimmering green waters reflected off the yachts' shiny hulls. Massive sugar maples cast shadows over the playground equipment, and a circular bandstand in the center only added to its charm.

The buddies dropped their bikes and raced to the teeter-totter and hopped on. After holding Davie hostage at the top, Mario leaped off, leaving him to crash to the ground. Davie rolled away, hurting and laughing at the same time. As Mario fled the scene, Davie shouted, "Hey, you creep! I'm gonna clobber you! You could have killed me."

The two meandered on the downtown sidewalk before cruising down Main Street, stopping to peek in the front window of Carson's Five and Dime. Dave admired the Mattel Sonar Sub Hunt Battle game and made a mental note to ask his mom for that come Christmas.

"Sandy, you wait here. Mario and I are going into the store."

While browsing, Davie saw Mario scrutinizing a senior gentleman pushing his shopping cart. "Davie! Look! See these ladies' underpants? I'm gonna throw them into his cart when he's not looking."

"No! Don't, Mario! You're going to get us in trouble!" Davie covered his eyes as he watched his best friend do just that. He wished he had Mario's brashness.

The unsuspecting mark removed his items at the checkout counter and saw the panties. He stood there perplexed, turning his head, peering to see if anyone was watching.

Mario and Davie were hiding nearby, covering their mouths to stop a severe case of giggles.

Sandy jumped onto Davie when they came out, happy to

see her young master. The trio rambled past the Rexall drugstore, where Mario saw the soda fountain. "Ya wanna go in and get a malted?"

"Nah. My mom only gave me five cents for the penny arcade."

On the other side of the street, they watched a drunk stumble out of Smitty's Bar. Mario glanced up at the marquee above the Majestic Theater. *The Absent-Minded Professor* "Hey, isn't your mom taking us to a matinee movie this weekend?"

"I think so. Mommy said it's about a professor who invents some flubbery stuff that makes cars fly."

They stopped in front of the deserted grocery store, which had been closed for about a year. Its windows had cracked and become covered with grime. Riley's Foodland had moved to a newer, larger facility on Vacationland Highway as the town continued its expansion.

Farther down the street, the boys walked into the penny arcade, where Davie could see a creepy fortune teller inside a glass case. They stood before it. The motorized wax mannequin appeared very lifelike. Davie noticed her strangely acute eyes above her protruding nose. She wore a red bandana on top of her long black hair, and, for just one cent, the mannequin predicted anyone's future.

Dave slid a penny in the slot, and Madam Valdoma lurched to life. Eerie lights within the case cast a glowing beam across her wrinkled face. The boys heard foreboding music, and she slowly turned from side to side while her piercing black eyes had stared straight into Davie's as if she was looking deep within his soul. A small card slid out and revealed his fortune.

You shall learn to live a slower life and be in the now. Not yet able to read, Davie pocketed the message to show his mom later.

Back at the park, the duo retrieved their bicycles. With Sandy leading the pack this time, they made it home for their suppers.

A LATE AUGUST heat spell had gripped northern Ohio, but Mario's mom and dad had promised to take the boys to Euclid Beach Park near Cleveland. Opened in 1895, it was famous for a rickety old roller coaster ride called the Thriller. The youngsters barely made the minimum height requirement, and considering it was their first time riding a coaster, they considered themselves fortunate to be front-seat riders. Rocco and Joyce were in the car directly behind.

After everyone strapped in tightly, the Thriller rolled away from the platform and slowly rounded a long curve. The mighty coaster began making clicking noises as it ascended to the top of the tallest hill. "Hey, look," Mario shouted. "You can see all over from up—"

Before he had a chance to finish, the Thriller crested the top and sped down the hill like a speeding bullet.

Neither boy realized its speed or its sharp twists and turns. Everyone held on and screamed for dear life. It raced back up a shorter hill. Dave thought he'd fly out of his seat and gripped the handlebar even tighter.

The second half proved milder than the adrenaline rush of the first hill and the series of shorter hills that had followed. The monster machine decelerated and jerkily stopped at the loading platform. When the handlebars released, they got out, and Mario asked his parents, "It's cool! Can we ride it again?"

Joyce suggested they all get a homemade ice cream cone instead. The ice cream cost ten cents a cone.

Davie realized he had no money. "I'm sorry, Mr. Panza, but I won't be able to pay for that."

Rocco laughed. "Don't worry, Davie; this one is on us."

"Really? Then I want butter pecan. It's my favorite."

"Whatever you'd like, partner."

Mario chose rocky road. Rocco and Joyce both settled for French vanilla.

At a park bench, they sat and lapped at their cones while Rocco removed a quarter from his pocket and a small tube of glue from the other.

"What's that for, Dad?"

"Shh, just watch!" Rocco affixed the quarter to the pavement.

They anxiously awaited their first unsuspecting prey, which turned out to be a young couple with a baby carriage. The father saw the quarter and bent down to retrieve it. His fingers slipped on his first attempt. He unsuccessfully tried picking it up a second time and told his wife, "Some smart-ass glued this down."

Rocco and the boys broke up laughing. The young couple shook their heads and continued down the midway with their baby.

"Rocco, *when* are you *ever* going to grow up?" Joyce appealed.

"*Never*, if I can help it."

Once finished with their treats, Mario asked, "Can Davie and I please go on the Rotor?"

"Absolutely not!" his mother replied.

Davie heard her and became nervous, as he probably should have. The Rotor was a mammoth wooden barrel that rotated at a high speed, pinning riders against the wall with centrifugal force after the floor had dropped away. It wasn't a ride for the timid, but Mario pleaded with Joyce until she finally gave in.

The thrill seekers assumed their places as the parents climbed the stairs to the viewing area above. With the last rider lined up, the entry partition closed, and the barrel slowly begun turning in a circular rotation.

Most everyone had closed their eyes.

The wheel spun faster and faster as the floor they'd been standing on magically disappeared below, leaving them all plastered to the wall.

Davie slowly opened his eyes. He was getting dizzy. The coaster had left him feeling queasy, and the spinning barrel proved no match. The fresh ice cream cone in his stomach decided it needed to come up.

He tried holding his breath and gulping it back, but it was useless. He turned his head as a stream of hot ice cream puke shot out of his mouth and into his best friend's unsuspecting face.

Mario gagged and wiped his eyes, then he started barfing. The rider next to him began throwing up. Across from them, the others had watched the appalling scene unfold, and they, too, became ill and upchucked. Soon, just about everyone on the spinning platform was heaving. Warm puke spun everywhere.

Rocco and Joyce could only watch in a horrific panic as the ride slowed. When it finally stopped, the boys stood looking up at them, covered in vomit from head to toe. The "barf-a-torium" had produced a mass of nauseated children, most of whom were now crying. Parents lined up to claim their offspring, not knowing what they should do with them once they had.

Rocco tried to bring levity to the scene. "Joyce, could we spray them off with a fire hose?"

"*Really*, Rocco? Will you get serious? Help me!"

He took the boys to the restroom to clean them up. Joyce purchased children's clothing from the gift shop and tossed their others into the trash.

It was a hot, humid, ninety-degree afternoon at Euclid Beach Park. It was an even hotter and smellier ride back to Cooper's Cove.

And Davie felt responsible for all of it.

SUMMER BREEZED BY, and before everyone knew it, it was time to return to school. On the bus ride there, Davie and Mario saw Miss Rossmore in her front yard planting purple mums. She wore a tasteful yellow gardening dress and wide-brimmed straw sun hat, and she dug into the soil on her knees.

She glanced at the bus as it passed. She saw the two little boys sitting together and smiled at them both.

"Lookie, Davie! She smiled at us! Now I'm sorry you helped get her fired."

"Me?" Davie exclaimed. "What do you mean?"

"You didn't know? My mommy and dad were talking about it. After you pooped your pants, your dad met with the school board, and he wanted her fired for not letting you go to the restroom."

Davie felt horrible. *If only I could have held it.* He'd become an unwitting scapegoat in the teacher's dismissal. Guilt and shame racked the young boy as he gazed out the window.

The bus turned into the parking lot and stopped to unload. Ida Mae said goodbye to them, the same as she did last year. Davie and Mario located their first-grade classroom, where their new teacher stood by her desk. She was their mother's age, and her blonde hair contrasted with the navy-blue dress she wore. But it was her smile that caught their attention and made them feel welcome.

The kids all found a desk, and she looked around at them. "Good morning, everyone! I hope all of you have had a busy summer. I have a gift for each of you." She presented them with a personal ink pen wrapped in shiny aluminum foil. The teacher had taken the time to tie each one with a red ribbon.

Davie, who didn't own a pen, was grateful for his gift.

She also gave them a piece of hardtack candy and informed them of more whenever they received A's on their report cards. Later that year, her kindness extended a step further when one of her students, a poorer Appalachian boy, wore holey socks. She discreetly reached beneath her desk and offered him the ones her husband had donated.

The boys learned how to read and write that session, but the school also introduced the concept of modern math, or "new math," as everyone referred to it. Dave could not grasp it. Last year, he'd learned basic arithmetic. But now, they forced him to learn a new approach to mathematics.

Dave struggled through the rest of the school year and barely passed, influencing his self-worth. By comparison, English proved to be his best subject and one at which he excelled. As he learned to write, he'd see his words on paper and marvel at them.

The more he learned to write, the more connected he felt with the world around him.

THE ENSUING WINTER seemed like it would never end. Gigantic snow drifts piled everywhere, and the usually busy tourist town lay dormant.

Dave's father faced a difficult decision. Larger competitors had been charging less for their peaches, making it difficult for small growers like him to profit.

He devised an idea and waited to share it with Kathleen, who was busy with the dinner dishes.

"I've been giving this much thought, and I can't see how we can make a living on the peach orchard alone. I'm considering demolishing the fruit stand and building one of those drive-in root beer places like Freeport."

"What, are you insane? Where'll we sell our peaches?"

"That's just it. We won't be selling them anymore. If my calculations prove correct, the drive-in should generate enough money during the summer that we won't have to kill ourselves in the orchards anymore. Besides, I have my ice taxi in the winter if we need extra cash."

"And what about the five acres of peach trees? Just what do you plan on doing with those, Frank?"

"Kathleen, I know the orchards have been in my father's family for years, but we just don't make enough money anymore growing peaches. I'm tearing the trees out and building a new mobile home park for the tourists. More and more of them are coming here yearly and need someplace to stay."

Kathleen couldn't believe what she was hearing. "You are out of your mind, aren't you? You can't be serious. You're willing to throw away everything we've worked for and risk taking a chance on a foolhardy stunt like this? We don't know the first thing about running a drive-in or mobile home park! I hate to think what your dad would say about all this if he were still alive."

Davie was listening from the other room and heard his parents arguing. He was worried. He knew money had been scarce in his family, and now he felt his world might fall apart. He felt powerless to do anything about it.

Frank was determined, and that spring, he plowed out all the peach trees to make room for his vision. Construction of the mobile home park would have to wait until he saved up a down payment for a loan.

He assured his wife, "This one's going to pay off."

AS HE'D PROMISED, Frank worked hard building Kathleen's Root Beer Drive-in, which stood in place of their old fruit stand and reached completion by the summer of 1962.

Dave could see the drive-in from his bedroom window at night. He envied the souped-up Chevies and Fords as they roared into the parking lot. He watched as teenage carhops wearing bright orange uniforms delivered the food on trays designed to fit over the edge of a car's windows. The menu included juicy, thick char-grilled cheeseburgers, freshly cut french fries served with vinegar and salt, and Coney Island hot dogs loaded with chili, raw onions, and yellow mustard. But the drive-in's mainstay was the Hires Root Beer floats served in chilled mugs, one of Davie's favorite daily treats.

FRANK'S AUNT BILLIE had moved to St. Petersburg, Florida, after cooking at the Woolworth luncheon counter in downtown Toledo for thirty years.

Frank telephoned her after deciding they could not handle the workload alone. "Hey, Aunt Billie! I haven't heard from you in a while. How are things down there?"

"As usual, Frank. Hot and humid with a lot of thunderstorms. I'd do anything to escape this god-awful heat and humidity!"

"Well, that's why I'm calling. We all miss seeing you here. Kathleen and I have opened a drive-in and could surely use you. Would you consider coming up to cook for us this summer?"

"Boy, would I!"

Soon after, she battened up her house trailer and boarded an Eastern jetliner bound for Ohio.

DAVE LOVED HIS Great Aunt Billie and always thought of her as cheerful and giving, always looking on the bright side of everything.

Dave may have loved his great-aunt, but his father feared her. Frank knew better than to cross her. When he'd been a little boy living on the family farm, his aunt had visited and would never let him get away with anything. Even now, when he did something that upset her, she referred to him as "Franklin," and Kathleen loved hearing her talk so sternly to him.

One morning at the family's breakfast, Dave noticed his toast was burned. He politely asked his aunt why.

"It's not burned, Davie; it's pleasantly brown." She used her butter knife to scrape off the burned portion. She had lived during the Great Depression when you threw nothing away.

She loved her job cooking, and the customers adored her as well. The drive-in made a modest profit its first year and closed for the season in October when it was time for her to head south, where the winter warmth of Florida beckoned her back home.

It saddened Dave to see his great-aunt leave, but he knew she'd return next spring. When Aunt Billie was there, things just seemed better around their home.

SEVEN-YEAR-OLD DAVIE SAT behind his school desk one October day and wondered, *Is the world going to blow up?*

The 1962 Cuban Missile Crisis brought the world to a standstill when Russian President Nikita Khrushchev installed nuclear missiles on the island of Cuba. It escalated into a standoff between the two nations. President Kennedy ordered him to remove them, and for thirteen days, the country was on edge as it waited to see who'd budge first.

Dave came home from school that day and asked his mom, "Is Russia gonna drop an atomic bomb on us?"

His mother had tried her best to comfort him, but he noticed the doubt in her eyes. "I hope not, honey. Try not to worry."

But worry, he did. Earlier that day, he'd been required to practice one of the duck-and-cover drills in case of a nuclear attack.

The standoff finally ended when Khrushchev backed down and removed the missiles.

Cooper's Cove and the rest of the world breathed a sigh of relief.

LAKE ERIE FROZE over completely that winter. Some said you could walk to Canada. The perch and walleye were plentiful, and Frank kicked off his ice fishing taxi. He built four ice fishing shanties, as everyone referred to them, constructed of corrugated tin walls attached to a wooden base on gliders, which allowed them to be pulled out onto the ice by the Doodlebug.

Nervous anglers climbed onto the back and held on as Frank wheeled the Model A down the boat ramp and out onto the frozen lake, honking the antique car's ahooga horn. Ten inches of ice was under them, and Frank felt relatively safe maneuvering the Doodlebug along the snow-covered pathway marked by discarded Christmas trees. He needed the markers to navigate back to shore in case a sudden snowstorm covered his tire tracks and brought zero visibility. He warned his riders that he might hit a thin patch and drop through the ice. "If that happens, fellas, be ready to leap off before she goes in!"

A few unfortunate drivers watched as their ice buggies floated to the bottom, where they'd remain until spring when salvage crews would haul them to the surface.

Frank often drove as far as a mile onto the frozen body of water, where total silence existed on the snowy tundra. He used an auger to drill holes in the ice and positioned the shanties over them. The anglers dropped their fishing lines through the small opening on the floor and waited for the fish to bite.

The huts had small coal-burning stoves to keep the anglers warm as they sat inside and fished in their shirt sleeves while they cooked cans of franks and beans. As a bonus, Frank included a bottle of wine from Panza Winery, which helped to keep the anglers even warmer.

He charged four dollars daily for the ice fishing package and pocketed nearly eighty a week. He felt proud of the money his concept had brought in. However, he needed more to fund his expensive project, and the land remained idle.

AS SHE'D PROMISED, Aunt Billie was back at the helm flipping burgers next summer. Profits had edged but still fell short of what Frank needed to secure funding. He also risked losing the property because of unpaid back taxes, so he made the painful decision to close the drive-in that fall.

He broke the news to all of them at dinner. "I'm sorry, but I have no choice but to close and sell. If I wait to do it, we might end up losing everything."

"No, Dad!" Dave shouted. "You can't do that! This is my home. Where'll we go?"

"I've been looking at a little house in town on Jefferson Street, Davie. It's only two bedrooms, but plenty big enough for the three of us."

"But there'll be no room for Aunt Billie!" He threw down his fork and ran up the stairs to his room, crying.

His dad looked at Kathleen with a defeated look.

Aunt Billie touched Frank's arm. "I'll go up and talk to the boy, Frank. He'll come around."

But Dave never really seemed to.

Frank sold the entire property that fall. He became more depressed after he witnessed the family homestead and everything they'd worked for disappear, as Kathleen had predicted. The stress added to the tension between his parents, which seemed to add to Dave's insecurities.

Ironically, a group of wealthy investors from Columbus who'd rented one of Frank's ice shanties that winter had overheard him discussing his plan to develop the property. They quietly purchased it and leveled everything. In its place, they built a massive five-acre mobile home park with three hundred lots, a swimming pool, and two tennis courts.

If only I could have gotten the loan, Frank thought. All of it could have been mine. I could have finally given Kathleen what that woman deserves.

AFTER LOSING THE homestead, Frank spiraled even further into depression, believing he'd let his family down. Even though he'd realized his "crazy" idea of building the park had become someone else's reality, it did little to soothe his bruised ego or ease his checking account deficit.

After paying of their debts and buying the house, little remained. It pissed Frank off every time he heard about the profits the developers had been raking in. Close to two thousand dollars a month! A fortune in his eyes! It only added to his desire to drink; he drank more often than he wished.

Kathleen became even more concerned with her husband's drinking and tried reasoning with him. "Honey, why are you doing this to yourself? It wasn't your fault things didn't work out the way you planned. The entire town knows it was your idea to build the mobile home park, and the developer stole it from you."

It seemed Frank was hellbent on self-destruction. He began drinking daily, and the couple argued more than ever.

DAVE AND HIS father drifted further apart. Dave hated what his dad's drinking had done to them and resented him for selling the orchard.

On a chilly late-fall day at Veterans' Park, Dave and

Mario played fetch with Sandy. Mario tossed the ball to the Labrador and asked his friend how he enjoyed living in town.

"I don't, Mario. It makes me sad. It was fun working in the orchard with Dad. And I miss Aunt Billie." That familiar empty feeling had taken up residence in his mind. He'd been writing in a secret journal where he could pen about his life. It helped him cope with his uncertain world.

His mom had told him to focus on his new home and the exciting opportunities life in town offered him. He couldn't quite see them yet.

UNEMPLOYED AND NEARLY broke, Frank's search for work ended when he finally secured a maintenance position at Cooper's Cove High School. The pay wasn't what he and Kathleen had hoped for, but Kathleen reminded him that a steady year-round job would offer security for the family.

Kathleen wanted to do something more with her time than sit around the house. She was reading the "Help Wanted" section of the *Courier* and noticed an ad. "Frank, it says here that Wilson McGuire is looking for an editor's secretary. I think I'll apply."

"No damn way, woman! It's bad enough I lost the goddamn peach orchard. Now you want to make me look like an even bigger fool by going out and getting a job? As if people don't already have enough to talk about in this town. There's plenty of work that needs doing around here. Besides, I hear he's catting around on his wife."

"Frank! I'm tired of you telling me what to do. I'm calling him for an interview!"

The following morning, she dressed in one of her classiest outfits and chose color-coordinated shoes for her interview. She drove across town to the twice-weekly publication to meet with the editor for an interview.

Wilson McGuire peeked through the slats in his office shades and saw the sharply dressed lady. When she went into his office, he noticed her down-to-earth beauty.

"How do you do?" he said. "I'm Wilson McGuire. Your application shows you have the required qualifications for the position. How soon can you start?"

"Uh, I'm ready whenever. If there's something I don't know how to do, I can learn. I'm a quick learner."

"I'm sure you are! I also appreciate you dressing up for our interview. It surprises me how some ladies dress when they come in and apply. And, if I may say so, you look beautiful in that dress. You'll fit in here well."

Kathleen thought the editor's comment rather improper. Like Frank, she'd heard the rumors. His wife had been his secretary, but after she'd caught him in bed with her best friend, she'd filed for divorce.

BERTHA MURKOWSKI WAS in the courthouse the day of the McGuires' divorce proceeding. She always followed the legal notices section in the *Courier*. When she heard of the couple's juicy divorce, she attended the hearings to derive the latest gossip.

Afterward, she telephoned her friend Verna Schmudabeck. "Why, his wife stood right up in court and told the judge she didn't give a damn what he did with his newspaper as long as she got half of everything!"

"So what happened?"

"Verna, she was just as nasty as she could be. You wouldn't believe the things she accused Wilson of. She let him keep the newspaper, and she got their pretty stone house on the cliff. Pity whoever gets involved with that man!"

"Oh, so true, Bertha!"

KATHLEEN HAD BEEN at the job for about two weeks and enjoyed being Wilson's secretary. She found him to be a personable and considerate boss. It not only got her out of the house; she now had her own spending money. She no longer needed Frank's permission to buy a new pair of shoes, which had always resulted in an argument.

"God damn it, Kathleen! You know we can't afford those! The shoes you have are just fine. You have too damn many pairs of shoes already," he always barked.

Shoes were her weak spot. Hoping he wouldn't notice; she'd buy them on sale at Nelson's and sneak them into the house. She'd slide them to the bottom of her massive stack of shoe boxes in the bedroom closet when she could.

She assumed he'd never looked, but he'd always had and smiled when he saw another box.

IN NOVEMBER THAT year, when Dave and Mario were in third grade, Lee Harvey Oswald was accused of shooting and killing President John F. Kennedy in Dallas. The president had been riding in a motorcade through Dealey Plaza when the shots rang down on him, his wife Jackie by his side.

The school principal entered Dave's and Mario's room later that day. The teacher stopped what she was doing, and the principal whispered into her ear: "Someone's assassinated the president." He left to continue informing the others.

Their teacher looked at the children. With her eyes watering and voice quivering, she announced, "Boys and girls, someone just killed our president."

A hushed silence fell over the classroom. They all stared at one another in disbelief. Some started crying. The teacher realized her phrasing was not the best way of informing a group of frightened eight-year-olds.

"Everyone loved the president," a girl cried out. "Why would anyone want to hurt him?"

Dave was wondering the same.

THE SCHOOL DAY ended early. Ida Mae wiped her swollen red eyes as Dave and Mario boarded the bus.

On the ride home, Dave asked Mario, "You think it could have been Russia? Maybe it was them, and now they want to take us out, too."

"Yeah, you could be right. Last year, they had us ducking and diving in case Russia nuked us." From the little Mario had seen on TV about nuclear blasts, he knew crawling under a desk would do little good if the unthinkable happened.

THE NATION MOURNED. All the flags in Cooper's Cove stood at half-mast to honor the fallen president. Two days later, on Sunday, November 24, a Dallas nightclub owner named Jack Ruby shot and killed the accused assassin in the basement of the Dallas Police Department while Oswald was being transferred to a more secure jail. The broadcast networks carried the shooting live. It was the first actual murder seen on television in America.

Dave was in their living room with Sandy napping at his feet. His father and uncle were watching coverage of the jail transfer on the black-and-white TV set when Ruby burst from the crowd and shot Oswald in cold blood.

Dave saw the entire event and yelled, "Someone just shot Oswald!"

Kathleen was in the kitchen with his aunt, basting the turkey. She dashed into the living room. She was still holding the turkey baster, the juices dripping onto her apron. She watched the events unfold. "My god, what is happening to this country?"

The family sat stunned. The terrible memory of the young president's death two days earlier flooded back and ruined everyone's appetite.

EVERYONE TALKED ABOUT the assassination for the next few weeks. People couldn't go anywhere in Cooper's Cove without hearing someone discussing it.

Bertha Murkowski was shopping at Riley's Foodland and saw Evie Crandall pushing her cart down the produce aisle by the turnips. Bertha wheeled her cart over to Evie. "Can you believe it? I was listening to my talk show on WLS in Chicago last night, and they're all saying it's a big government conspiracy."

"Oh, I know, dear! I heard the Mafia might have had something to do with it."

The Rexall druggist told his customers he'd heard Cuban president Fidel Castro was behind it.

Cooper's Cove and the rest of the country moved on from the tragedy. But questions remained in everyone's minds, and no one would ever forget where they were and what they were doing the day of the assassination.

MARIO AND DAVE still hung out every day after school, but Dave needed help making new friends. He often felt alone in the presence of others and had become a mama's boy, seeking his mother's counsel when he needed advice or had questions he wanted answered.

Kathleen often used him as her emotional sounding board, and Dave had become a surrogate spouse. If something upset him, he tried talking to his mom about his feelings. He often confided in her that he disliked the way his father treated her, only to be told, "Why, Davie, you shouldn't feel that way. Your father means well."

Kathleen seemed unable to validate her son's feelings, and Dave learned how not to feel. He discovered how to keep his emotions bottled up. He became uncomfortable in his father's presence and had little to say to him. He viewed his dad as a stranger. His father never told him he loved him; Dave could never express those words.

An overachiever, he had a lingering feeling in the pit of his stomach that he wasn't good enough and should do better.

THE TOWN EXPERIENCED growing pains as the sixties progressed. The Cooper's Cove Chamber of Commerce launched a new ad campaign that helped boost the population to over 12,000 people during the summer, and many of the 1,200 year-round residents didn't like it.

The owner of the Sudsy Clean Laundromat was one who attended a special session called by the town council to address the ongoing traffic concerns and other issues during the summer. "I'm happy. If it weren't for them tourists, I wouldn't be able to stay in business. Y'all don't patronize me in the winter cause y'all got your washer and dryers. The tourists don't, and they are welcome in my place anytime!"

Louise Shamp, the Curiosity Seeker's Gift Shop proprietor, echoed his comments. "Everyone knows summer is my only chance to make money. Few tourists are looking to buy walleye tank tops in February!" Like the other merchants, Louise closed her shop in late fall when the number of tourists dwindled.

But those opposed to the continued expansion of the town had their say as well. Cora Jensen was next to speak, and the eighty-three-year-old was upset. "I'm sick and tired of all those damn Michigan drivers who don't know how to drive and about run my Nash off the road. I can't wait till Labor Day when we can wish them all good riddance!" She also said she didn't like standing in line at Riley's Foodland to buy groceries while the tourists cut before her to get their beer and fishing tackle.

Cora was a colorful character, indeed. The retired telephone switchboard operator seemed stuck in a time warp from the thirties. She always dressed in clothes from the era. The locals waved as they passed her 1939 Nash Lafayette. Cora insisted on driving a safe fifteen miles per hour, even on the busier streets.

The town's minister had been next to stand and speak to the council, claiming his tax dollars had been used to hire additional police to control the drunken tourists in the summer. He also pointed out that the boaters who used the town's services paid no taxes like the property owners were required to.

An out-of-town couple who owned a quaint summer home on the way into town were weary of listening to the constant roar of traffic in front of their house. "It's so bad we can't even sit on the front porch," they complained. "Too many tourists are coming to Cooper's Cove in the summer. The town's charm is going right down the toilet. Something has to be done!"

The mayor noted they were residents of Tiffin. "Now, you folks know as well as we all do that you're tourists yourselves and only use your place on weekends. What are we supposed to do? Tell the others they need to get out now because there are too many of them?"

The audience laughed, and the disgruntled couple shut up and sat down. Everyone in Cooper's Cove knew that the town wouldn't be there if it weren't for the tourists.

The council voted unanimously against any new laws limiting further expansion.

3

THE SEVENTH GRADER sat inattentive, staring out the window at the church across the street.

Dave wasn't interested in what the algebra teacher had to say. Thanks to America's new math program six years earlier, he'd never learned how to solve the most straightforward equations. And he'd received an F on his exam two weeks ago. He worried about failing math and not advancing to eighth grade with the rest of his class.

The teacher noticed Dave daydreaming. "Mr. Meyers, if you find something out there more intriguing than what I have to say, you're welcome to come up here and share it with the rest of the class."

Dave slid down in his chair and blushed. He'd hoped the teacher wouldn't ask him to solve last night's homework question. He hadn't even opened his algebra book. None of it made sense, anyway. When he took multiple-choice tests, he randomly chose and correctly answered enough questions he kept floating by with D's and a few F's. The teachers liked him, and he'd always passed. *This year could be different,* he'd thought.

Just as Dave feared, the teacher had indeed called on him.

"Dave, why don't you come here and see if we can solve this?" He pointed to what he had written on the chalkboard:

$7x + 9 = 23$

Dave let out a deep breath. He stood up and thought, *It might as well be in Greek,* and made his way to the front.

The instructor smiled at him and handed him a piece of chalk. Dave knew he couldn't solve it. He also knew everyone was watching him, so he tapped the chalk against the equation on the board as if that would help. In his mind, he saw the 7 with an *x* and the 9 equaling 23.

In kindergarten, they had taught him two plus two equaled four. So, why had they found it necessary to replace a number with an *x*? It made no sense to him.

The other kids shifted in their seats, wondering why it was taking Dave so long to solve something simple. He felt embarrassed.

But the caring educator was kind enough to walk Dave through step by step, using calculations he hoped Dave could comprehend.

It was useless. The teacher told him to return to his seat.

Dave felt like an idiot and sat back down as he felt everyone's eyes still on him. *Capable of doing better* was always on his report cards and in his mind.

AFTER CLASSES ONE day, the boys were rooting around the old town dump looking for treasures when Mario discovered an old *Playboy* magazine. He opened the magazine's centerfold and whistled to Dave. "Man, look at the titties on that one!"

Dave felt a stirring below, but he didn't understand it. Mario's older brother, Anthony, had told them what to do when that happened, but Dave had thought it sounded stupid.

A few weeks earlier, he'd heard his father breathing heavily in his parents' bedroom. He'd thought his dad might have been having a heart attack.

Dave was about to go in to render help when suddenly he heard his father whisper to his mother something about coming.

Dave froze. He couldn't believe it. His father had been having sex with his mother! He'd never thought about his parents having sex. Neither of them had ever broached the subject since he was four years old, when he and his mother had been in the family's 1955 Pontiac Star Chief in front of the Western Auto. Out of nowhere, Dave had suddenly blurted out, "Mommy, where do babies come from?"

His mom, startled by her son's sudden query, had thought about it before answering, "Well, they are just there."

The four-year-old had wondered where *there* was, but for the moment, it had to satisfy his young curiosity.

Dave had never given the lack of discussion much thought until hearing his parents. He'd tried not moving a muscle. He stayed completely still and held his breath. *What if they hear me? They'll know I was listening to them have sex. How would I ever be able to face them again?*

In the morning, at the breakfast table, his father had asked him to hand over the *Toledo Blade* newspaper.

Dave made no eye contact with his dad and gave it to him as he thought, *I can't believe you two were doing it! Aren't you a little old to be having sex?*

Never again did he feel the need to talk about sex with his parents.

AT ABOUT THE same time, Dave developed a crush on his young English teacher, who wore tight dresses and a fragrant perfume that reminded him of the one he gave his mother each Christmas, Chanel No. 5.

Unlike algebra, he enjoyed learning about literature and composition and understood lessons about phonics and vocabulary building, increasing his desire to write. English was the one class where he stood out above his classmates, including many math whizzes who talked about him behind his back, making him feel vulnerable.

No one ever chose him first for any of the teams in phys ed class; he was always the last to be picked. The phys ed teacher seemed to poke fun at him as well.

Dave was up to bat in a softball game, and the teacher pitched the ball to him. "Grit your teeth, Charlie Meyers!" The teacher of course, was referring to the famous *Peanuts* cartoon character Charlie Brown. Dave struck out and wished to melt into home plate.

It embarrassed him to shower after gym because of his skinny body. Some mistook his sensitivity for something more feminine. One boy on the junior varsity football team called him a queer. Dave knew he liked girls and brushed off the demeaning remark, but it made him more determined to grow stronger because of his lack of male prowess. He empathized with those who didn't fit in, underdogs like him who may have been different.

It only made him more determined to help others.

HIS BUDDY MARIO considered himself the class stud. His developing physique and dark Italian features had given him a significant advantage over the other boys. Along with his body, he'd also developed an arrogant personality. "Come on! Everybody knows Italian men are God's gift to women!" Mario had earned his title as a chauvinist thanks to his father, who'd passed on some undesirable traits Mario seemed to have absorbed.

His bitter grandmother only fueled their attitudes. She egged on Rocco, often in Joyce's presence. "Rocco, all Italian men have a mistress. Joyce doesn't need to know anything about it."

Joyce overheard the remark. It was another reason to dislike her problematic mother-in-law.

Since coming to America, Giovanna had stayed alone in

her carriage house by her choice. Like the martyr she'd become, she liked to whine. That was all she seemed to do. "No one ever comes over! No one ever calls! Why bother?" she often said.

Joyce visited her every morning and invited her weekly for Sunday dinner. At one of those, she took her place at the table, assessed Joyce's delicious spread, and sneered. "I'm not hungry. I'll have dry toast with black coffee."

Rocco ignored her. Joyce rolled her eyes. And both boys laughed at the older woman's comment.

She eventually picked up her fork and cleaned her plate.

She died in her sleep a week later, at ninety-one. She'd hoped to be laid to rest next to her husband.

Rocco and the boys made the trip to Italy to bury her. Joyce stayed home.

SOME SUMMER VISITORS to Cooper's Cove became year-round residents, and the locals didn't care for them. They felt the newcomers threatened their way of thinking and their beliefs about how things "ought to be."

Dave kept up on current events. He read a *Cleveland Plain Dealer* article about the nearby Detroit riots of 1967. That summer, Detroit police raided an unlicensed after-hours bar where eighty-five African American patrons were celebrating the return of two Vietnam veterans. Several people were outside watching the raid, which turned into full-blown riots that killed forty-three people.

When it was all over five days later, 400 stores had burned, and they'd estimated the damage at $40 to $45 million.

It surprised Dave to learn only fifty African American police officers served on the Detroit police force. He already knew the city's Black residents lived in cramped housing, and poverty and crime had become widespread after the downturn in the auto industry. Racial tension was at an all-time high in Detroit and other cities.

President Lyndon Johnson appointed a National Advisory Commission to investigate the nation's riots. It concluded the US had been moving toward two societies, one black and one white, separate and unequal. The report also said discrimination and segregation had long permeated much of American life and threatened the future of every American.

Most Cooper's Cove residents felt differently. They placed the blame squarely on the backs of the rioters who'd caught the attention of everyone watching the networks' evening news broadcasts.

Verna Schmudabeck had lived in Cooper's Cove her entire life. She watched Chet Huntley and David Brinkley report the riots on NBC as scenes of burned-out buildings and violence against the police played out on her TV.

She picked up the phone and dialed Evie Crandall. "Evie, it's just terrible that all those negroes can run rampant and burn and loot all those stores. My cousin used to live in Detroit and moved out because too many were moving into his neighborhood. And look at what they're doing now. Just burning it down. It's a disgrace!"

Evie agreed. "Let's just be thankful that none live here in Cooper's Cove. Except, of course, Amos, and everyone loves him. I talk to him each time I see him at Riley's, and he's so pleasant. Nothing like those I see breaking windows and throwing bottles at the police. Why do they have to act the way they do?"

AMOS LIVINGSTON WAS the lone African American living in Cooper's Cove. He served as a butler to Justin and Mary Beth Roby, the owners of Roby Tool and Die, for thirty years.

The Robys were the wealthiest residents in town and lived in an old Victorian mansion built by descendants of the town's namesake. Amos cooked for them, cleaned their house, maintained their gardens, and ran their errands. They paid him one dollar per hour, with Thursdays off, and provided his room and board. He even sailed with them on their yacht and accompanied them on their flights abroad, serving as their chef.

Amos cared about his employers, but he was aware of his place in the pecking order at the Roby home. He may have been their friend, but he was their servant first. On his days off, Amos smoked a cigar at the front of Riley's, greeting all the customers as they came in.

Kathleen and Dave were grocery shopping one day and saw him.

"Well, hello, Ms. Kathleen. And how are you, Dave? My, you've certainly grown up."

"Thanks, Amos; I guess I have."

DAVE REMEMBERED THE first time he had met Amos. He couldn't stop staring. He'd only been four, and Amos's dark skin had intrigued him. He'd whispered to his mother, "Mommy, why is that man's skin so dark?"

Kathleen hushed the boy and told him she would explain later.

Amos offered his large hand to Dave. "Well, hello there, young man. And what's your name?"

"Davie." He noticed the inside of Amos's palms were almost the same color as his.

"Well, Davie, it's a pleasure meeting you! And my skin may appear to differ from yours because many years ago, they took my family from a faraway place called Africa, where people look the way I do. But we are the same as you in every other way."

"Do you have dark blood, too?"

Kathleen looked embarrassed at the little boy's question.

Amos laughed. "No, Davie. We don't. Our blood flows red, the same as yours."

A FRIENDSHIP BEGAN, and Dave spent more time at the Roby mansion. He'd ride his bike there, where Amos would meet him at the kitchen's side door with freshly baked chocolate chip cookies and milk. Dave would sit on a stool and watch Amos prepare the Robys' evening meals in his white chef's hat.

The Victorian mansion impressed the young boy, and he marveled at its magnitude. The mansion had six bedrooms, each with a private bath. The builder had graced the home with mahogany woodwork, and a marbled entryway gave way to a spacious living room with plush white carpet and red velvet furniture.

In the dining room, a sparkling crystal chandelier hung from the ceiling above a Duncan Phyfe dining table. A separate parlor with pocket doors was used to welcome and receive guests. Mary Beth, an accomplished pianist, would entertain them at her baby grand.

Amos confided in Dave that the couple slept in separate bedrooms. He explained it had been an option for many of the wealthy. Mary Beth's bedroom held a white queen canopy bed with pink lace curtains. She'd chosen a white flocked wallpaper with New England purple asters for her wall coverings. Justin's more masculine room bore geese, mallards, and Lake Erie fish on the walls, and he slept in a mahogany Chippendale king-size bed.

Dave's favorite room was the library, with its thick, rich oak paneling and bookcases that lined the walls with leather-bound literary classics. The Robys allowed Dave to borrow one on each of his visits. The talents of Tennyson and Hemingway enthralled Dave, while many of his friends preferred hanging out at the Rexall Drug soda fountain.

He visualized himself someday living in a home as majestic as this.

CIVIL STRIFE AND the Vietnam War continued to divide the country further. Dave felt the world seem to unravel around him.

In April 1968, a sniper shot and killed Dr. Martin Luther King, and two months later, Bobby Kennedy fell to an assassin's bullet. The North Vietnamese launched the Tet Offensive against South Vietnam. Public opposition to the war grew, and Dave agreed.

A young man from Cooper's Cove, Thomas Waverly, became one of the war's victims. He'd been the star quarterback for the Seafarers, the town's high school football team. He enlisted in the Marines after graduation and died while on patrol in the Battle of Khe Sanh, just south of the Demilitarized Zone.

The town labeled him a hero, as he'd saved the lives of two other men by carrying them to safety before a bullet from a North Vietnamese rifle ended his life. The Marines returned his body with military honors, and the small town mourned the loss of one of their favorite sons.

As the war dragged on, the protests mounted, and thirteen-year-old Dave questioned why the United States was involved. He watched Walter Cronkite report the daily carnage each night on CBS.

Unknown to his parents, Dave took an anti-war stance. One night, he and his dad listened to Cronkite's commentary declaring the war mired in stalemate, and Dave agreed. "We don't have any business being there in the first place!"

His dad had served on an aircraft carrier in World War II and had no use for those leaving for Canada, those who'd applied for conscientious objector status, or anyone who opposed the killing. "What the hell are you talking about, boy? The Waverly kid volunteered to fight and died for his country. All those long-haired, drugged-up hippies out there protesting are nothing but a bunch of damn cowards!"

"Dad, when you went to war to fight for your country, Japan attacked us, and we had to defend ourselves. Don't you realize this war is political? They dragged us into it, and now there doesn't seem to be any way out while thousands of our soldiers have died. And for what?"

That pissed his father off, who'd been drinking. "You're only thirteen! How the hell can you sit there and talk about something you're too young to know anything about? Go over and tell the Waverlys what you think about the war and see what they say. I'll tell you one thing. Life's a shit sandwich, and every day you're gonna take another bite and not like it!"

Dad, I may only be thirteen, but in five years, I'll be eighteen, and it could be me coming home in a body bag." Dave had seen Mrs. Waverly at Riley's Foodland that morning. He knew what she'd probably have said by the expression on her ashen face and the dull stare in her eyes.

Later that night, Dave penned his thoughts in his journal. *All of this seems so wrong. So unfair. We're killing black people, and brave guys are dying in Vietnam. Haven't we learned anything? Hate and war seem to control our world.*

"THAT'S ONE SMALL step for man, one giant leap for mankind."

The Meyers were gathered in their living room, watching Neil Armstrong become the first man to walk on the moon in July 1969. Dave wondered what lay next in America's space exploration program. *Maybe Mars?*

He grabbed his AM transistor radio and rode his bike to the library, the trending hit song "One" by Three Dog Night. At the library, he read James A. Michener's *The Bridges at Toko-ri*, a novella about the fighting during the Korean War. The book was required reading for his upcoming English class.

Dave finished the short novel in one afternoon. After reading Michener's vivid narrative, he pictured Lieutenant Harry Brubaker standing alone in a dirty ditch with death and dying all around him. It only made Dave more indignant about the war in Vietnam.

A few days earlier, he asked Mario while they were hanging out at the marina, "Why are all these guys dying?

This war has nothing to do with us. I think we're being misled into believing we need to be over there to defend democracy here in the US. Think about it. In four years, they could draft us. What then?"

Dave knew his father would never speak to him again if he became a conscientious objector. He hoped he could afford college; if not, he stood the chance of being drafted if the war hadn't ended by then. He would not fight and die for something he felt was such an unjust cause. Too many young men had already died, and he believed Americans had grown numb to everything happening around them.

Mrs. Waverly, the dead soldier's mother, was at the public library while Dave was there. He noticed her reading a book about grief and healing.

SHE'D BEEN IN constant emotional pain since receiving the news the enemy had killed her son. Thomas had wanted to fight. His father had been proud, but his mother secretly felt differently. She'd never wanted her son to be involved in a war so far from the soil of the United States.

She needed to read an atlas to understand where Vietnam was. *The French have turned the whole mess over to the United States*, she bitterly thought. And now, her son was dead. She hated all the politicians.

Even her husband, who'd admired his son's bravery, was now questioning the validity of being in a war he'd realized the US had no chance of winning. He cried more often than his wife and told her, "If only we could go back in time and start over, Tom might still be alive."

DAVE HAD SEEN the mother wiping away her tears and felt desperately sad for her. He wished he could ease her suffering.

On his bike ride home, Dave listened to the CKLW Golden Oldies program and heard Jackie DeShannon singing "What the World Needs Now Is Love." Dave couldn't help but think, *Hal David and Burt Bacharach hit the mark on that one.*

THE ROBYS RECEIVED rather disturbing news that summer. Mary Beth had been having breathing difficulties and feeling ill for a few weeks. She finally met with a physician who diagnosed her with a pulmonary breathing disease. The doctor informed her she was living in the worst climate for her health. Knowing of their affluence, he suggested Hawaii, which he'd recently visited.

After considering their limited number of years left on the planet, the couple decided that moving to paradise wasn't a bad idea. Mary Beth's cousin in Cincinnati, Charlotte Brookstone, admired their home and offered to buy it, so that wouldn't be an issue. The more pressing need would be finding someone to purchase the tool and die, which was now worth a tidy sum.

Justin listed the manufacturing plant, hoping to find a suitable buyer. His employees seemed like family to him, as the couple had no children. He wished to find the *right* buyer—one who would treat the workers the same as the Robys had.

An entrepreneur from Flint, Michigan, was interested in purchasing the business and requested a meeting to review the books and tour the facility. He told them he'd make a cash offer. They set the meeting for the following week, and Justin made sure the factory appeared in top-notch condition, operating at total capacity. He'd mentioned nothing of the potential sale to his employees. He reasoned with Mary Beth, "Why tell them anything at this point? What if we can't sell it?"

The Robys waited in the conference room for the buyer to arrive. Mary Beth and Justin were startled when they saw the tall, distinguished gentleman walk in the door. Justin, who'd never prepared for such a scenario, gathered his composure and shook the hand of the conservatively attired African American man standing before him. "Justin Roby here. And this is my wife, Mary Beth."

"I'm Benjamin Austin, but please call me Ben."

Mary Beth felt faint. She sat down. "It's a pleasure to make your acquaintance, Mr. Austin." She never offered her hand and wondered, *Where is this man getting all this money?*

Introductions exchanged; Justin showed Ben the company's balance sheet.

Ben liked what he saw. "Well, let's say I look at the place. I want to see your machine placement, cutting tools, and output potential."

Justin worried that would entail taking the man onto the toolroom floor, which may have raised the workers' suspicions. Instead, he suggested, "Why don't we go up to the office? It has observation windows overlooking the plant."

Ben thought it a rather odd request, but having lived in Flint, he'd dealt with enough covert racism from affluent white people like the Robys. They went upstairs, and Ben peered through the glass opening and looked down upon the white artisans at work on their trade.

Mary Beth anxiously peeked over his shoulder to see if anyone had noticed him in their office. *Well, if anyone sees him, they'll just assume he's here applying for a janitor's job,* she reasoned.

Ben, satisfied with everything, informed them, "There's no need to quibble over the price. I like what I see. I'll take it!"

The couple was shocked. Mary Beth sat down again. Justin, aware of the potential legal ramifications if he refused a full-price offer, stuck out his hand. "Well, Ben, it looks like you're the new owner of Roby Tool and Die."

Mary Beth fainted this time.

AFTER JUSTIN CONVINCED his wife selling the business to Mr. Austin would be in her best interest, as well as his legal interest, they began preparation for their upcoming move to Oahu. The Robys learned more about their mysterious buyer, Benjamin Austin. After growing up in Detroit, the son of an auto worker and seamstress, the young man received exceptional high school grades and a scholarship to Michigan State. He later graduated from the Howard University School of Law in Washington, D.C. After working his way up in a Detroit law firm, he purchased a small factory in Flint that manufactured parts for the auto industry there. Ben transformed the underperforming parts facility into one of the best in Flint.

He married a woman named Grace; the couple now had a fourteen-year-old daughter, Nora. The previous summer, the family had visited Cooper's Cove on vacation and fallen in love with the charm and peacefulness of the small town. They'd shopped at Riley's Foodland, where they'd observed a black man standing alone. They'd introduced themselves and discovered he was the Roby's butler, Amos. The men traded stories, and Ben learned Amos had been the only black resident living in Cooper's Cove.

Ben wanted to know more. "So tell me, Amos. What is it like living here in Cooper's Cove? I mean, with you being the only person of color?"

Amos smiled at Ben. "You know what, sir? I don't have a problem with white folks living here with me."

THE ROBYS POSTED a notice in the employee break room informing everyone of a special announcement the following weekend at the high school auditorium, which they'd reserved for the event. Word spread quickly throughout Cooper's Cove, and dozens of residents, including most employees, turned out, since the plant was closed on weekends.

Rumors floated around the plant. One was that they would all receive a well-deserved pay raise, which the Robys had promised them. The Robys paid their workers well, but less than what the union-scale workers earned in Toledo or Detroit.

Trish Higgins was there with Heidi Rossmore. She'd heard there would be a significant retooling of the plant, and the Robys would need to hire an additional two hundred workers.

The owners came out on the stage to the appreciative applause of their audience. Justin thanked them for coming and relayed the unfortunate news of Mary Beth's illness. "So, upon the advice of Mary Beth's physician, we are moving to a warmer climate. We've sold the plant to a Flint business executive who will assume ownership next week. Now, without further ado, I'd like to introduce you to the Austin family."

The family strolled out onstage.

You could have heard a pin drop in the auditorium that morning as everyone sat in disbelief, mouths hanging open, eyes frozen on the African American family standing before them.

Before they witnessed any backlash, the Robys left the stage escorted by bodyguards. A chauffeur waited to whisk them to Cleveland Hopkins Airport, where they'd board a flight bound for Honolulu.

THE ROBYS PURCHASED a four-bedroom, three-bath estate overlooking Diamond Head Beach with breathtaking views of the Pacific Ocean from every room. Glass sliders offering open-air living led to a saltwater pool, and terraced gardens cascaded down from the lanai to the ocean. Colorful and fragrant plumeria trees dotted the landscape, and tropical orchids hung from the pergolas.

Mary Beth had known the island style would not complement her stuffy Victorian-era furniture and wished to start anew. She decided upon white rattan furniture with koa wood accent pieces. She planned to create a tropical theme in their new home to reflect the peaceful tranquility of the islands.

They began the aloha life without a butler. Amos was now seventy-five and wished to retire and live with his younger sister's family in Toledo.

Their former business and everyone back in Cooper's Cove were the last things on the Robys' minds as they jetted off to their new home in paradise.

The headline in the next day's edition of the *Cooper's Cove Courier* read, *TIMES ARE A-CHANGING.*

4

WHEN THE ATTENDEES witnessed the Robys being led from the premises by men in suits, everyone assumed they'd arrested the couple for even considering selling their factory to the Austins.

The auditorium erupted into shouting, and the raucous mob scrambled for the exits, knocking one another over on their way out.

If the phone lines could have caught fire overloaded with callers, it would have happened that day. No one had expected an announcement such as this. *How could they do this to us?* and *What in the world were they thinking?* were the two big questions being asked of the Robys.

Verna Schmudabeck was on the phone with Evie Crandall. "You know, if the Austins weren't filthy rich, they wouldn't get away with this. The idea! Thinking they can waltz in like this and take over the whole place."

"Oh, I know, dear. My husband has already said he will not work on Monday. Said he wasn't becoming anyone's white slave."

No one seemed to have had a problem with Amos living among them. As Verna explained to Evie, "At least with Amos, he knows his place. But I can assure you, the Austins will never tell us what to do! And that doesn't mean we have to be the least bit happy with it!"

But the simple fact was that the sale had happened, and there wasn't a single thing anyone could do about it except for maybe quitting their jobs. Considering the newly named Austin Tool and Die employed close to half of the town, that wasn't happening.

MONDAY MORNING'S FIRST shift at the plant looked like the setting for a funeral. Employees came into work and punched in for their shifts as usual, minus any of the frivolities usually exchanged. All at once, the tooling machines rumbled to life.

Fifteen minutes into the shift, the supervisors walked in with Mr. Austin and shut the equipment down. Everyone gaped at one another. No one seemed to understand what was happening.

Ben picked up a bullhorn. "Good morning! It's nice to see all of you, and I hope you'll enjoy working here for us. The Robys have done a magnificent job of giving back to this town, and we intend to continue the tradition. So, I'm happy to announce Grace and I are donating the funds to complete the high school natatorium."

Silence filled the factory.

"I've spoken with your supervisors concerning your pay and working conditions—"

The workers cut him off and began shouting. Dale Crandall screamed at the new owner, "There's no way you're coming in here and cutting our pay!"

Ed Persty echoed his coworker. "We're going to get the union in here. You'll be sorry!"

Ben smiled and raised both his hands to calm his objectors. "I was about to say that your supervisors and I have discussed the substandard wages you've been receiving from the Robys compared to your union counterparts in Michigan. Grace and I want you to know that effective with your shifts today, we're increasing your hourly rates to five percent more than the union scale. We're also increasing your vacation allotment from one week to two and offering company-paid medical coverage for you and your families. We ask that you put in a good day's work. When employees perform well for their employers, we believe everyone should reap the profits."

As at the school auditorium on Saturday, a pin drop could've been heard inside the Austin Tool and Die Company. The workers soon began hooting and hollering at one other, stomping their feet and slapping each other on their backs. Dale, who'd said he wouldn't go into work that day, shouted over to Ed working the stamping press, "See Ed? I told you these folks were going to be nice people!"

It took the town a while to settle down. Many in the community welcomed the newcomers. But a few most likely would never change their distorted view of others. A sense of newfound hate seemed to envelop the town, causing unease.

However, some knew love would eventually change the hearts and minds of others.

FRESHMAN YEAR WAS a new beginning for Dave. His love of writing had floated to the surface. The more he wrote, the more he uncovered about himself. He seemed to have grasped more of his emotions. He'd been acing his English classes but still lagged everyone else in math. This continued to affect his self-worth, even though he'd proven his writing talents.

The young writer looked forward to becoming a junior when he'd finally be able to drop all math requirements and do what he loved doing: writing.

Mario, meanwhile, barely kept up a two-point GPA. He was more interested in girls than any textbook, except for maybe anatomy, where he ogled women's breasts.

Nora Austin joined them as a freshman. Dave noticed her in the hallways between classes. He always smiled at her and thought he'd seen Nora smiling back at him, but he wasn't sure. He sat beside her in his art class elective and was too shy to say anything. Nora seemed aloof to him, so he kept his distance but maintained a secret fascination with her. Nora appeared so much more mature and intelligent than those who ostracized her. She paid no attention to them, which made Dave like her even more.

Mario wanted nothing to do with her. He used a derogatory name in front of Dave more than once, and Dave didn't like it. Mario's mother tried changing her son's perception of race to no avail. Rocco possessed some personal sway over his son. Rocco, whose tendencies had been racist, didn't care for the Austins either, although with his olive skin, Cooper's Cove's German-born grape growers thought he looked like one of the migrant workers.

It was difficult for Dave to comprehend why Mario and his father harbored hatred toward the Austins when their ancestors were victims of discrimination. He'd learned in history class that American workers had loathed the poor Italian immigrants coming to this country in the late 1800s searching for a better way of life. The laborers had called them "wops" and "dagos." And now, Mario and his father treated the Austins with the same disdain.

History repeats itself, and people forget, Dave thought. *Why can't we all coexist?*

IN THE SPRING of 1970, the war in Vietnam shifted toward Cambodia. President Richard Nixon ordered bombings there against North Vietnamese forces occupying the region.

Following his election in 1968, Nixon promised to de-escalate the war and begin the gradual withdrawal of troops. But in late April, he addressed the nation and told everyone he'd commit U.S. combat troops to Cambodia to battle the North Vietnamese forces.

Major protests broke out across the country. At nearby Kent State University, Governor James Rhodes called up the National Guard to handle the anti-war demonstrators. Those soldiers fired upon a peace rally being held at the college and killed four unarmed students.

A front-page photograph in the *Cooper's Cove Courier* depicted a student kneeling over the dead body of another. When Dave saw the photo, he saw the rage and grief in the girl's eyes.

It triggered his own. "See this, Dad?" Dave showed his father the front page of the *Courier*. "Now do you understand? Too many young men are dying in a never-ending unpopular war, and now four innocent students are shot and killed by soldiers who thought they were defending their country."

"God damn it, Dave! There ya go again. Standing up for a bunch of spoiled brat college kids trying to hold the campus hostage while our soldiers fight for our freedom. I don't blame the governor for sending in the National Guard. I hope they've learned a lesson!"

"Fuck you, Dad! You're the one who hasn't learned the lesson! Like everyone else, do you think what happened that day at Kent was justified? Did you ever stop to think maybe that could have been me lying there dead in a pool of blood for all the world to see? What was the governor thinking when he sent them in there?" Dave stormed out of the room.

His father just sat there shaking his head and took another swig of his Canadian Club.

The next evening, Dave and his mom waited at the kitchen table for his father to leave work. His dad telephoned. "It's been a rough day here at school, Kathleen. I think I'll stop at Smitty's for a drink before heading home."

"Just be careful, Frank. You know how I feel about you drinking and driving."

"Don't worry, honey. I'll see you soon."

Two and a half hours later, they heard a knock on their front door. Dave got up to answer it.

"Hello, Dave; is your mom around?" The Cooper's Cove Chief of Police stood in the doorway.

Kathleen got up from the table.

He looked at her uncomfortably. "Kathleen, I'm afraid I have some bad news. There's been a terrible accident on Vacationland Highway, and Frank's injuries were fatal."

Kathleen's knees buckled, and the police chief steadied her as he helped her back to her chair.

Dave stood there, not knowing what to think. "What happened?"

"Frank was coming home from Smitty's. His car crossed the center line and hit an oncoming car head-on. He wasn't wearing his seatbelt. He flew through the windshield and hit his head on a tree. He died instantly."

"What about those in the other car?" Dave asked. Are they okay?"

"The driver was wearing his seat belt. It looks like it banged him up pretty bad, but the doctors say he will make it." The chief tried comforting Kathleen, who was sobbing as if wracked with guilt.

"Damn you, Frank. You're not coming home for dinner tonight. Or ever again. If only you would have listened to me!"

Dave couldn't put the image of him and his father arguing out of his mind. The last thing he remembered was telling his father to go fuck himself.

The police chief held the hand of the distraught woman. Dave tried comforting her as well. He placed his arms around her and kissed the top of her head.

She wept louder, and Dave felt her love for his father. His eyes welled up, and he cried for the man for the first time in his life.

He knew he'd never again have the chance to tell him he loved him.

THEY SET THE funeral for the following Friday, with calling hours to be held at the Woesten Funeral Home the night before. Kathleen and Dave went to the mortuary the morning after the accident to begin preparations for the funeral.

In the lobby, they could see the funeral home director, Donald Woesten, standing in horn-rimmed glasses. The effeminate man wore an expensive-looking black silk suit.

He extended his sympathy and showed them into the casket room. As they approached, they could see the dead face of their husband and father. Dave couldn't help but notice the fillers and several layers of makeup attempting to conceal the damage caused by being thrown through a car's windshield.

"I worked from a photograph," Donald proudly told them. "I wasn't sure we could have an open casket when he first came here. I trust you're both satisfied with my work?"

The man grossed Dave out, and his mom thought it morbid to say to grieving family members.

DONALD CONSIDERED EMBALMING to be an art. Like an old master creating a beautiful canvas, he'd learned how to recreate youthful features in mortuary school. He beamed when told the deceased looked like they'd just been sleeping, proud of the realistic effects he created with the proper application of makeup. He, too, enjoyed wearing makeup.

Gertie Reynolds from the Perfectly Quaffed Beauty Salon styled the deceased's hair and never realized she had misspelled the French word Coiffed. At one session, she noticed the red rouge on Donald's cheeks and asked if he wore makeup.

Her inquiry had offended him, and he'd snapped, "I only use a light bronzer on my face with just a touch of mascara to highlight my eyelashes."

But Gertie told all the girls at the salon she thought he used more makeup than she ever had.

⁓

THE TOWN SHOWED up to pay their respects. Dozens of their friends filed by Frank's casket, surrounded by endearing arrangements of red roses, white carnations, and yellow mums designed by Rose Petals Florist.

Kathleen and Dave stood on either side of the coffin. Every time someone new approached the casket, they began crying again. Kathleen looked up and saw Wilson in the reception line.

Dave noticed the expression on his mother's face change when she observed her boss. She wiped away her tears and seemed happy to see the man. He also noticed their embrace seemed to last longer than usual, but he gave it little thought. As he observed the grief in the room, Dave realized how much he loathed funerals. The first time he'd seen a dead body lying in a box of eternal rest, his uncle's, he couldn't understand why families put themselves through agony. But he needed to respect his mother's wishes and stood there not feeling anything.

As a young boy, he'd often wondered, *What would aliens think if they visited Earth and observed what humans do with our dead? Most likely, they'd assume it's an odd custom. Perhaps the aliens most likely know the souls have already left their bodies and moved on to the next dimension.*

When it would inevitably become his time to transition,

Dave preferred cremation. He could only hope his mom would make it through in one piece.

FRANK'S FUNERAL TOOK place the next day, and the volunteer firefighters' engines sprayed dual streams of water across the sky to honor their friend. Frank was laid to rest at Cooper's Cove Memorial Cemetery, where Kathleen planned to join him upon her death.

Later that evening, Dave was alone in his room, writing in his journal. The all-too-familiar feelings of guilt and shame occupied his mind as he wrote:

Dear Dad,

Once again, you got the last word in. You would have to kill yourself and leave Mom and me alone here to pick up the pieces of our shattered lives.

What were you thinking when you got behind the wheel of your car after another drinking binge?

Were your last memories of me telling you to fuck yourself?

Or were they of Mom warning you about drinking and driving as you crossed the median and almost took someone else's life as you ended yours?

I have many unanswered questions for you, but there is one thing for sure I want you to know.

I love you, Dad.

I'm sorry it took so long for me to say those words. I know that somehow, somewhere, you can hear them.

I know it wasn't your fault you were the way you were, and I hope you have found peace.

I hope Mom and I can find the same.

Love, your son Dave.

PROGRESSIVE CHANGE MOVED on in Cooper's Cove. The Chamber of Commerce launched its annual advertising blitz, designed to attract new business to fill the gap between the post office and the First National Bank.

Two men signed a leasing agreement to take over the empty storefront previously occupied by Riley's Foodland. They turned out to be a gay couple, fifty-eight-year-old Steven Conrad and his thirty-eight-year-old partner, Christopher Brighton, from Key West.

STEVEN HAD GROWN up in Cooper's Cove. His real name was Steven Zaremba, and his wealthy grandfather had raised him after his parents died in the 1918 Spanish Flu pandemic. The grandfather never exploited his wealth and had wanted his grandson to grow up with modest values like his. No one had known otherwise.

As a young boy, Steven knew he differed from others his age. He possessed urges he was unable to identify or act upon. He grew up confused and felt empty inside. He learned to hate what society taught him to hate. He felt a part of him was evil, as the association had led him to believe.

His best friend was Diane Gale; he took her to their senior prom in 1930. They sat in his car afterward, and he leaned over to kiss her goodnight. Diane put her hand on his lap and caressed his penis.

Steven froze. "Diane? What are you doing?"

Embarrassed, Diane moved her hand away.

After graduation, Steven knew he needed to escape and discover who he was. With his grandfather's fortunes, he enrolled in Northwestern University in Evanston, Illinois, to major in theater drama. He'd been in several high school plays including the Northwestern production of *A Farewell to Arms,* adapted from the Hemmingway novel set in Italy during World War I.

In the play, he portrayed Lieutenant Frederic Henry, a role initially performed in the 1932 film by ruggedly handsome film star Gary Cooper. Henry, an American medic in the Italian army, falls in love with English nurse Catherine Barkley. In one scene, Steven kisses the nurse. Being a convincing actor, he smiled at all the women in the audience to solicit an emotional response.

During his sophomore year, Steven fell in love with his roommate, a heterosexual man from Santa Monica, California. After a night of drinking heavily, Steven advanced toward the handsome young man, who rejected him outright. "What the fuck are you doing, Steven? Are you a queer?"

Steven felt the same shame as Diane had seemed to the night he'd rejected her. He knew he could no longer live with the lie and needed to tell Diane the truth.

He telephoned her to reveal his surreptitious identity. "Diane, there's something you need to know. I'm homosexual."

There was a moment of silence. "I understand. I knew there was something different about you."

Steven admitted that if he'd been born heterosexual, he'd wish to spend the rest of his life with her.

DIANE ALWAYS HOPED he would. She never left Cooper's Cove. She never traveled outside the state of Ohio. She was content living there in her domain and once told Steven, "Why should I leave? Everything I need is here, except you, of course."

STEVEN'S GRANDFATHER DIED his senior year of college, and he was willed with an annuity that would keep him comfortable for the rest of his life. He wished to pursue acting, and after he graduated from Northwestern in 1935, he moved to Los Angeles to fulfill his dream.

It was the height of the Great Depression, but he used part of his endowment to purchase an imposing English Tudor on Chislehurst Drive in the hills of Los Feliz. Well-known actors' residences surrounded his sprawling estate, which featured a secluded black marble swimming pool and grotto in his backyard.

His drama professor from Northwestern had seen talent in the aspiring actor, and, at Steven's request, called one of his friends, a writer at MGM. He told him about Steven's acting abilities, and the writer met with Steven two weeks later.

"The first thing we need to do is change your name. Fans won't identify with a name like Zaremba. From now on, you're Steven Conrad. It's very competitive out here. I suggest you become a freelance actor unattached to any particular studio. I think you'll fare better. Allow me to make some calls."

The smaller parts paid little, but Steven didn't care. He had his grandfather's money. He held gala affairs, invited his neighbors, and got to hobnob with those he envied. He became their friend as a means to an end. With their connections, he thought he'd go far.

The handsome, muscular, black-haired actor had little trouble meeting agents, and he made several B movies before World War II broke out. He was drafted into the military, where he served as a personal chauffeur to a general at the Pentagon.

After the war ended, Steven returned to LA to continue his career. But by then, his star had fizzled. He met with the writer again and asked for help restarting his career.

"Steven, you're a good actor, but I believe your real talents lie in writing. I've watched how you become the character you're playing. You give it your all. Why not write the words instead of acting them out?"

Steven agreed to the suggestion and began writing scripts for the DuMont Television Network, a new broadcasting platform. He especially enjoyed writing bit parts for character actors like he'd been.

At one of his Los Feliz galas in 1955, Steven and a group of his Hollywood gay friends were enjoying a pool party. Steven was lounging on a pool float when he noticed an attractive twenty-three-year-old flamboyant blonde man standing by the cave with a cocktail glass. Steven locked eyes with him, and the feelings exchanged were intense. He learned Christopher was a hairdresser from Warner Brothers and the two swam into the private grotto, where Christopher performed oral sex on the writer.

They ended up spending the night together, and a relationship ensued. After moving in with Steven, Christopher quit his job to spend more time at home while Steven worked at the studio. Their relationship had a twenty-year age gap, and Christopher became bored. He often cruised Santa Monica Boulevard in the couple's Ford Thunderbird convertible.

Christopher made no secret of his sleeping around, and the two adjusted to an open relationship, although Steven was in love with Christopher and felt no need to stray beyond it. He allowed it because he feared losing his younger partner.

~

BY 1966, THE thirty-four-year-old Christopher had tired of the LA lifestyle. Steven placed their Los Feliz estate on the market and sold it at a handsome profit.

Christopher wished to move to New York City, so they purchased an impressive brownstone in Greenwich Village, the core of the 1960s counterculture. Steven freelanced while Christopher frequented the gay hangouts. One night, Christopher was about to enter the Stonewall Inn when he observed patrons being led away in handcuffs. He and dozens of others began protesting, and that started a series of riots.

Christopher became a gay militant in the Stonewall uprising, unafraid to speak out for his cause. The catty man participated in several of the resistance gatherings. They arrested him for coming to the defense of one of his friends, a drag queen being harassed by the police. They accused Christopher of throwing a beer bottle at a police cruiser.

A year later, Christopher was ready for yet another change. Steven sold the brownstone and they moved to Key West, where they felt comfortable living as openly gay partners but soon tired of the long and humid summers.

Christopher suggested they seek a seasonal reprieve in

the north's summer coolness and return to Key West for the winter. They agreed to move to Cooper's Cove, where Christopher planned to open an antique store specializing in Baldwin brass.

STEVEN FELT APPREHENSIVE about going back. He recalled the painful memories of his youth, but Christopher was very convincing.

"Steven, don't you realize most of those women still remember you from the pinnacle of your Hollywood acting days? They still watch you on late-night black-and-white TV movies! They think you're Hollywood royalty!"

They purchased a bungalow with a waterfront deck and were required to apply for a zoning permit. At the zoning hearing, there were no objections, but Steven overheard someone in the audience whisper, "That's all we need. Two fags want to open an antique store. What's happening with this town?"

The Brass Buckle premiered in the summer of 1971. The couple hired an LA interior designer to create the shop's interior. The nautically themed business was reminiscent of those in Key West, and the partners traveled the country antiquing and filled their store with collectibles.

Christopher, as he'd promised, proudly displayed his vintage Baldwin brass in the front window. He also accepted consignments, and the store seemed a successful concept for the tourists to fancy. At their grand opening, the ladies of the town lined up down the block, waiting for their chance to get the autograph of the former Hollywood actor.

BERTHA STILL THOUGHT the maturing writer sexy and pictured herself in his brawny arms as he made love to her. She shared her fantasy with Evie Crandall. "I can see my-self riding the man while he lies there looking into my eyes."

Evie visualized her rotund friend on top of Steven and thought, *In your dreams, sweetheart. You'd probably crush him.*

AS A HIGH school junior, Dave signed up for a forensic speech class taught by a thirty-six-year-old divorcee who displayed malicious intent toward Dave from the first day of class.

He didn't care for her, either. She wore an ivory hair clip in her Lucy Ricardo red hair. Dave thought she looked a lot like Wilma Flintstone from the Hanna Barbera television cartoon.

She was lecturing on the art of public speaking when she observed Dave daydreaming as usual. "Mr. Meyers? I'd pay attention if I were you. Your oratory skills could use some honing. Your diction sounds sloshy, and you speak as if you have marbles in your mouth." With no warning, she picked up the book she had been lecturing from and hurled it across the classroom, striking his right temple, where it left a small cut.

Dave glared at her, then got up and walked out. His classmates, stunned, all sat staring.

Blood trickling down his face, he headed to the principal's office and reported the attack. Several of his classmates later testified about what they'd witnessed, and the school board quietly dismissed "Wilma" for assaulting a student.

Dave's mother wished to bring legal action against the teacher, but Dave refused to participate. "Mom, she just didn't like me! I don't know what I did to provoke her like that, but I feel I'm responsible for getting her fired. Just like I did with Miss Rossmore. Leave it alone. Just drop it!"

WILSON MCGUIRE LISTENED intently as his secretary told him what the speech teacher had done. "I couldn't believe it when Dave came home. She tossed a book at him! She could have injured his eye! And to make matters worse, he somehow feels responsible for it!"

"This is a terrific news story, Kathleen. I want to headline it in tomorrow's edition."

"Please, don't do that. Dave wants to focus on his writing. He wishes to put it behind him. You know, Dave is seventeen now and becoming an excellent writer. With Frank gone, we could use some additional funds around the house. Would you consider hiring him as a reporter after his classes?"

Wilson gave it some thought. "I think we could use him around here."

AFTER HIS MOTHER told him the good news, Dave's excitement occupied their house over the weekend. The thought of writing for a newspaper intrigued him. Maybe now he could put some of what he had learned about writing into a professional format.

He showed up for work on Monday afternoon. When he walked in, the smell of newspaper printing ink permeated his nostrils.

Wilson provided him a tour, beginning with the front office, where his mom worked at a desk. "This is where you'll work as well, Dave. The desk in that corner is for you to use." Wilson then led him through a swinging door to the press room.

Dave saw what appeared to be an obsolete printing press and another odd machine with someone sitting at it typing. Giant newspaper rolls lined the walls, and the floor appeared slippery with ink. He could see the pressman operating it for that day's edition. Dave watched as the finished product rolled off in newspaper form, waiting for kids on bikes to deliver the papers to subscribers.

Wilson spoke loudly over the roar of the press. "As you can see, Dave, we still print the Courier using the old linotype hot metal typecasting method, but it does the job with our twice-weekly publication."

"Thanks, Mr. McGuire. It's cool seeing the back-of-the-house operation. I never knew that much work goes on behind the front-page stories. I look forward to my first assignment."

"You already have it. You'll cover the fall festival at Veterans' Park this weekend. And even though I'm now your boss, you may address me as Wilson. Listening to your mother talk about you, I already know you."

Dave's first story read:

By Dave Meyers, City Desk Reporter.

The Cooper's Cove Annual Fall Festival was at Veterans' Park this past weekend. It was a perfect day for the celebration. The fall trees were crimson red, set against the cerulean blue skies. The day's festivities began with a parade down Main Street, concluding at Shoreline Avenue.

This year's homecoming queen rode on the back of Steven Conrad's 1955 Thunderbird convertible, and they both waved to the crowd.

The song "Everything Is Beautiful," written by Ray Stevens, echoed from the Cooper's Cove High School marching band. Members of the VFW post and the Elks Lodge marched in unison.

The Riley's Foodland float, a captivating live wild turkey display, won first place for the most creative category until the turkeys escaped and lurched onto the sidewalks.

Newly elected mayor Ben Austin addressed the crowd. Afterward, complimentary cider and donuts were served at the park bandstand, where Bertha Murkowski took to the stage. She reminded everyone of the rummage sale to benefit the dog pound next weekend.

DAVE AND HIS mom were watching an ABC springtime episode of *All My Children*. "Man, I sorta dig this show, Mom. Erika Kane can be ruthless!"

"Susan Lucci is a clever actor. I'll give her that. I wish I had her talent." Kathleen glanced up from her knitting and noticed a distant lightning bolt outside. "Dave, it looks like a storm is brewing. You know what to do with Sandy, right?"

The dog, now age eleven, slept soundly by his feet. Her silky yellow coat had transitioned to white, and her muzzle was now gray. She seemed to have grown old and tired so quickly.

The thunderstorm soon raged outside their home. Lightning flashed, and the television reception faltered. They both heard a loud clap of thunder, and Sandy began trembling.

Dave moved to the floor to calm his upset pet. As the storm moved away, she lay back down and fell asleep. Dave softly caressed the top of her head and whispered into her ear, "It's okay, baby. The storm won't hurt you. Daddy loves you!"

Dave noticed her rib cage was no longer rising. Her breathing had stopped. He realized his companion was dead.

Tears ran down his cheeks as he held onto her and cried while Kathleen watched from the sofa. "Mom! Sandy's dead!" An overwhelming grief came over him, and he refused to believe she was gone. They'd been through so much together. The passage of time had gone unnoticed as his dog aged. To Dave, Sandy had always been the puppy he'd brought home from his aunt and uncle's litter.

He relived the pain of losing his father. He couldn't imagine life without his beautiful, sweet friend, protector, and confidant. But he knew it was time for her to cross the rainbow bridge.

KATHLEEN REALIZED HER son's pain. She wished to hug him and take it away. As she stood there massaging her only son's shoulders, she somehow heard the words, *Pain equals suffering, but suffering equals growth.*

Suddenly, she realized Dave could live his own life. She knew it was time to set her emotional hostage free.

DAVE DUG A deep grave in their backyard and wrapped Sandy's body in his father's old navy blanket. Gently, he lowered her into the grave, along with her favorite rubber ball that she had played fetch with so many times at the orchard and Veterans' Park.

Mother and son said their final goodbyes, and he shoveled dirt over his deceased partner's body while he continued weeping. He chiseled Sandy's name and her dates of birth and death onto a piece of limestone he found.

The grieving boy's tears stopped for the moment, but later, when he found one of her toys, they came rushing back.

5

THE STATE'S ATTORNEY closed down the whorehouse after Sheriff Dodster got caught with his pants down. Literally.

As the locals referred to it, Pearl's Cider House sat on the far side of town near the Coast Guard station. The cathouse had been operating as a house of ill repute since the 1940s; until now, no one had a problem with it. Pearl kept her girls "clean," treated them well, and paid them well. She'd also been paying Sheriff Jeremy Dodster well. The sheriff had been taking bribes from Pearl since the residents elected him. Before that, Jeremy's father, also the sheriff, had been getting his cut for several years.

The gig would have continued to pay off until one of the Coast Guard men caught a case of VD, which reached the commander's desk. The commander contacted the state attorney general's office, and they conducted a raid on the establishment. They found Sheriff Dodster in a room with a lady of the night.

Dave was at the courthouse the day the story broke and got the first scoop of his young career. His headline for the next day's edition read:

PEARL'S CIDER HOUSE RAIDED
By Dave Meyers, City Desk Reporter

Armed with a search warrant, state police raided the well-known establishment yesterday. Sheriff Jeremy Dodster pled not guilty to solicitation of a prostitute.

Police also accused the sheriff of accepting illegal bribes from Pearl Tweedsley, the alleged mistress of the operation, who they charged with operating a house of prostitution. Two of her female employees also face charges.

The Courier news desk attempted to reach the sheriff at his residence for comment on the charges. However, Mrs. Dodster informed us her husband is no longer living at that address.

The sheriff wasn't the only one drinking cider at Pearl's. Following her arrest, Pearl threatened to spill the beans on everyone. She had been keeping an informal log of guests visiting the cider house over the last thirty years. That list included the judge, the clerk of court, other prominent upstanding citizens, and most of the all-male jury, which found everyone not guilty of all charges.

Pearl was back pressing apples at the cider house the following week.

FINALLY! DAVE HAD become a high school senior. He took whatever subjects he wished, which gave him more time to focus on his writing.

Walking with the others on their way to their next class. Nora Austin had smiled at him again. This time, he knew he was going to say something. He turned and yelled, "Hey Nora, you wanna go out sometime?"

DID DAVE MEYERS just ask me out? The first time he'd sat beside her in their art class, Nora thought the blonde, white guy was cute. They'd acknowledged each other that day, just nodding and smiling. Nora saw something in Dave she hadn't seen in any of the other boys she'd dated in Michigan, all of whom were Black.

Before she agreed to his shouted question, she needed to ensure his intentions were sincere, not those of a con- siderate white boy who was friendly to the only Black girl in his class. "How many Black girls have you dated?" she asked him.

"Ahh, none so far."

"And how many Black friends do you have?"

"One. And now two, I hope."

Nora's frown turned into a smile. "Sure, Dave. I'd love to go out with you. Thanks for asking."

DAVE BLUSHED. "I was just waiting for the right time." He'd always wanted to say something to the enigmatic girl, but he didn't think he stood a chance with her. Nora seemed to emit a magnetic attraction that pulled him closer.

The other students stopped to stare at the biracial couple.

Fuck all of you, Dave thought. He'd never understood bigots and asked himself, *What would cause a human being to reach beyond the depths of despair to harm another?* He recalled his visits with Amos, who never noticed a difference. Dave knew Amos had seen him for who he was. A human being. He remembered Amos telling him a story during one of their visits.

"Dave, if you place a two-year-old African American baby and a two-year-old white child into a play crib, do you know what happens?"

Dave, his mouth full of cookies, shook his head.

"Why, the innocent children play together. They don't care about a difference in their skin tone. They're color-blind. They both know only love. It's ingrained within them. Truth is, Dave, love is within all of us. Humans teach hatred. It's my belief we were born without hate and learned how to. Unfortunately, it then becomes part of our lives. But I also believe humans can change how they think or feel about one another. Then, and only then, Dave, can the planet change. And only if everyone is willing."

When Amos finished, Dave opened his journal and wrote, Amos knows the secret.

Now, he stood in a daze while recalling his conversation with Amos.

"Dave? Are you okay?"

"Yeah, I am. It's all beginning to make sense now."

"What's beginning to make sense, Dave?"

"I'll tell you some other time. Here's my phone number. Could you give me yours? I want to go out on Friday night. If you're sure you want to."

Nora took out her spiral notebook and jotted down her number. She tore it off and handed it to Dave, and they both said goodbye. Dave moved on to his English literature class.

His twelfth-grade English lit instructor was popular with all the students. She was in her late fifties, an attractive, proper, and prim southern lady who seemed to enjoy teaching. Dignified and aging gracefully, she related to her students, which most likely helped make her a good teacher. Everyone thought she was excellent. She could be stern, but her students sensed she had their best interests at heart. She wanted them to immerse themselves in creative literature with the same passion she had.

Those taking her class had to memorize and recite part

of Chaucer's The Canterbury Tales, a collection of stories written in Middle English in the late 1300s. She'd have the boys kneel on one knee while reciting.

Dave knelt before her and looked into the fostering mentor's eyes. Visualizing his first line, he began, "Whan that Aprille with his shoures soote." He had memorized the required eighteen lines from the prologue.

Mario, a dumb football jock by now, was lucky if he could recite the first two words of the magnum opus.

It didn't seem to bother the teacher. She allowed the football jocks to slide by with poorer grades. She knew their vocation was playing college or pro ball let them advance into the colleges and universities. Football was more important than their academics. She cheered them on at their home games, and one talented wide receiver confessed he would never have made it to the big leagues if not for her kindness.

But it only went so far. She didn't like troublemakers in her classes. Such was Mario, who thought he was a comedian and wanted to interrupt her lectures with his smart-aleck wisecracks.

At first, the educator laughed at his witticisms, but she quickly cut him off when he bombed. "Mr. Panza! Please! Join me."

Mario smiled at all the girls as he approached the front of the classroom. In his most innocent voice, he asked, "Yes, ma'am. Is there something I can do for you?"

Not at all amused, she coyly answered him, "Yes. There is something you may do for me, Mr. Panza. Drop and give me forty!"

Everyone broke out laughing. Mario did his push-ups. And she brought the class back into the present and continued to tell everyone about Chaucer.

THAT FRIDAY AFTERNOON, Dave telephoned Nora and asked if she wanted to go to the screening of Peter Bogdanovich's movie *The Last Picture Show* playing at the Majestic Theater. The movie had premiered a year earlier, but the small conservative theater lagged in showing many films, especially one considered offensive and controversial.

"Dave, I've always wanted to see that movie!"

"Great; I'll pick you up at seven, if that's okay with you." Dave showered for his date and jumped into his classic 1964 Ford Mustang he had recently bought. The red convertible with its V-8 engine was the envy of his friends when they saw it parked on Shoreline Avenue in the summers with the top down. An unexpected January thaw had settled in that day and with the mercury at fifty-six degrees, he thought he'd lower the top to try and impress Nora.

Dave pulled up in front of the Austin home and waited at the passenger door for Nora. When she came out, he saw she wore a mod blue pantsuit with a red and green polka-dot blouse. He also saw her sunglasses perched on top of her afro. "Man, you sure look groovy, Nora." After closing her door, he got into the other side.

"Thanks Dave. You look super in those maroon bell-bottoms and brown suede vest. I admire your taste in clothing."

Dave revved the car's 289-horsepower engine. They headed into town. As he approached Shoreline Avenue, they saw the expressions on everyone's faces as they drove by. Dave realized he may be making Nora uncomfortable. Nora smiled at him and turned up the volume on the radio. "Treat Her Like a Lady" by the Cornelius Brothers and Sister Rose was playing. Two men in front of the barbershop stood shaking their heads at the biracial couple.

Ed Persty looked at his good friend Pete York, who owned the bait and tackle shop down at the marina and poked his ribcage. "Hey! Isn't that Frank Meyer's boy in his car with that Austin girl?"

"It sure as hell is," Pete admitted. "Pity. What would Dave's father say to him if he could see this spectacle?"

"I know he wouldn't like it one damn bit, Pete. He raised that boy with better morals. I heard he's also been attending those anti-war protests at Oberlin College. Of course, that doesn't surprise me. Those liberal college professors are filling those kids' heads with all that communist bull-shit!"

Dave parked at one of the meters in front of the Majestic, and the couple joined the line at the box office. They both felt the stares of onlookers. They smiled and held hands.

A fellow student at the ticket window asked for IDs for the R-rated movie.

Dave angrily responded, "Come on, man! You know we're all seventeen."

He grudgingly handed Dave the tickets, and the couple went inside. Dave bought a large popcorn with melted butter and two Cokes at the concession stand. They chose seats at the very front of the theater. "You get the idea everyone is staring at us?" Dave asked Nora.

"You better get used to that if we go on another date. You'll get an idea of what Black people face every day of our lives. Let me rephrase that, Dave. We never get used to it. We've learned to tolerate it."

Nora's comment caught him off guard. It triggered something within. He felt angry toward those who harbored hatred toward different people, like the Austins and the gay men who owned the Brass Buckle. The world seemed so unjust. "I'm sorry, Nora. I wish there were something I could do."

"You think you're that powerful, Dave? Systemic racism is ingrained in our society. Look around you. Do you find any of these people staring at us accepting? Let's give them something to stare at."

"Like what?"

"Like this." She gingerly held his chin and kissed him.

His eyes closed. Her kiss was sweet and sensual, unlike any he had imagined. Dave hugged her and returned an even deeper kiss, then glanced over his shoulder to see the shocked expressions on everyone's faces.

They let go of each other as the lights went down for the movie. They held hands as the whispering behind them continued.

After the movie was over, Dave and Nora heard others

carrying on as they left. Some were shocked at Dave's and Nora's behavior, but more were upset about the controversial coming-of-age film.

MANY OF THE town's residents thought the movie's language was filthy. Even Bertha Murkowski said the sex scenes were too raw for her to watch. She told her friend Evie, "And that handsome young man, Timothy Bottoms! Imagine! Having sex with a middle-aged woman like Cloris Leachman! That was disgraceful!"

Evie knew Bertha would have given anything to be in Miss Leachman's shoes, playing the part of Ruth Popper, the middle-aged woman in the film.

DAVE AND NORA sensed that the residents of Anarene, Texas, the fictional setting for the movie, were like many in Cooper's Cove. Judgmental energy seemed to exist in both towns.

"Would you like to grab a bite to eat? The diner has great burgers. Reminds me of the ones Aunt Billie used to make at our drive-in."

"Sure, Dave. Whatever you crave. Who was your Aunt Billie?"

"She's my great aunt. And she's still alive and lives in

Florida. She used to fly up every summer to cook at my mom's drive-in root beer stand. But that was a long time ago." They walked over to the eatery. The stares continued unabated when they entered.

Molly Kingston greeted them. Dave knew her from high school, and she had once had a date with Mario. "Hi, Dave!" she said. "Table for two?"

Dave noticed the booth in a corner. "How about that one?"

They sat down and he introduced Nora. "Molly, I'd like you to meet Nora Austin."

"Nora Austin! I dug all the uproar it created when your dad bought the factory. Nice to meet you. And may I add Dave has impeccable taste?"

"Thank you. I think he might be a keeper."

Dave felt his cheeks turning red.

MOLLY MADE IT no secret to anyone: she detested the bigots and hypocrites in town. She'd gotten pregnant her junior year and told her parents, the Reverend Horace Kingston and his wife Eleanor, that she wasn't sure of the father. Upon hearing the unwelcome news, they banished her to her grandparents' home in Chillicothe, where she remained until the child was born. Her parents ordered her to put the child up for adoption before she could return home.

After a short contemplation, Molly decided to keep the baby and return to Cooper's Cove. She later gave birth to a handsome baby boy and named him Alex. Molly thought her parents would forgive her once they saw their new grandson.

Holding Alex in her arms, she knocked on the front door.

Her father opened it and looked into the eyes of his grandson for the very first time. The minister asserted, "You are no longer welcome in our home. Not only have you disgraced us; you have disgraced the church."

Her mother stood there with tears in her eyes. She did not condone her husband's callousness, but she respected the word of her lord.

Molly's heart broke. She felt alone and abandoned. She left, vowing never to return.

The diner's owner, Russ, offered her a furnished one-bedroom apartment above the restaurant in return for waiting tables. The town wasted little time in passing judgment on her.

A testy salesclerk from Nelson's Clothing Store was getting her hair done at Perfectly Quaffed. She sat in her chair smoking a Camel cigarette while gossiping with Gertie, who was also smoking while styling the woman's hair.

Gertie always told it like it was. "Well! The way I hear it, the father isn't even from around here! He's some weekend boater from Youngstown and had his Chris-Craft docked down at the Erie Marina. I heard Molly saw the guy walking through the park one night and followed him back to his boat. Everyone in town knows what a slut that girl is! She's no different from the girl over in Brooksville who got

pregnant in eleventh grade and ran off with that car mechanic back in fifty-eight."

Molly couldn't have cared less what any of them thought. Proud and determined, she believed it was no one's business but hers.

MOLLY TOOK THEIR orders: two well-done hamburgers with lettuce, tomato, ketchup, and mustard, and one large portion of french fries to share.

"Nora, I admire your family's tenacity in moving here. I can somewhat relate to what you go through. Don't pay any attention to the narrow-minded idiots here. You're more than welcome in Cooper's Cove, and you should know there are a lot of kind, considerate folks in this town who feel the same as I do. You're sitting across from one."

"I'm realizing that; thanks."

Molly took their menus and gave Russ their order at the service window.

"Dave, she's charming," Nora said. "Molly's the one with the grit and determination to return. I admire her for that. You mentioned your parents owned a drive-in?"

"Yeah. And we had an incredible peach orchard, too. That's what my dad did before he lost it all. You know of the Cooper's Cove Mobile Home Community?"

"Sure; it's near where we live."

"Well, that was my dad's idea, but someone else beat

him to the punch. Then, he began working as a custodian at the school. And, well, I'm sure you've heard the rest."

"Tragedy seems to befall everyone in their lives, Dave. I hope you can take comfort in knowing him as you did."

"That's a story for some other time. I know about your parents and the factory. Tell me more about you."

"Hmm. Let's see. I grew up and attended school in Flint before moving here. I consider myself even-keeled—most of the time. I like a good murder mystery, the smell of newly fallen rain, and Good and Plenty licorice candies. There's more, but I feel self-conscious talking about myself. My parents taught me to love myself, no matter what. Dad always says what others might think or say about me is none of my business. I like it here in Cooper's Cove. It's a beautiful place. I find a lot of inspiration for my art here."

"Is that what you wish to do?"

"My dad wants me to assume his responsibilities at the Tool and Die. I don't want to be an executive. It's what my father wants."

"What do you want, Nora?"

"I want to sculpt and be an artist."

"Then talk with them."

"You don't know my father. Once he's made his mind up about something, it's quite a challenge getting him to change it."

"What about your mother? Maybe you could talk to her instead."

Nora sighed and laughed. "You don't know my mom

either. She goes along with what my father says. Like the book I'm reading, *The Stepford Wives*."

"I think you owe it to yourself to talk to them and tell them what you want. Don't allow yourself to be swayed by the opinions of others, just like your father told you. As Shakespeare wrote, 'To thy own self be true.'"

"You speak as if you are a writer, Dave."

"That's what I want to be, Nora. I'm trying to determine if I have what it takes to be one. They've accepted me at Oberlin College with scholarship for the tuition. Mom doesn't make enough at the newspaper to send me to school. And I figure the money I've saved from working as a reporter will cover my room and board."

They continued their conversations into the evening, getting to know one another better. Dave told her more about Oberlin and why he wanted to attend. They felt like they'd known each other for a lifetime, or perhaps many. Dave felt entirely at ease in her presence.

When he took her home, they could see her father peering through the curtains, concerned about his daughter's welfare. Dave kissed her goodnight as Ben watched.

BEN HAD ADMIRED the boy's doggedness in asking his daughter out on a date. He knew the challenges Dave would face. But he also knew Dave was cognizant of that before asking his daughter out.

Once inside, Nora told her parents, "I like him. There's

something about Dave I can't put my finger on. He seems different from other white boys."

"I'm concerned about you dating him, Nora," her mother said. "Some in this town seem set in their ways, and I'm not sure you should rock the boat."

Nora thought about what Dave and Molly had told her at the diner. "I'm not trying to rock the boat, Mama. I'm claiming my rightful place in society! It's no one's business who I choose to date!"

"Nora! We're just trying to look out for your best interests. Your father and I don't want you getting hurt."

"That's a chance I'm willing to take, Mom. I'm almost an adult and quite capable of making my own decisions! And while we are on the subject, I need to say something. Daddy? I don't want to take over for you at the Tool and Die."

Ben paused before he spoke. "Well, this is something I hadn't expected, honey. I've always assumed you wanted to assume my responsibilities. If not, what do you want to do with your life?"

"I want to be an artist, Daddy. It's all I've ever wanted to be."

Grace had known of her daughter's career ambitions, but she'd been afraid to broach the subject with her husband. She knew Nora's first love was art and always had been. "You've never noticed your daughter's creative, expressive side?" she asked her husband. "Who do you think painted those beautiful acrylics hanging in our bedroom?"

"Nora? Is this true? I know you enjoy painting, but you want to be a professional artist?"

"I was afraid I would disappoint you if I told you the truth, Daddy. You seemed so intent on your wishes for me."

Ben took a deep breath. "Sweetheart, we want you to be happy. If a career in the art world or whatever else you desire to do makes you happy, we're happy."

Nora liked what Dave had told her about Oberlin. She realized this was her opportunity to talk with her parents about attending college there. "Dave told me tonight they've accepted him at Oberlin College. He's chosen to focus on creative writing and has worked part-time as a reporter at the *Courier* since his sophomore year."

"Yes. I've read some of his articles, and it appears he has talent. But why creative writing? Isn't journalism more to his liking?"

"Dave's true desire is to become a writer. He's enjoyed covering the news but told me writing is his passion. He shared with me he has some ideas for his first novel but won't tell me what they are.

"I want to go to Oberlin as well. Dave told me it's an excellent school for the arts, and they've committed to a minority enrollment program, one of the first colleges in the nation to do that. I bet you didn't know Oberlin was one of the first colleges in the nation to admit African Americans and the first to award a degree to an African American woman? And Dave told me both of those happened as far back as 1835 and 1841!"

"Sounds like he's done his homework. And it also sounds like you're firm in your decision. Oberlin sounds great, but your mother and I must discuss this."

Grace had no problem with Nora pursuing art. Still, she decided to withhold her opinion of the couple's relationship until she got to know the young man better.

Ben remembered reading something else about the school. "And one more thing, young lady! I understand Oberlin has had coed dorms since 1970. There'll be no coed dorms for you!"

"Don't worry, Daddy. We'll live in separate dorms."

WHEN DAVE GOT home a short time later, he found his mom waiting for him, watching *The Carol Burnett Show* on CBS. As he entered the den, his mother laughed at Carol's portrayal of Stella Toddler, the klutz. She looked up as he came in. "So, how was your date?"

"Groovy! We both enjoyed ourselves. I was a little nervous at first. Nora's very confident. We had a good time. She also met Molly. The two of them seemed to hit it off well."

"Dave, I must confess, I'm a little concerned about you and Nora. You'll come up against many haters if you know what I mean."

"We got a few stares tonight. What do you think Dad would have to say if he'd known I'd go out with an African American girl?"

Kathleen gave it some thought. "If you want me to be honest with you, I'd have to say he wouldn't be supportive. Try to understand, Dave. His was a different generation. It's not that I found your father prejudiced. It's just that he didn't know any Black people personally, except Amos. He most likely would have had difficulty not seeing Nora's skin color. Like others our age he may have been afraid of someone who looked so different from him."

"Mom! That's the problem with Cooper's Cove. They look for the differences in people instead of the similarities! What about you? What do you think of us? Even though it is just our first date."

Kathleen furrowed her brows. "I think you'll both face adversity in your relationship. But I know you can overcome any obstacle put before you."

The eleven-p.m. news came on. Secretary of State Henry Kissinger was on his way to Paris to sign the peace accord to end the Vietnam War. The US Supreme Court had also agreed on abortion rights. On the same day, former President Lyndon Johnson died at sixty-four.

"Busy news day," Dave commented. "Nixon told us the war was ending back in 1970. What's taken him so long?" Dave had recently turned eighteen and no longer faced the prospect of being drafted and having to decide whether he would go. Kathleen was grateful she no longer needed to worry about Dave being sent to die in Vietnam.

"Mom? What do you think about abortion? Do you think the Supreme Court made the right decision?"

"I believe it's past due, Dave. I've always felt that choosing an abortion was between a pregnant mother and her own personal god. No one else. I don't believe anyone can dictate what a woman may do with her own body."

"Well, the largest court in the land has finally put this

to rest. As you said, it's been a long time coming. Women have been fighting for their reproductive rights for years!"

He kissed his mom goodnight and went up to his room to contemplate. Before falling asleep, he wrote in his journal. *I think I know what I want my book to be about now. Nora's the inspiration for my story.*

IN THE MORNING, he met Mario at the diner for breakfast, where Molly Kingston was working behind the counter.

"Well, look what the cat dragged in!" Molly glared at Mario before acknowledging Dave. "How are you this morning, Dave? It was so nice meeting Nora! I hope you two hit it off."

"Thanks! And she enjoyed talking with you."

Molly turned her attention back to Mario. "So! I see Dave brought along trouble."

"Hey!" Mario snapped. "You're the one who seems to get into trouble."

Molly handed Dave his menu, tossed the other into Mario's lap, and walked away.

"I just don't get the two of you, Mario. She never did like you, did she?"

Mario goaded Dave. "What? Do you still have a crush on her? You always thought she was pretty. You sure you're not the father?"

"You know, Mario, you can be a real asshole. You don't care about other people's feelings. I also know you don't like Nora, either."

"Come on, buddy; I was just kidding with you. You know I care about Molly. She had the guts to return here and face everyone. But you dating an African American girl in this town? Well, that's another story."

" Mario. I don't give a shit what anyone thinks, and that goes for you, too, buddy."

Molly brought their food, and they ate it in silence.

A MYSTERIOUS MURDER took place in Cooper's Cove that winter. The police received an anonymous phone call and discovered Donald Woesten dead at the bottom of his staircase. The unfortunate Donald had taken a tumble and broken his neck. But evidence at the scene suggested it may have been intentional, but they had no suspects, and they charged no one with the crime. It became an unsolved murder.

With no heirs, the director's residence and business were to be auctioned. An out-of-towner, Nick Foster, had recently graduated from the Quagmire School of Mortuary and was the winning bidder for the funeral home. A trendsetter, he modernized the business and installed a drive-up viewing window.

Grievers were no longer required to leave their cars in inclement weather. Friends and relatives could drive their autos to a curtained window where they pressed a call button to notify Nick of an automobile's presence outside.

He'd draw the curtains, and the sorrowers could see their loved one displayed in the coffin, which tilted slightly, offering a better glimpse of the corpse. After one last look, the mourners nodded to Nick, who'd open the teller's drawer containing the guest registry. They'd sign and put it back, and Nick would slowly draw the curtains closed as the auto moved away.

Cora Jensen, ninety by now, couldn't see well enough to find the call button, so she blared the horn on her Nash until Nick opened the curtains.

April 20, 1973
Mayor Benjamin Austin
Cooper's Cove, Ohio

Dear Ben:

By now, you've had time to grow accustomed to folks' ways in Cooper's Cove.

When Mary Beth and I first met you and your lovely wife, Grace, we were concerned about the town's perception of you both. I'm sure it came as quite a shock, and we sincerely apologize for our rapid departure from the stage that day.

Reverse discrimination occurred upon our arrival here in the islands, where most folks have darker skin. Some locals frowned upon white people, referred to us as Haoles, and some shunned us. However, once we gained their trust, they

proved to be the most compassionate human
beings and accepted us with loving, open arms.

The Hawaiians and other ethnic races inhabiting
our little corner of the world are remarkable. They've
taught Mary Beth and me the meaning of aloha,
and I can only hope you've found the same true for
many of the good people there.

Sincerely:
Justin Roby
Honolulu, Hawaii

May 1, 1973
Justin Roby
Diamond Head Road
Honolulu, Hawaii

Dear Justin:

Thank you for your eloquent letter. Grace and I
know it was from your heart, and we appreciate
your kind and considerate words.

Now that you understand how hatred feels,
you can do your part in helping to change the
world. You certainly are in a beautiful place to do
that!

In case you haven't heard, I ran for your
former office and won the election by a three

percent margin. Slowly but surely, things appear to be changing here.

Aloha!

Ben Austin

Mayor, Cooper's Cove, Ohio

THE ROBYS MAY have been basking in their retirement, but after purchasing their old home, Charlotte Brookstone, Mary Beth's cousin, wasn't faring as well. She'd become a hermit. No one had even seen the woman since she'd moved from Cincinnati. Riley's Foodland delivered her groceries every week. She'd told Buster Riley, the owner, to have the driver leave her groceries on the back steps and ring the doorbell before leaving. Charlotte promised, "I'll be glad to include a weekly ten-dollar tip if you agree never to reveal the contents of my order to anyone."

But Buster got drunk one night at Smitty's and revealed most of her orders were nothing more than junk food. He told everyone, "Charlotte's favorite is Ballreich potato chips and French onion dip." Buster also said a typical weekly order comprised six dip containers, six bags of locally produced potato chips, and five boxes of Little Debbie chocolate cupcakes.

Buster took another sip of his Blatz beer and laughed. He choked and spat his beer out on the bar top before blabbing, "Oh yeah! One more thing. Charlotte makes sure I remember her bottle of castor oil each week."

No one ever observed Charlotte outside her home. She kept the shades pulled, even during daylight hours. Everyone assumed the senior widow had become a loner who minded her business and wished to be left alone.

That didn't stop the beauty shop girls from offering their takes on the mysterious transplant. Everyone seemed to have a different opinion.

Bertha and Verna sat under the hair dryers at the Perfectly Quaffed. Bertha had been looking over her latest copy of *The National Enquirer* and reading about a grossly overweight woman who couldn't leave her bed. "Hey, Verna! That Brookstone woman must weigh a ton if what Buster said is true. He told everyone at the bar she only eats crap!"

Verna peered at Bertha over her bifocals, thinking, *You're one to talk.*

Sadly, Charlotte cared little about her once-beautiful mansion. The plush yard Amos had once proudly maintained became overgrown and hadn't seen a lawnmower in months. She left her bushes untrimmed to hide her house from the street; the gardens lay bare during the summer, and the mansion's antique green shutters hung from their rusty hinges.

Dave shook his head when he drove by the ornate Victorian. He could only think, *What is wrong with this lady?*

6

MARIO'S AND DAVE'S estrangement continued, and the crack only seemed widen. To fill the void, Dave sought a new friend and found one in Warren Holtzman, his auto shop class partner.

The young car enthusiasts shared a common interest: their 1960s muscle cars. Warren even rebuilt the engine of his 1963 Pontiac LeMans custom convertible he'd discovered sitting on a used car lot in Lorain.

Holtzman maintained a four-point grade average and was class valedictorian. But the high-intellect scholar had little interest in continuing his education, even though his parents expected him to attend Harvard, one of three Ivy League colleges they'd chosen.

As a little boy, Warren had tinkered with toys, taking them apart to discover what was inside and piecing them back together. His parents seemed oblivious to his desire to become a car mechanic, and Warren had to hide his true self from them.

The gifted technician secretly worked in Dave's garage while his mother and father assumed their scholar was studying at the library. Not wishing to put his wants above those of his parents, Warren couldn't tell them his natural aspirations.

The teenagers were changing the Mustang's spark plugs when Dave came out and asked, "Warren? Why haven't you told your parents? You dig cars, man, and you know you do! Someday, you may reflect on all this and realize you've spent your entire life doing something you've never wanted."

"Dave, since I was old enough to talk, Dad has bragged to everyone about me becoming a lawyer."

"You sound like Nora Austin. She thought the same about her father."

Dave tried reasoning with his misguided friend, but it was useless. Warren had already chosen not to follow his true path.

EIGHTY-TWO COOPER'S COVE High School class of 1973 members accepted their diplomas on a late spring day. Warren delivered his valedictorian speech and lied to those assembled, "We've tremendous choices before us today. The decisions we make will influence us for the rest of our lives. May we all choose wisely!"

His mom and dad sat proudly in the audience. They had no way of knowing how much their son would hate Harvard.

After the ceremony, most of the graduates partied, but Dave and Nora preferred a more low-key celebration and drove to secluded Barnes Harbor for a picnic and their first swim of the season in Lake Erie. The long-awaited spring temperature had reached seventy-four degrees for their graduation, but the lake was still a chilly fifty-seven.

They changed into swimsuits and waded into the frigid water, shivering as the icelike ripples lapped at their legs. Dave looked around the deserted beach and suggested they go in naked. Nora, not at all prude, peeled off her swim top first, revealing her supple breasts. Dave shyly admired them and then pulled off his bathing trunks. Nora glimpsed his prominent member. Dave knew the frigid water would not keep it that way for long and dove into the lake.

Nora did the same, and they floated into each other's arms and kissed, their teeth chattering from the cold. They noticed another couple in the parking lot wanting to do the same as they had, so they crept out of the water and ran to hide under a large Colorado blue spruce.

They slipped back into their clothing, and Dave spread a blanket in the sunniest spot in the park. Nora had brought a picnic basket her mother had prepared: chilled pepper steak salad with homemade baked beans. As an added surprise, Grace had included two pieces of her fresh strawberry pie, which Dave quickly scarfed down.

He licked his fingers. "Your mom's a terrific cook."

"I think she is. Dad does, too. He's always telling her to cut back, or he will get fat."

Her parents were in great shape. Ben ran five miles a day, even in the winter. At forty-three, he had nearly the same physique as when he'd graduated from college. Forty-year-old Grace was a fitness enthusiast as well. She played racquetball at the country club and occasionally jogged with her husband.

Nora possessed the same beauty as her parents, and that didn't go unnoticed by Dave.

They returned the leftover food to the picnic basket, and Dave lay on the blanket. Nora sat beside him. He placed the back of his neck on her lap and stared at the sky with its curious cloud formations. "How come we're not doing it by now?"

Nora stroked the platinum blonde hair on her boyfriend's forehead. "I don't know about you, Dave, but I wouldn't risk getting pregnant. I have other things I want to do before I get married and even think about having children, if I ever will!"

Dave wasn't prepared for that. He hadn't considered having children, but now he knew Nora had doubts. Perhaps he'd never be a father. Dave wasn't sure he even wanted to. What kind of father would he be? Distant like his own had been to him? He wondered if he could even fulfill the responsibilities of being a dad.

For now, he had two wants: to go to college and to write his book. He decided to change the conversation. "Nora, there's something I've been meaning to ask you. I'm thinking of writing my book about discrimination in society and its effects on people like you and your family."

"No, no, no! Dave. Just hold it right there! The last thing we need is some *Uncle Tom's Cabin*-type author writing a book about how my people have been the victims of discrimination! How could a white man ever know how *my people* feel? If I read one more book written by a white guy trying to tell us what it is like being Black, I'll pull my hair out! Thanks for trying to help us, but no thanks."

"Nora! I've seen how it is when we walk past people in public. You seem to have your eyes glued straight ahead, staring, not looking at anyone." But he stopped what he was about to say. He realized he may have just discovered a way to write a book Nora may approve of.

But he wasn't about to share any of the *secrets*.

"WHAT DO YOU think of my artwork, mama?" Nora asked while Grace washed dishes at the kitchen sink.

Her mother laid her dishrag on the counter and removed her pink rubber gloves. "I think you're very talented, Nora. And your work reflects that. Why do you ask, honey?"

"I thought of asking Christopher Brighton at the Brass Buckle if he'd accept my artwork on consignment. It'd be a creative way to make money while Dave works at the newspaper this summer."

Grace looked out the window at the birdbath in their

backyard, crowded with robins bathing. "Baby, I think that's an excellent idea." Then she noticed her husband lying in the hammock enjoying an afternoon siesta. She yelled out the window, "Benjamin Austin! You promised me you'd mow the lawn today, and now I've caught you sleeping."

"Okay, okay! I'll get to it!" Ben got up and took the power mower out of the garage.

Nora was proud to witness her mother's spark in scolding her father. Maybe she'd evolved from always agreeing with him to not being afraid to voice her opinion. It was a side of her mother she wasn't used to.

Later, Nora drove to the antique store with an acrylic she'd painted of the Rocky Point Lighthouse. She'd sat alone at a picnic table and painted, capturing a realistic effect on the canvas.

Christopher was ecstatic when she showed it to him. "Darling, I simply love it! It looks fabulous! Just like a photograph! The more you can bring me, the better. If that works for you, I charge a fifteen percent seller's fee."

"That's perfect! I'll have more for you in three weeks."

The lighthouse painting sold the first weekend for twenty dollars, and she prospered. Nora never felt as if she was working while painting. Instead, she considered making art as getting paid for something she loved to do.

THE FUTURE COLLEGIANS drove to Oberlin to check out the campus before their classes began in a week. After turning off Route Ten and heading into town, they went down College Street with its stately older homes.

Nora told Dave that Oberlin reminded her of Cooper's Cove without the lake. Much of the housing was reminiscent of that same era. Two Presbyterian ministers had founded the town in 1833, just a few years before Cooper's Cove.

"You're right, Nora. This place might as well be back home. They cater to college students in the winter, as we do with tourists during our summers. And look at this downtown. Doesn't it resemble ours?"

They parked the Mustang in front of the Ben Franklin store. Nora saw an exciting shop next door and wanted to stop in. They read the sign above the door: *Sage Gallery.*

A bell rang as they entered, and a smiling woman with curly gray hair greeted them and introduced herself as Holly. "You here to see the kittens?"

Dave and Nora squinched their eyebrows and looked around at the distinctive artwork and pottery on display. "I thought this was an art gallery?" Nora asked.

"It is," she told them, "but I also rescue kittens. The students come here to pet them. I've owned this place since I graduated from Oberlin in 1953. Most of the kittens would die if it weren't for me. When anyone finds the abandoned strays wandering about the streets in the summer, they call me. It's a shame, but most die during the winter before I can rescue them."

Holly's kindness toward animals touched Dave and Nora, and they asked if they could see the kittens.

"Well, if classes were in session, I'd ask you to take a number. This place has gotten so overrun with students I had to start a number system! But go on back."

As they walked into the storeroom, they saw cage upon cage of kittens stacked almost to the ceiling. Every color and size imaginable. More fur babies were sitting on the laps of the "Obies," as the locals called them in reference to the town.

Dave and Nora watched as one of them, a rugged Oberlin Yeoman football player with tears in his eyes, pet a sick mother cat that some cruel and thoughtless person had abandoned along with her litter of six.

"Oh, he's been in several times," Holly told them. "The mother cat reminds him of his cat back home."

Sauntering around the gallery, Nora saw Holly's selection of art supplies and knew where she'd be purchasing her paints and brushes. After thanking her for the tour, they contributed to her kitten rescue fund as they left.

A few doors down, they discovered an eclectic thrift store named The Enlightened One in Progress. Inside, they focused on a vast array of New Age items and collectibles gained from the college's heritage. Old books, magazines, lamps, knickknacks, and clothing adorned the boutique. Dave found an issue of *Life Magazine* from 1939 and an original map of the campus from 1928. He picked up a calendar from 1936 that listed the downtown merchants that existed then. They noticed antique pins, emblems, and Oberlin collectibles inside a glass display case.

A young lady dressed in black jeans and a black T-shirt approached and asked if she could help them find anything.

"No thanks; we're just looking. My girlfriend and I are checking things out before classes begin."

"Sure! If you need anything, I'll be right over there. My name's Lauren."

NORA WAS APPRECIATING Lauren's collection of vintage clothing when she saw Lauren approach Dave.

"Excuse me," Lauren asked him, "but are you, by chance, an Aquarian?"

"Ah, yeah. But how'd you know that?"

"You appear to me as one. Many Aquarians can reflect on a time they may have lived before."

"So, you believe in reincarnation?" he asked.

"No, not necessarily. But I believe we were before. That we are now and that we will be again. In some place or form. Many customers find what I sell here intriguing. They're drawn to these clothes and seem connected with these old photos. A sense of déjà vu, if you will. I'm also a psychic and can read auras." She handed Dave a card. It read *Lauren Edwards: Mystic and Psychic*, and it had her telephone number.

Lauren's revelation fascinated Dave. Nora thought her strange, and they were ready to leave the store.

"Before you go, I'd like to give you each a complimentary reading."

Nora politely refused, but Dave said, "Why not?"

Lauren led him and Nora through a draped curtain into a darkened room containing illuminated crystals and candles. They could smell burning incense. Dave and the Lauren sat across from one another at a small table. Lauren asked Dave for one of his items.

He removed his wristwatch and handed it to her. She placed it in her right hand and closed her eyes. She leaned her head back, and it appeared she was listening to someone communicating with her.

Lauren opened her eyes. She took Dave's hands in hers. "You were born a very lonely child. I see pain with your father. You're a creative soul sent to our planet with a specific purpose. You'll discover contentment and happiness." She also told him he would marry and become a father.

Dave rationalized she may have been doing nothing more than generalizing, but as

he stood up to leave, Lauren looked at him and told him one more thing.

"Oh yes, I forgot to tell you. They said you'll write and publish a book."

They? Dave thought as he walked away.

But Lauren's book prediction impressed even Nora, who wondered, *What are the chances she could have known something like that?*

Once outside, they peeked at their pocket campus map. "This restaurant sounds fun, Dave," Nora said.

They walked to Wilder Hall for lunch at The Rathskeller. The Bavarian-themed restaurant in the building's basement sold food to the students and the town's residents. It was one of those places where the townies could mingle with the Obies.

They squeezed into a dark wooden booth that looked like it had been there forever. They looked at the menu on the wall and both agreed on a hamburger and fries.

After they finished, Dave suggested to Nora, "Hey, let's scope out the Carnegie Library. That's where we will do most of our research work."

At the circulation desk, an extremely helpful supervisor introduced himself and went on a short dissertation. "Well-known philanthropist Andrew Carnegie gifted this noble sandstone building to the college in 1908. The Chicago architects Patton and Miller designed it. You'll do most of your research in the biographical library room, and there's also a large reading room. You'll find more information on the wall directory."

Dave looked at the supervisor. "I need to know where the restroom is located, but thanks for all that."

"Dave, I want to go see the Allen Memorial Art Museum," Nora said.

As they approached, she recognized the ornate Italian Renaissance-style facade with its district fountain in front. "This dates to 1917. It's one of the country's best college and university art museums. I read that its collection includes paintings, sculptures, decorative arts, and so much more. I'm finding myself more interested in sculpting."

After finishing their self-guided tour, they roamed Tappan Square and sat on a park bench to compare students.

"Do you notice the clothes they're all wearing?" Nora asked. "Everybody seems to have on jeans and T-shirts, Dave." The two had already purchased trendy new clothes for the semester, but they decided they may have wasted their money if few students wore them. The boys had longer hair, and the girls favored granny glasses.

Walking back to their car, they beheld a group of young Asian students taking photographs of a large stone memorial. Dave read the bronze plaque on the monument. "Nora, it says *Memorial Arch, Dedicated in 1902*."

"I read that they erected the stone arch to honor the thousands of missionaries with Oberlin connections who died in the Chinese Boxer Rebellion of 1900."

With the start of classes less than a week away, and excited by what they had seen, the two drove home to Cooper's Cove.

⁓

STEVEN CONRAD AND Christopher Brighton were enjoying cocktails on their waterfront deck after closing the antique shop for the evening. Steven was unhappy in Cooper's Cove. He still harbored unpleasant memories of what it had been like growing up gay there. Many times, he still felt like an outcast. He knew how the Austin family must have felt when they arrived in town. Many still snubbed him, and he'd be grateful for their return to Key West in the fall, where he could be his true self.

Diane helped make the summers a bit more bearable.

They met for coffee twice a week at the diner. She enjoyed bringing him up to date on the whereabouts of their former classmates, and the two rehashed the olden days. Diane laughed at his jokes, and he sometimes felt it was 1930 all over again. Little did he realize she still harbored feelings for him.

"So. What's been going on with the two of you?" she asked.

"Not much, other than the business at the store is doing great, and I'll give Christopher credit for that. I've been working on another script for a writer's friend in LA. Most of us have retired by now, but we keep in touch."

"Do you ever miss acting? What was it like being in front of the camera, knowing millions of people could watch you?"

Steven laughed. "Well, I don't think it was millions, Diane. I was only a B-list actor, you know. But, yes, sometimes I miss it. I've found that being a writer is just as rewarding as being an actor. Without our words, they wouldn't have a job!"

"I forgot to tell you. Bertha Murkowski has been nagging me to ask her over when both of you can be there."

"Bertha Murkowski! I can't believe you're still friends with her. Isn't she the town gossip?"

"Yup," Diane told him. "She tells me all the latest dirt I must share with you."

Steven just shook his head.

UNLIKE HIS PARTNER, Christopher had taken a liking to Cooper's Cove. He inventoried the antique store and chatted with the tourists when they shopped. He knew it embarrassed Steven when he flaunted his gayness in public and told his partner, "Girl, there's no way I'm going back in the closet for anyone! If they can't handle someone like me being in their face, it's their problem, not mine!"

Since the riots at Stonewall, Christopher had allowed no one to tell him how he was supposed to act or who he was supposed to love. He'd made unexpected new friends during his summer liaisons in the town. One of those was Bertha. The two first met at the Brass Buckle's grand opening while she was waiting in line to get Steven's autograph.

She told Christopher, "You know, honey, your boyfriend, or whatever you call him, was the most handsome man in high school back then. Were you aware of that?"

Christopher lowered his rose-colored sunglasses to the tip of his nose. He adjusted the white ascot around his dusty rose satin shirt and told her, "No, honey, I didn't. But did you know he has a big penis?"

Bertha roared with laughter and knew she had just found her new best friend. Few people had been any match for Bertha's crude mouth until she'd met Christopher. He'd mistakenly told her he had been a hairstylist at Warner Brothers, and Bertha wanted to know all the secrets of the stars. "Was Marilyn's hair really that blonde, or did she bleach it?"

"Oh darling, I've sworn to secrecy on that one," he teased.

"You know, we have a couple here in town that have been married and divorced four times," she divulged.

"No, I didn't know that. Tell me all about it."

She began. "Well, it's Louise Shamp and Ed Persty. She runs the gift shop, and Ed runs the stamping press at the tool and die. They both lost their spouses about fifteen years ago now. They lived right across the street from each other. And, after their spouses died, they started seeing each other.

"They'd known each other for years, anyway. They found out they both enjoyed the same things and got hitched. The first marriage lasted about a year, then Louise told him she'd had enough and was moving back across the street into her old house.

"About two months later, they began speaking to each other, and before ya knew it, they were married again. That one lasted three years, until Louise found out Ed had been doing the coat check gal at the Elk's Lodge, so she filed for divorce and moved out.

"Another two years went by, and they got lonely for each other. They ran off to Niagara Falls to get married for the third time. Louise told everyone this one was for keeps. Well, only six months passed, and Ed told Louise he'd had enough of her bullshit this time, so he filed for divorce and sent her packing back to her house.

"And, just like their three previous marriages, they decided they couldn't stay away from each other and got hitched for the fourth time. That was about two years ago. But this time, they stayed in their own houses, just in case."

After contemplating the implausible tale, Christopher told her, "I'll have to make sure I tell Steven about that one. It sounds like it would make a fabulous screenplay!"

"Oh honey, you haven't heard the best of it," she told him. "I have more where that came from."

"Darling, I'm certain you do!"

BERTHA WAS THE biggest gossip in town and had a foul mouth that would make a trucker blush. After her husband died, she spoke to the Reverend Kingston after the funeral. "He was a wonderful soul. He was always so kind and thoughtful," she admitted. "Oh, and the dick on that man! He sure made me happy all those years."

The Reverend hurried away with a red face. Bertha couldn't understand what she had said to offend him.

Most of the time, she sat in her La-Z-Boy watching television. Her favorite game show was Match Game with Gene Rayburn. She told everyone she loved watching it. "And that Fanny Flagg! She puts me in stitches with her innocent Southern charm and dirty little sense of humor. She's always sitting in the bottom right-hand corner next to Richard Dawson, and I laugh my ass off when those two go at it."

One sweltering summer afternoon, the mailman had a special delivery package for Bertha that she needed to sign for. He knocked on the door. Bertha was hard of hearing and hadn't heard him.

He peeked in. Bertha was sitting in her recliner in front of the window air conditioner. He later told Dale Crandall, "There she was, laying in that big old recliner with her legs spread. She had her house dress hiked up to her panties, and that air conditioner was blowing nice cool air up there."

That was too much for the poor mailman, so he signed her name and dropped the package at her doorstep.

Her neighbors and friends knew Bertha to have a heart of gold. She liked to cook and share her Polish recipes with her neighbors. Pierogies, cabbage rolls, and schnitzel were her favorites, and she gave everyone her prize-winning makowiec, a Polish poppy seed cake, every Christmas.

She weighed nearly 200 pounds, most likely the result of sampling her cooking.

THE FALL SESSION at Oberlin got underway, and the first-year students found themselves acclimating to college dormitory life. Dave shared a room at Burton Hall with Matt, an expected psychology protégé from Berkeley. Dave thought he was a blast.

Nora and her roommate, Veronica, lived in the all-female wing at Dascomb Hall. Her fellow art student was from New York City. The pair discovered they shared an interest in more than their skin color and college majors. Both liked to collect beach glass and were fans of the Beatles. They even attended some of the same art classes.

Dave and Matt were studying in their dorm room. Matt was lying on his twin bed, perusing a psychology text. Dave was at his student study desk typing on the Royal Aristocrat typewriter his mother had given him as his going-away present. He'd spent the day at the Carnegie Library researching the Underground Railroad's history and was compiling his notes. He'd discovered Oberlin had been a major stop for formerly enslaved people on their trek to freedom from the southern plantation property owners.

Matt glanced over at Dave. "Do you think we are alone here?"

Dave looked around their room. "Seems like we are."

"No, I mean, do you think humans are the only ones who inhabit the planet? Think about it. We speak different languages in different parts of the world to communicate. Who do you think taught us those languages? They've most likely been here and probably still are."

Dave already knew his roomie was a Trekkie who meditated for one hour each morning. "You mean like an alien life?" he asked.

"Yeah. I wonder if they may be here among us at this very moment. How do we know if the privileged people of the planet who control so much aren't members of another race with higher intelligence? They want to ensure we don't blow ourselves up in a thermonuclear blast."

"Well, then, maybe they were here in 1962. Matt, are you an alien?"

"No, just a normal dude who likes to probe and ask questions."

"I like the wild things you come up with, man. It might be true. People need to listen to what their hearts are telling them and trust in themselves." After his session with psychic Lauren, Dave had a newfound respect for New Age theory.

Matt approached life from a more noetic view. "I believe humans rationalize what you just told me. They don't always think or do what their heart tells them. They become humans doing, instead of human beings. Hey, you wanna get high?"

Dave knew he wasn't talking about alcohol, which was forbidden on campus. He'd never tried weed. The out-of-town summer kids got high back home, but in Cooper's Cove, the subject remained taboo for anyone who lived there. He admitted, "I'm curious what the stuff does to you."

"What do you say we go smoke a little?"

They walked off campus to a deserted alleyway. Matt pulled a joint out of his shirt pocket. He lit up and handed it to Dave. "Just be careful. Don't inhale too much your first time."

Dave took it and took a deep puff. He started hacking, and his eyes began watering.

Matt just stood there laughing. "Dude, I told you not to inhale that much!"

They passed the joint back and forth while they walked, and Matt continued expounding upon life. "Too bad everyone doesn't use Mary Jane. If all the world leaders tried it, more wars probably wouldn't exist."

Dave couldn't believe the sensations he was experiencing. Every negative thought in his mind was gone, replaced with an incredible awareness of being present. Even colors appeared more brilliant. He noticed the azure sky contrasting with the chromatic leaves of the changing fall foliage. "Man, I can't believe I waited this long to try it. I feel energized and alive. I guess people who shun it have never tried it. I want to go back to the dorm and write some more."

"Nothing wrong with that, dude. I bet you find you're more originative on the shit."

Slowly, they strolled back through Tappan Square. Dave noticed other kids in the park with smiles who seemed happier than others. Now he understood why.

LATER IN THE semester, Nora played matchmaker. She suggested to Dave a double date with Matt and Veronica. "I think they'd hit it off well. I've seen Matt looking at her with more than just a casual glance. And I know she feels the same. She told me she thought he was an intellectual cutie who reminded her of John Lennon."

That week, Dave asked Matt, "How do you feel about women of color? Nora seems to think you have an interest in her roommate. She wants us to double date."

"Sure. She's one foxy chick!"

THEY MET AT the Tap House, a popular eatery along College Street, and ordered low-alcohol beer and shared a fourteen-inch sausage and pepperoni pizza with black olives and mushrooms. Oberlin was a dry town, with no liquor served, but some restaurants served the lower alcohol beverage to those under twenty-one.

Matt and Veronica seemed to like each other. Dave and Nora listened intently as Veronica revealed more about herself to Matt. "I believe nothing is unattainable if you put your mind to it. Why settle for second-best when you know you can finish first?"

"I agree. Self-worth plays a role in all of that, Veronica. Too often, people seem to give up before the miracle they were hoping for happens. It's a matter of perception. It's never too late to change how we see ourselves."

Dave contemplated Veronica's message as he sat watching his girlfriend. He found himself ever more in love with Nora.

The four gobbled down their pizza.

"Dave?" Veronica asked. "How are you coming with your book?"

He glanced at Nora to gauge her reaction to Veronica's inquiry. He'd been poking around, inquiring about her experience with social injustice and those who festered their hatred toward her race. He later wrote what she told him in his journal. "I'm still in the research stage. I am coming up with my plot and storylines. I'm trying to flesh out my characters and always editing and re-editing. But I promise, you guys will be the first to know when it's finished."

After pizza, they went to the Apollo Theater to see *The Exorcist*. After seeing Linda Blair's head spin around and vomit on the priest, all four agreed to swear off horror flicks for a while.

7

MARIO STILL MISSED his old pal. He'd known Dave for what seemed like an eternity, and now Dave wouldn't even take his calls. Mario was surprised to hear Dave's voice on the other end of the telephone line after the phone rang and he had answered it.

"Hey, douchebag, you feel like hanging out tonight?"

"Dave! Hey buddy. I've missed you! Let's grab a couple of brewskis and hash things over. Ah, you meant me and you, right?"

"Nora's coming along too, man. What, you think I wouldn't ask her to come?"

"Look, what you do with your girlfriend is your business, but I don't want to hang with her if you catch my drift, Dave."

"Yeah, I catch your drift, Mario, and I've had it with you. I thought I would give you another chance. You're a fucking bigot, and I don't want to hang with you anymore, either!" Dave hung up and vowed not to call him again.

Mario moped around for a few weeks before he realized Dave was serious about not being seen with him.

Screw him, Mario thought. *Who needs him, anyway?*

He went to drown his sorrows at Smitty's Bar, getting drunk and hoping to replace his trusted ally with someone else. He saw an attractive girl, a few years older than him, place a dime in the jukebox, and Charlie Rich began singing "Behind Closed Doors."

Mario was winning at a game of pool and noticed the girl return to the bar. She appeared drunk and was getting sloppy with a man much older than she who was buying her drinks.

Mario was drunk by now and tottered over. "You need me to rescue you from this dude?"

She looked Mario in his eyes and told him, "I can fend for myself. Thank you."

Mario took a place on the empty stool on the other side of her. "I'm sure you can, but I think you can do much better than this old troll."

The older gentleman gave him a nasty sneer, got up, and walked away.

"Look, cutie; I just want to be left alone. I had a fight with my husband. We're always arguing, and it seems like all we can do is stay home and watch TV. Shit! He doesn't even want to have sex with me anymore! We're too fucking young to act like an old couple."

Mario heard his cue and moved in. His eyes glistened

with desire. "So, your husband's not much in that department, huh? Maybe you're looking for a hot, younger surrogate to step in and help?"

~

HE'S SO VAIN, she thought. *But he is hot.* The dark-haired, cocky Italian seemed the opposite of her pasty, boring husband at home. "Pretty straightforward, aren't you?" she asked.

"I believe in getting straight to the point. I have my dad's van from the winery in the parking lot. The cargo department is empty, and it's carpeted. Does that work for you?"

She chugged the rest of her drink. "Why not?"

They went outside, where Mario banged her in the van. She got off four times as the virile Mario did things to her that her husband never had. He was a "three pumps, a squirt, roll over, and go to sleep" kind of guy.

Afterward, they went back inside. Mario kept looking at her and finally seemed to recognize her. "You're Christy Peters. You went to Cooper's Cove High, and your boyfriend Kevin Jamison was on the football team in sixty-eight when they won the state championship."

"I am. And he's not my boyfriend anymore; he's my husband." Christy had sobered up and realized Mario may also have known her parents owned the Pizza Shack, which she managed. Kevin was the dishwasher there, the same job he had held since high school.

They both agreed the entire evening was better off

forgotten. Christy assured him he had nothing to worry about since she was on the pill. She added, "Kevin probably wouldn't care, even if I told him."

When she got home, he was asleep on the couch in front of the TV, as usual. Johnny Carson was delivering his one-liners on NBC's *The Tonight Show*.

She thought of telling him what she had done but shook her head and went to bed.

DAVE AND NORA went home for Thanksgiving to celebrate the holiday, and Grace invited Dave and his mother for a Thanksgiving dinner. She pulled out all the stops with her menu, including seared duck breast with lingonberry sauce, twice-baked potatoes, a green bean casserole, and a homemade sweet potato pie with whipped cream.

After dinner, they enjoyed their dessert in the living room. Kathleen told her, "Grace, everything was delicious, and this pie is addictive! Where did you get the recipe?"

"Thank you! It was my mother's, and it's been in my family for generations."

"It's also my favorite," Ben said. "It's one of the many reasons I asked this phenomenal lady for her hand in marriage."

The couple had met while he was attending law school. She'd been a cook at a popular off-campus eatery, Ben's Chili (no relation to him), and he'd asked her for the secret ingredients.

She told Kathleen, "He tried charming the recipe out of me, and when that didn't work, he asked me to marry him!"

"Not only is she a terrific cook; I don't think I would have made it through law school without her. I consider her my most trusted advisor."

The couple's devotedness touched Kathleen. "You seem like a perfect match. My husband, Frank, and I also complemented one another."

"Yes, we heard of his untimely death. Everyone's told me how well-liked he was here."

Dave and Nora had been listening to their parents' conversation. "Nora and I have something to tell you all," Dave announced. "I've asked her to marry me. With your permission, of course, sir."

Ben asked his daughter, "Nora? Are you in love with him?"

"Yes, Daddy. I am, and I want to marry him."

"Dave! I'd consider it an honor to have you as my son-in-law." Ben stood and shook Dave's hand. He turned and hugged his daughter. "It's hard to believe our baby girl is getting married. We're both so happy for you."

Grace still had doubts about the biracial couple becoming man and wife, even though she'd seen how much they loved one another.

Kathleen already knew they did. She'd assumed the couple's announcement would be forthcoming; she just didn't know when.

"But we haven't set a date yet," Nora reminded everyone.

Dave joked, "I guess this means we are past going steady, right, Nora?"

"Yeah Dave. I guess a little."

MARIO WASN'T IN a festive holiday mood. The day before, Christy had called the winery and told him she needed to see him, that she had something essential to talk to him about.

They met at the diner where Molly worked. She noticed the pair walk in and she wondered, *Why are they together?* They sat at the counter, and Molly gave them menus and poured their coffee. She knew Christy was married to Kevin. "So, what brings you guys in?"

"The town council has granted Dad a liquor permit for the Pizza Shack, and Mario has been so kind as to help us select a wine menu."

Molly wondered if that was why they were there or if it could have been something else. She'd heard that Christy had been alone on more than one occasion getting drunk at Smitty's, and she surmised it might have to do with that. "Would either of you like to order something?"

"No, thank you," Christy answered.

Molly went into the kitchen.

Christy glanced around to see if anyone was listening. "I'm pregnant," she told Mario.

"What? How can that be? You said you were on the pill!"

"My doctor told me it doesn't work one hundred percent

of the time, and I guess when you and I did it, that was one of those times."

"But how do you know it's mine? What about Kevin?"

"Like I told you, Kevin and I haven't had sex in months. It has to be yours."

"And you haven't slept with anyone else, right?"

"Of course I haven't been with anyone else! Only you. And I'm keeping the baby."

Mario freaked out. "What are you talking about?"

"Relax, Mario. Kevin knows it's not his. I told him what happened and, as I said, he didn't care. He just told me he would not be part of raising it." Christy had concerns about who the baby might look like. If it looked like Mario, people might wonder how a fair-skinned couple had an olive-skinned baby. But she already had an excuse for that. If the baby looked like Mario, she could tell everyone it resembled her grandfather, who was also Italian. "Mario don't worry! I don't want you more involved with this than you already are. No one needs to know about it. I'll handle it on my own."

But Mario had a different scenario playing out in his head. He may have just found the perfect replacement for his friend Dave. A child! He was going to be a father! His parents had told him he needed to grow up and accept some responsibility. What more responsibility than being a father? He couldn't contain his enthusiasm and told her, "I think this is great news! This is the best news of my life! I'm going to be a dad!"

Christy moaned, "No, Mario, you don't understand! I

thought it was only right to let you know you got me pregnant, but I don't want anyone to know what happened between us. I'm going to raise him." But then, she thought, *This could work out to my advantage. Kevin doesn't care. Mario's dad is rich, and Mario gets whatever he wants. He can pay for the expense of raising a child. I know Kevin's not going to.*

THE MONTHS WENT by, and Mario was acting manic. More than he usually did. He knew he couldn't tell anyone he would be a daddy come July, but that didn't stop him from acting like one. He bought expensive baby gifts Christy told him she needed.

Bertha Murkowski was shopping at the new Kmart store recently opened at Riley's shopping plaza. She saw Mario studying the strollers in the baby department and went over and asked, "Mario, why in the world are you looking at baby carriages? Is there something I should know?"

"Hi, Mrs. Murkowski. I heard Kevin and Christy Jamison are expecting. I know they earn little working at the Pizza Shack, so I thought I'd help them."

"Why Mario! How considerate of you!"

IT SEEMED LIKE Mario was over at the Jamisons' house every day to talk about the baby. Kevin, at first, had resented him being there, but he couldn't help but like the guy. They'd both played football, and he thought Mario had great humor. The shyer Kevin appreciated Mario's straightforwardness. And the idea of Mario footing the bill made it easy to allow him to hang around. *So what if the baby isn't mine? Mario keeps Christy busy and out of my face. I didn't want to be a father.*

But it also made Kevin feel like a loser. He was twenty-five and still washing dishes for a living. He didn't have the initiative to do anything else.

CHRISTY HAD GROWN tired of that. Kevin no longer resembled the attractive football star she'd once known. Looking at him, she saw a sad, overweight, pathetic young man she no longer found desirable.

But she knew Mario had no place in their lives besides the financial aspect. Mario had become a control freak, driving her batty! She told Kevin, "If he had his way, he'd probably move in with us."

INSTEAD, SEEING THE vacant lot for sale next to the Jamisons' house, the wheels turned in Mario's head. He asked his parents if they'd give him the money to build a new home.

Rationalizing it to his father, Mario explained, "Dad,

Anthony got his place and moved out when he was eighteen. There's an empty lot for sale here in town. I could build a house. It'd be a great investment, right?"

His proposal impressed Rocco and Joyce. They both thought it was a good idea. Perhaps their work-shy son was finally growing up and willing to do something more with his life. They hoped Mario would display some of the same initiative his older brother had.

Anthony was now the general manager of the winery. So far, Mario had been content with working a part-time shift on the loading dock and spending most of his time hitting on cute girls at the wine tastings.

Mario knew building a new house would take too long. He needed to speed things up. He ordered a prefabricated modular home that would be ready for the lot in two weeks. The schemer seemed to have everything scoped out.

His dad seemed oblivious to the sudden devotion his son had developed to the Jamisons. But Joyce took notice. She assumed her son was putting someone else's needs before his, and that he may have moved away from his self-centeredness.

His former friend's peculiar behavior also intrigued Dave. While home from college, he drove by Mario's new digs and saw him in the Jamisons' yard. *What is he doing?* Dave wondered. *He has nothing in common with the Jamisons. If I know Mario, there must be something in it for him.*

Little did Dave know, the growing baby in Christie's womb belonged to his erstwhile friend.

"PUSH, CHRISTY, PUSH!" Mario pleaded as she gave birth to a healthy baby boy. He held her hand in the delivery room while Kevin sat in the expectant fathers' waiting room watching a Cleveland Indians baseball game.

Kevin had called Mario and told him they were leaving for the hospital. At the admitting desk, Mario had looked at Kevin and told him, "I think I should be with Christy. Why don't you go watch the game?"

Kevin glanced up and saw the game tied at the top of the ninth. He shrugged and sat to watch.

Christy was in no mood to argue with anyone, so Mario got his way. The attending physician and nurse thought it odd that Mario was by her side instead of the father. They assumed it was none of their business.

When Mario saw his son, he blurted, "Christy, he looks just like your grandpa! Let's name him Dino."

The doctor and nurse inspected the olive-skinned baby and the Italian holding him. Now, they knew for sure it was none of their business.

THE BIG NEWS of the summer of 1974 was the resignation of President Richard Nixon in August. The botched burglary of the Democratic National Headquarters in 1972 had finally led to his fall from grace, and he announced to the nation he was stepping down as president.

Vice President Gerald Ford assumed office the next day and unconditionally pardoned the ex-president. He said the nation needed to move on and heal from the Watergate affair.

Wilson McGuire decided Dave should write the editorial about Nixon. He told his young colleague, "You've been following Nixon since sixty-eight. You've been active in the anti-war protests and pro-choice rallies as well. I think you should write this editorial."

Dave was proud his editor had such confidence in him. He gathered his thoughts and devised the editorial for the next edition.

THIS WEEK'S EDITORIAL COMMENT
BY DAVE MEYERS, CITY NEWS DESK

Nixon has resigned, and the nation can move on from the scandal that has plagued the administration for two years. Nixon attempted to cover his lies and even told us he wasn't a crook. He may not have been a crook in the conventional sense of the word, but he knew about the break-in, then attempted to cover it up.

Our President lied and got caught. Most of us know he is guilty, Republicans and Democrats alike.

Nixon only has himself to blame. He acted deceitfully and tried to cover everything up in the hope the public would believe his claim that the press was the enemy of the people. He also fired the special Watergate prosecutor and his attorney general.

The people did not believe him. They felt no president was above the law.

Ford may have done the nation a great injustice by pardoning the man. However, Nixon's previous supporters should be commended for refusing to stand behind him.

For that, justice may have been served.

A NASTY RECESSION gripped the nation that year, and the oil price skyrocketed following the Arab Oil Embargo. The economy tanked, and stores such as Western Auto and Rexall Drug went out of business, leaving two more vacant storefronts downtown.

Trish Higgins had accepted early retirement from Austin Tool and Die and told her friends she had too much time on her hands. She joked, "Heidi may enjoy gardening, but the closest I want to come to planting a peony is watching my lover do it."

She missed not working and realized she'd made a mistake. Trish was fifty-eight, and Heidi was now seventy-six. The perception of their age difference seemed more significant.

While Trish's face may have aged, she still maintained her youthful physique.

Heidi had become frail. Her memory had also been failing.

Trish entered their kitchen after supper one night and found her mate had left the stove burner lit again. Another time, she discovered Heidi's car keys inside the freezer.

Heidi also sensed something was wrong. She got lost while driving home from the grocery and had to ask for directions home. The days seemed to rush by, and she paid little attention to the time, other than knowing her own was slipping away. She often stared into the mirror, where she saw a split face. On one side was a beautiful young woman with youthful skin; on the other, the wrinkled older woman she had become.

She asked the reflection of the older side staring back: "What happened to the beautiful young girl you once were? Where has she gone?"

Her only concern was her companion of the last twenty-five years. She wished to ensure Trish would be okay without her.

Trish acted as Heidi's personal trainer in their basement workout room, encouraging her to practice light resistance training exercises to increase her muscle strength and tone and protect her aging joints from injury. Occasionally, the couple drove to a new gym that had recently opened in Cleveland. On their ride home from there one day, Heidi told her girlfriend, "We need a health club like that in Cooper's Cove."

Trish thought it was her usual babble. "There's just one problem, Heidi. We need money to do that."

"Well, that may not be a problem. I've invested wisely over the years, and I have the means. We both know the population grows daily and for God's sake, they crowd the high school weight room and pool at night. A modern gym makes perfect financial sense."

"Babe, you would do that for me?"

"You know I would. I love you. I loved you the first time I saw your beautiful eyes watching me at that golf tournament."

Trish, touched by her partner's uncommon display of affection, replied, "I love you. And it's you who has the beautiful eyes."

Once back in Cooper's Cove, they stopped at the traffic signal on Main Street in front of the vacant stores. Heidi gazed at the empty businesses and admitted to Trish, "It's such a shame. I remember shopping at those when I was younger and look at them now." She continued staring into the empty buildings. "Trish, we may have the perfect location for your new health club."

JUST AS STEVEN and Christopher had been required to do, the women applied to change the zoning to permit the construction of a new health club. A good deal of the townspeople opposed progress, but the council approved it after another hearing.

Ed Persty and Pete York were having breakfast the next day at the diner. Ed picked up a copy of the *Courier* and noticed the headline announcing the permit approval. "You know Pete, it's bad enough the Austins took over this town, and those two queers opened the antique shop. But now we have two dykes running a gym. What the hell is next?"

Pete looked up from reading the sports section. "Probably one of them queer bars."

THE DYNAMIC HEALTH Club became a reality in the spring of 1975. The facade fit the trend of the changing town, and they demolished interiors to make room for a 7,500-square-foot gym with separate men's and women's workout areas. Cybex and Universal Weight Machines took up most of the space. An indoor pool, jacuzzi, and saunas were in the new addition behind the original structure.

Nora purchased a couple's gym membership and finally talked Dave into going. "Come on, Dave, just try it?" she pleaded.

Lifting weights had never inspired him. He thought bodybuilders out to impress everyone were idiots. He'd been to the gym at Oberlin. "Haven't you ever noticed the muscle dudes, Nora? They seem to get off on flexing in front of the mirrors. They go to the gym in hoodies, even in hot weather, then pull them off to show off their physiques. And why are they constantly tugging on their weenies through their gym shorts while talking to each other?"

Nora looked at him strangely.

"What? Is it a macho thing, or do those guys think it will make their dicks bigger? Who are they trying to impress?"

When they got to the gym, "Philadelphia Freedom" by Elton John thundered across the multi-speaker sound system. Nora curiously glanced around to see if Dave's description of bodybuilders was accurate.

"Nora, I feel out of place here."

"Everyone has to start somewhere. Let me show you how to use the cable crossover machine."

Dave took hold of the handles. As Nora instructed, he pulled them together, gathering all his strength, gritting his teeth as he did so. He watched the dormant muscles in his chest, shoulders, and arms contract while he observed himself in the mirror. Nora led him through a series of sets, and Dave seemed to enjoy it.

After their workout, they soaked their sore muscles in the Jacuzzi. "Nora? Maybe I do want to get bigger. My muscles hurt, but it's a good hurt. I want to look like him." Dave pointed to a chiseled muscle hunk by the side of the pool who was flexing his biceps for his girlfriend.

"My, haven't we changed our attitude?" She moved closer to him in the bubbling whirlpool and felt his penis through his swim trunks. She teased, "Don't get too big. You're plenty big enough where it counts."

THE TWO DEDICATED their summer to daily workouts. Nora was already in beautiful form, but with a change in his diet, Dave added thirty-five pounds of solid muscle to his 140-pound frame in three months. He added two inches to his chest and an inch and a half to each arm.

At one workout, he was wearing a tank top and bench pressing close to his body weight when he heard someone on the weight bench next to him. "Looking good, Dave! Keep it up!"

He glanced over and recognized his junior high physical education instructor. Recalling his Charlie Brown humiliation at the hands of the coach, Dave grabbed his workout towel and sat to face him. He was about to mock him like the coach had done to him. Instead, he used his towel to wipe his brow. "Thanks, coach!" He shook the coach's hand, then he and Nora walked away.

"Dave? I'm so proud of you. You could have let him have it."

"Why? Shaming the shamer never works. It's better this way."

THINGS GOT EVEN weirder between Mario and the Jamisons. He went all over town with Dino, and people talked. He doted on the toddler more than Christy ever did.

She freely surrendered Dino whenever he asked. It gave her more time to enjoy her wine, courtesy of Mario, and blot out her reality.

Bertha saw Mario with Dino at the post office. "Mario, I notice you've not only bought the Jamisons a baby stroller, but you're also pushing him around. How nice it is to see you helping. And look at the cute fellow's eyes." Bertha stopped short of saying anything further, even though she thought the child had too many similarities to Mario. But, using the grandfather look-alike excuse, Mario was very convincing.

Bertha still had her suspicions.

Christy knew it had been wrong to lie to everyone. But she had no choice. The entire affair had evolved into a complete mess. She'd never dreamed Mario would take it this far. She couldn't further complicate matters by admitting the child belonged to him. Mario had already taken the boy to his parents' house, and they often treated the child like a foster grandson.

Her parents acted strangely in the baby's presence. Christy knew her mom had her doubts. Her grandfather may have been Italian, but her mother had told her daughter the now-deceased man had blonde hair, which a small share of Italians do.

MOLLY KINGSTON'S SON Alex was three years old. She was grateful for her job at the diner and for the kindness Russ had shown her, but she told him she needed to do more with her life and planned on opening a child's day-care center. As a working mom, she knew how vital child care was, and she saw an opportunity to prosper with a new career in demand.

With her boss's encouragement and financial support, she leased space and started Happy Faces Day Care Center.

Christy suggested to Kevin it might be a good idea for Dino to attend Molly's child care. "This way, Mario can't spend as much time around him. People are getting suspicious."

"Whatever you think." Kevin turned back to his favorite episode of *Scoobie-Doo*.

DAVE AND NORA came home for another break between semesters their junior year. They'd been shopping at the plaza, and Dave saw Mario with Dino.

"The dude's been acting so weird taking this Jamison kid everywhere! I just don't get it, Nora."

Nora wasn't as naïve. She'd had suspicions from the very beginning. She'd recognized right off the likenesses between Mario and Dino and seemed to understand his preoccupation with the child, but she felt it wasn't her place to say anything. She knew Dave had cut Mario out of his life because of her. She also knew the duo had been inseparable buddies since kindergarten.

Mario's bigotry had become a non-starter for Dave, so she kept quiet when Dave talked about Mario and Dino. She knew someday Dave might figure it out, but until he did, mum would be the word.

8

 it out there in the universe, and his dream became a reality in early 1977 when the highly respected publishing house Simon & Schuster offered to buy his book.

He planned to spring the excellent news on Nora, Matt, and Veronica at The Tap Room. Everyone in the eating establishment was watching the coverage of President Jimmy Carter's inauguration. As they sat down, Dave joked, "Who would have thought? We've elected a peanut farmer from Georgia as our president. I think he's going to be good for this country."

They chose the manager's unique pizza, a combination of pepperoni, sausage, mushrooms, black olives, green peppers, and onions with extra cheese, and four low beers.

Dave couldn't contain his enthusiasm any longer. "Okay,

you're all aware I've been working on my book for a while now, right?"

Nora bit into a slice and tried talking with her mouth full. "It's been more than a while."

Dave looked amused. "Okay, I probably deserved that. But I sold my book today. One of the best publishing houses in New York picked it up! "

Nora practically choked on her pizza and threw her arms around her fiancé. She wiped her mouth with a napkin and kissed his face several times.

The other diners were watching. "Stop, Nora! You're embarrassing me!"

Matt shook his index finger. "That's radical, dude." Veronica offered her congratulations.

"Why did you feel you needed to keep something like this from me, Dave?" Nora asked.

"It wasn't as if I was trying to keep it from you, Nora; it's just that if I said anything about finishing the book, I might jinx myself. And I didn't want to jinx myself. Especially after all the time and effort I put into it. It's been several years now. Guess I'm a slow learner."

"I never thought you were slow, Dave. You've taken your time to write. It's probably going to have everything you envisioned. Finish telling us about your story."

"Well, I completed the book on Halloween and mailed a copy to my creative writing professor from my sophomore year. I learned to write with passion in his classes. He told us to put ourselves in the scene when we were writing.

Show our readers what we want them to imagine. He was such a cool teacher. I greatly admired the guy and knew he would give me an unbiased critique. After he read it, he told me he thought it was an original manuscript that went beyond his expectations for a new writer like me. He's also a good friend to a literary agent in New York, Maurice Donovan. I submitted a query, and he signed me. I just heard from him about Simon and Schuster's offer."

Nora cut him off. "Dave! Tell us what he said to you!"

"The publisher offered me a $1,000 advance for my manuscript and another two percent in royalties."

"Very cool, Dave!" Matt shouted. "Now can you finally tell us the title and what it's about?"

Dave turned to Nora. "I know you told me not to write a book about racism from the viewpoint of a white author. You said there was no way I could relate to the plight of the disenfranchised and forgotten here. I understand why you told me that. But after seeing firsthand the prejudice you and your family endure and the disdain for gay couples, the town's injustice infuriated me. I had to do something with my anger. The only way I could deal with it was to channel what you told me and let you tell the story. I did nothing more than type the words. These are your words, Nora, and your experiences portrayed by my characters.

Nora looked touched.

"*We* named the book *Above the Rainbow*." He smiled at her. "*Our* story is that of an impoverished southern Black girl who felt alone, forgotten, and unloved. *Our* central character was one of five children born in Mississippi to an alcoholic father and a codependent mother in 1945. An older neighbor raped her when she was twelve, and she became addicted to drugs by age sixteen. Surmounting the hate and challenges she endured, the young girl eventually becomes the lead facilitator at a large treatment center for troubled youth in Atlanta.

"When I listened to you tell me about your experiences drifting about in a sea of hate, I envisioned a book I hoped would enable readers to see life through the eyes of an African American. I wanted them to feel what a curious African American child must feel when she looks into the eyes of a white man and fears retaliation for her smile. Nora. You were the impetus for my writing. After listening to your stories, I feel like you co-authored it. At least let me name you as a collaborator in my foreword."

Veronica cut in. "Dave, I'm moved. But even though you used Nora as your inspiration, it will take more than just you writing a book. Racism is so prevalent in our society and continues unabated. Please stop and think about it. Abraham Lincoln supposedly granted us freedom more than a hundred years ago, but some people's attitudes have not evolved, and things are not much different from what they were then."

Nora agreed with her. "Dave, I'm also touched. But change has been slow in coming, and unrest has been brewing,"

"I understand completely. You are both correct. But if I get just one person to change their mind about how they feel about this, I'll achieve what I set out to do. It all begins with one. And there's power in numbers."

"Dave, I'm stoked, dude!" Matt said. "When's the next one coming out?"

"I hope I'm able to write another, Matt. Maurice says the publisher is offering me another book deal, but I don't think I can work under that pressure."

Somehow, Nora knew he would find a way.

OBERLIN HELD A graduation ceremony at Tappan Square for the class of 1977. Dave and Nora bid their farewells to Matt and Veronica, who were going back to their respective homes. The couple had dated intermittently over the past four years, but they both felt the distance between them would be too great. Berkeley Matt wanted to pursue his psychology master's degree on the west coast, and Veronica's art history major would keep her domiciled in New York.

Dave and Nora went home to live with their respective parents. They knew their parents would not permit them to live together, so marriage remained their best option. Both were sure by now. They already felt as if they were soulmates, but their relationship wasn't perfect.

Like many young couples, they argued—and did so often. They clashed over the most insignificant issues. Sometimes, the debates got heated, with each saying things they didn't really mean. Nora thought she was always right, and Dave felt the same about his point of view.

After insulting each other more than once, they'd have

a flash of nowness and realize how silly they were even to argue. They'd both laugh about it later.

Until their following argument.

THEY BEGAN LOOKING for the perfect spot for their wedding. Dave had been reading *Frommer's Hawaii,* in which he'd learned many couples have a kahuna, a Hawaiian priest or priestess, bless their weddings, most of which were performed at a beach or other breathtaking sight found there.

They thought such a union more befitting. Neither wanted a conventional church wedding, and they did not want Reverend Kingston officiating their vows after he'd rejected his daughter.

During one of his catch-up calls with Justin Roby in Honolulu, Ben told him of Nora's intention to wed Dave, and that the couple had settled on Hawaii as their destination.

"That's wonderful, Ben! We remember Dave very well. Mary Beth and I have seen many obvious newlyweds strolling around the beach. It's an enchanting place to spend a honeymoon. There's so much to do. I realize it's their honeymoon, but they can stay with us. We have more than enough room."

"Thank you, Justin; that's very kind of you to offer, but Grace and I have already reserved an oceanfront suite at the Royal Hawaiian as a wedding gift."

"That's a gracious wedding present. We locals call it the

Pink Palace of the Pacific. It dates back to 1927. We've stayed there ourselves for our anniversary, and I must tell you, it is a destination of unparalleled luxury and romance. The kids will enjoy chilling on the beach at Waikiki. Make sure you tell them to get in touch with Mary Beth and me."

"Thank you again, Justin. I'll let them know that. Good talking with you."

A MONTH LATER, the bride and groom left for Cleveland Hopkins Airport in a chauffeured limo, courtesy of Justin and Mary Beth. At the United Airlines ticket counter, the agent handed them their tickets, and they realized Justin had graciously upgraded them to first class.

They completed the short hop to Chicago, where they boarded United's Flight One to Honolulu. Onboard, the twenty-two-year-olds enjoyed pre-departure mimosa cocktails as Don Ho's signature melody, "I'll Remember You," serenaded them over the airplane's entertainment system.

The boarding door closed, and they witnessed the professional safety demonstration by the colorfully attired flight attendants. The women wore floral-patterned muumuus, and the male flight attendants wore traditional long-sleeved Hawaiian shirts.

The Boeing 747 taxied out and roared down the runway to begin its ten-hour flight to Honolulu. After the plane leveled and the captain explained the Halfway to Hawaii game, the flight attendants reappeared in the dual-aisle jumbo jet, and the renowned first-class royal Hawaiian meal service began.

Dave and Nora were savoring Mauna Loa macadamia nuts with their Mai Tai cocktails when their flight attendant, Leilani, approached. Dave noticed how beautiful she appeared. She was striking!

Tall and slender like Nora, the flight attendant of Hawaiian descent wore a yellow plumeria in her silky black hair. "Aloha nui loa," she remarked. "Would you care for a hot towel and menu?"

Dave appeared confused by her unusual greeting.

Leilani smiled. "It's our way of expressing our happiness that you chose the friendly skies. It means to love so much."

They selected the prime rib that would be carved in the aisle next to their seats. Leilani offered them a selection of cold and hot pupus, Hawaiian appetizers. The sample included sashimi, caviar, teriyaki chicken skewers, and Chinese egg rolls with a hoisin dipping sauce.

After clearing their china, Leilani reappeared, pushing a linen-lined serving cart with a tropical floral arrangement accenting the prime rib. "Aloha again, Mr. and Mrs. Meyers. How do you care for your roast to be served?"

Dave laughed. "We are not Mr. and Mrs. yet, Leilani. We're on our way to get married."

"Oh, what a beautiful, happy couple you make! Have you chosen your locale yet?"

Dave told her, "Not yet," and asked for suggestions.

"My, we have so many beautiful spots to choose from. Have you heard of Diamond Head?"

"We have. We know friends who have a house there."

"Oh my, how blessed! If it were me, that would be my choice. It's *u'i loa.*"

"Wait, don't tell me," Dave said. "That means beautiful, right?" They'd seen photos Justin had sent and envisioned themselves committing to one another on the gracious Roby estate, with the Pacific Ocean as their backdrop.

Later, the couple watched the inflight movie, *Smokey and the Bandit,* starring Burt Reynolds and Sally Field. The flight attendants conducted a second service before landing, and they dined on sliced almond chicken salad with tropical fruits served in a carved pineapple bowl garnished with fresh coconut flakes.

Leilani returned with their refresher towels. "Mahalo to you both! I hope you enjoyed being with us today."

The plane descended into Honolulu, and the captain pointed out the extinct volcano Diamond Head and Waikiki Beach. After landing, the plane taxied to the gate, and the agent welcomed the weary travelers. "Aloha! Welcome to Honolulu. You may claim your luggage at carousel seven."

They boarded the Wiki Wiki Shuttle, which transported them to baggage claim. An older couple, casually attired in island wear, held a sign that read *Meyers Newlyweds.*

Dave and Nora both recognized them. Dave waved his hand. "Hello, Mr. and Mrs. Roby. We're surprised to see you. Do you remember my fiancé, Nora? And we aren't newlyweds yet."

"Of course we do, Dave!" Justin looked at Nora. "You're as pretty as I remember you. We wanted to make sure you saw us. We told your dad we would surprise you and offer you a ride to your hotel. I guess he may have forgotten to tell you."

Mary Beth placed Puakenikeni leis around their necks and kissed them lightly on their cheeks.

Nora detected the potent smell of the yellow-orange tubular flowers. "Thank you; they are lovely. So fragrant!"

"Their aroma is powerful. One of the sweetest-smelling flowers in Hawaii." Mary Beth asked Dave how their flight was.

"It was an incredible experience, Mrs. Roby. And thank you both for your generosity."

"We understand you'll be exchanging your vows while you're here. Do you know where?"

"Our flight attendant mentioned Diamond Beach on the flight over. From what we saw in the air, we understand why."

"That's just what I wanted to hear," Mary Beth exclaimed. "Oh, please! Let us offer you our home for your vows. It's a wonderful setting, and we won't take no for an answer."

"That's most kind of you, and we wholeheartedly accept your offer. Nora and I must adjust to the jet lag for a day or two. Can we plan it for the middle of the week?"

"That sounds marvelous! We'll handle all the arrangements. I even know of a kahuna to bless your vows. Don't worry about a thing."

They gathered their luggage from the carousel, and

when Dave saw the Roby's automobile, a 1976 white Jaguar XJ6C sedan, he let out a cat whistle. "Man, oh man, Mr. Roby. Those are some wild wheels!"

"You like it? We have three vehicles. You kids are welcome to use it for sightseeing while you're here. And please, call us Justin and Mary Beth. This is Hawaii. We're not that formal over here!"

JUSTIN MANEUVERED THE luxury sedan down Nimitz Highway. On their way to Waikiki, he briefly described what they were passing. "That's the Ala Moana Shopping Center, and when it opened in 1959, they considered it the largest shopping mall in the United States. Right across the boulevard is Ala Moana Beach Park. Its beach is over a half-mile long and great for swimming and jogging. There are one hundred acres in that park!"

He dropped the pair off at the entrance to the Royal Hawaiian Hotel. After checking in, the valet escorted them to their room and opened the door to their opulent ocean-front suite.

"My god, Dave, isn't this astonishing?"

"Nora! Look at this view of the ocean!" The sun was about to set. On the horizon, the evening sky's yellow, red, and orange colors were mesmerizing them.

Dave tipped the valet.

The man thanked him. *"Mahalo. Hau'oli i kou noho ana."*

Dave said, "So, I already know *mahalo* is thank you. I bet

the rest of it means you hope we have a good time while we're here. Or something like that?"

The valet laughed as he closed the door and gave Dave the shaka sign. "Right on, braddah!"

They eyed the inviting, luxurious queen-sized bed. Then they noticed the six-hour time difference between their watches and their ten-hour flight. They both yawned and lay down on the soft duvet.

An early consummation of their vows would have to wait. They fell asleep in their clothes, holding one another, listening to the tranquil sounds of the ocean waves rolling in.

IN THE MORNING, Dave woke to doves cooing in the expansive gardens beneath their windows. He kissed Nora as she lay there, still sleeping. "Morning, sunshine. How are you this incredible morning?"

Nora opened her eyes. "What time is it?"

"It's seven a.m."

"Seven a.m.? Dave! Can't we go back to sleep for a little while, baby? It's too early."

"Nora, it's one in the afternoon, our time. You want to sleep our honeymoon away?" He pulled back the curtains, revealing the tranquil turquoise waters of the morning ocean gently lapping against the shore.

They donned their swimsuits and flip-flops and went down to the beach. Holding hands, they drifted along the ocean's edge as the warm water ebbed in between their toes. Dave inquired, "A little warmer than Lake Erie?"

"A lot warmer!" Nora studied the ocean and saw the morning's surfers catching their waves. They make it look so easy. "I don't think I could even stand up on the board."

"I read the Waikiki beach boys give lessons, honey. Maybe we can take in one while we're here." They walked to the opposite end of Waikiki near Queen's Surf before turning around and heading back. Dave saw one of the local surfers. "Hey, man. Do you know of a good place to grab breakfast?"

"Eggs and Things, braddah. Over on Ena Road, yeah? Best fish and eggs breakfast on the island." The surfer grabbed his longboard and ran into the water.

"That's the second time we've heard that, Dave. What does 'braddah' mean?"

"Leilani told me about that while you were sleeping on the plane. The locals speak what's known as pidgin English. 'Braddah' is slang for brother. The longer you are here, the easier it is to understand. I'm starved! Let's try that place, yeah?"

Nora laughed. "Sure, braddah!"

They ate breakfast, and on their way out of the obscure eatery, Dave admitted, "I was hesitant about ordering fish for breakfast, but I'm glad I tried it. That place was awesome! The spicy Cajun ahi was so good, or 'ono' as I heard one local call it. It means good to eat."

"Then my macadamia nut pancakes were 'ono' too. The coconut syrup was decadent. What time are the Robys bringing the Jag over?"

"Around noon. What say we hit the beach until they get here?"

THEY SPENT THE rest of the morning swimming and taking in the rays. Dave suggested they try a surfing lesson as they lay there basking. Paddling out was a piece of cake, but coming in was a different story. Despite their best efforts, they couldn't stand on the boards. After five attempts, the duo chucked their idea.

Once they were back at the hotel, Justin delivered the Jag, as promised, and later that afternoon, Dave planned to drive Nora to the other side of Oahu, where they'd view a sacred Hawaiian burial site he had read about in Frommer's travel magazine. "The place I'm taking you is what the locals call 'Pu'u o Mahuka,' which means hill of escape. It's a sacred heiau, a sacrificial temple site constructed by the Hawaiians hundreds of years ago. Some say a powerful presence exists there. It sits on a 300-foot bluff overlooking Waimea Bay and has incredible views of the coasts."

Not far outside Honolulu, they saw the Dole plantation workers harvesting pineapples to be shipped to the mainland. "You know, Dave, imagining something as serene as this exists so close to Waikiki is difficult. We've gone from an urban setting to a peaceful Hawaiian paradise in minutes. And look at that ocean! It's captivating!"

After they rounded the curve at Waimea Bay, they turned and drove up Pupukea Road to the sanctuary. They stepped out of the Jag and walked along the red dirt paths surrounding a massive rectangle of stacked lava rocks.

Nora saw a stone altar covered with flowers and other offerings left by the natives. Dave noticed four native islanders, their heads bowed in prayer, standing before the altar. They respectfully moved away and walked down a path leading to the bluff's edge where they took in the sweeping panoramic view of the coast.

"Can you feel it, Nora? It feels as if hundreds of years of sacrificial worship have occurred here. Legend has it the Hawaiian goddess Pele leaped from here to Molokai. There's something special up here."

Nora closed her eyes and held onto his hand. She envisioned herself as an ancient Hawaiian girl harvesting her catch from Shark's Cove below them. The whispering winds sent chills up her spine, and she opened her eyes to take in the views of distant Ka'ena Point and the Waimea Valley surrounding them. "I feel it as well, babe."

Dave told her he had another surprise on the drive back to Honolulu. A short time later, the luxury automobile slowly ascended the twisting turns and bends of the road leading to Tantalus Lookout. "Nora, you are about to see one of the most incredible sunsets you'll ever witness!" Dave parked the car before a hidden clearing and killed the engine. "They named this spot after an ancient Hawaiian god."

The sun was slowly melting into the ocean, and they both gazed outward, hoping to glimpse the green flash as it dropped below the horizon. The hypnotic twilight skies soon changed to darkness, and the city's bright lights sparkled below. The rich, aromatic smell of Eucalyptus trees enveloped the thick evening air.

Dave turned to Nora. He had tears in his eyes. "Do you know how much I love you? I've never felt like this with anyone."

"I love you too, Dave. It feels as if I have forever. Let's get married tomorrow. Why wait?"

Alone with their thoughts, they noticed how near the heavens above appeared. It was as if they could reach out and touch the stars.

Dave had to interrupt their meditation. "Honey, we better get going. If we're getting married tomorrow, we have much to do before then."

At the hotel, Nora telephoned Mary Beth. "I'm sorry to do this, but we want to get married tomorrow."

Mary Beth laughed. "No problem, dear. I'll notify everyone."

The same as the evening before, the soon-to-be newlyweds found themselves exhausted from the day's sightseeing and fell asleep with Dave cradling his fiancé in his arms.

This time, they remembered to undress first.

IN THE MORNING, Dave woke first and nudged his still-sleeping bedmate. "Good morning, princess! Time to get up!"

Nora looked at the clock and realized it was eight a.m. "Dave, must you always be so cheerful in the morning? Don't you ever wake up in a bad mood?"

"Why? It uses less energy to be happy." He kissed her forehead before jumping in the shower.

Nora called after him. "Just one more reason I fell in love with you!" She remembered her conversation with Mary Beth the previous evening. "Dave? Can we go to that shopping center Justin showed us on the way here? I need a new dress for the wedding. Mary Beth says mine is too formal."

Dave pulled back the shower curtain and yelled, "Nora, you don't have to come up with a reason to go shopping. We all have our fetishes."

When he came out of the bathroom wrapped in his towel, Nora tossed her pillow at him. "You think you're funny, don't you? Smart ass!"

They ate breakfast again at Eggs and Things before heading to the mall. Dave parked the Jag on the upper parking level, and they explored the massive shopping enclave.

Nora noticed a sign: *Reyn's Men's Wear.* "We need to go in there. Mary Beth told me an Aloha shirt would be the most appropriate for you."

"But I brought along a tux! What's an Aloha shirt?"

"You are about to find out."

They looked around the store, and Dave liked what he saw. "These shirts look casual, but they also have a formal air. They're pretty cool looking."

A Caucasian sales clerk nearby overheard. "Yes, that's what our founder had in mind when he started the business in the fifties. He combined a casual inside-out look with an Oxford shirt flair, and our classic Reyn's Spooner shirt was born. No need for suits over here. Too hot, yeah?"

"Not at all. Your weather's perfect. My fiancé and I are getting married at a beachside ceremony, and I'll need one of your shirts."

He checked Dave out and smiled. "I have just what you need. It will look perfecto on your muscular physique."

Dave's face turned red, and Nora grinned.

"This is our traditional Hawaii tapa design. You'll notice it looks faded, but it is supposed to look like that. There's even a pocket sewn on the left-hand side."

"Very cool. It looks like I'm headed to the beach and a wedding simultaneously."

"That's the idea, exactly! Nifty robin's egg blue Aloha shirt for blonde haoles like us."

Dave appeared confused again.

"Oh, I mean white person! That's a name locals use when they refer to us. No biggie. Mostly a friendly term here. But if they don't like you, watch out!"

Dave looked at Nora and thought, *Even here, in a beautiful Eden like Hawaii, people discriminate. I guess it's part of who we are.*

Nora had Dave's purchase in hand as they left the store. "Okay, now it's my turn! Let's see what I can find."

They passed dozens of open-air shops, and Dave noticed a large department store. "Look! There's a Sears store!"

"Dave! We can splurge on something a little flashier than a dress I'd get from a mail-order catalog!" Nora noticed the mall's store directory, which included Liberty House of Hawaii. She read its description. "Yes. This one will work. It sounds like Macy's we have back on the mainland."

The couple traversed to the opposite end of the mall, where they could see the locally known department store.

Dave sat and watched Nora go from rack to rack, searching for the right outfit. "Hmm, something beachy, but with a touch of elegance…" She noticed a mannequin attired in a stunning blue bat wing sleeved blouse with white hibiscus flowers. "It will go perfectly with those white cotton culottes I saw."

Nora came out of the dressing room in her chosen garb and pirouetted in front of Dave. "So, tell me, monsieur. How do I look?"

"Ravishing! Like you always do! Everyone will think we've blended together with me in my blue Aloha shirt and you in that pretty blue top. But, then again, I guess that's what we're here doing."

~

MARY BETH RAN around like a chicken with her head cut off. She'd meticulously planned everything but felt nervous she may have omitted some vital detail. She telephoned her friend Mindy Kalani and advised her of the date change. The state of Hawaii had ordained Mindy to perform marriages. The two ladies had met while attending Unity Church in Honolulu.

Mary Beth had also visited Mindy for a reading and learned Mindy possessed the great wisdom of Hawaiian culture passed down by her Hawaiian grandfather. During Mary Beth's session with the medium, Mindy had seen into her past and communicated with Mary Beth's deceased mother. During the reading, Mary Beth said Mindy told her details only her mother could have known, and she'd provided comforting messages from beyond the grave.

Justin contributed by erecting a temporary pergola on the beach. He also secured a photographer to capture images to share with the couple's parents back on the mainland.

Mary Beth called the Liliha Bakery and requested a guava chiffon wedding cake, and she ordered native flowers and leis. A local caterer would provide light pupus for after the ceremony.

She assured Justin it would be a splendid occasion.

"YOU LOOK ADORABLE in that." Dave admired Nora's classy ensemble as they got in the Jaguar to drive to the Roby's.

"You don't look bad yourself, hottie! I'd swear I was marrying a cute blonde surfer boy." Nora had no doubts Dave was the one for her. She knew how much he loved her and would treat her with respect. He'd already proven that.

"Dave? Wouldn't it be wonderful to live here like the Robys? I seem to blend right in like you said we did."

"Yes, but consider this. Over here, I'd be the minority. But then again, no one here seems to pay much attention to people's color. It's such a melting pot. I guess it's about how you treat people. Be nice to them. They'll be friendly back to you. Like the Golden Rule. Besides, wouldn't you miss Cooper's Cove if we ever moved? We'd be so far from home."

"I would, but we could always go back to visit. That's what airplanes are for."

"Maybe," Dave said, "in a perfect world. For now, we belong in Cooper's Cove. I miss it, and we haven't been gone for a week!"

They passed by Kapi'olani Park on Kalākaua Avenue and were supposed to turn right onto Diamond Head Road, but Dave turned the opposite way.

Nora caught it. "Dave! You made a wrong turn! You should have turned right!"

"No, I did not, Nora! I know where I'm going, and I don't need you telling me how to drive! Mind your own business."

Nora's temper took over. "Don't talk to me like that, mister. I'm soon to be your wife. Remember?"

"Well then, maybe we shouldn't get married!" Dave immediately heard what he had just said and stopped dead in his tracks. He started smiling. "Nora, listen to us. We were arguing right before we exchange our vows. I'm sorry. I didn't mean any of it."

"I'm sorry too." But she still got the last word in. "Did you notice I was right?"

Dave laughed as he turned the car around and headed in the correct direction. When they saw the classic Hawaiian beachfront homes, they recognized the distinctive gates at one of them and knew they had found the valid address.

Dave pressed a call button. The adjoining copper gates, both etched with porpoises, swung wide. He maneuvered the Jaguar into the *mauka*, or mountain, side of the beautiful white beachside villa. It reminded him of Mr. Roarke's home on ABC's *Fantasy Island*. He parked in front of one garage, curious about which cars sat behind the other two doors.

As they got out of the car, Justin and Mary Beth were there to greet them. "*E komo mai!*" said Mary Beth to welcome them. "You're almost right on time."

"We would have been, but Dave made us late!"

"I did not, Nora!"

Justin and Mary Beth laughed. "You know Mary Beth, I think they'll suit each other. They're not even married, and already they're arguing. Please. Come in! Let us show you around." Justin opened the monkeypod wooden door.

Inside, they paid little attention to Mary Beth's gracious furnishings. Instead, their eyes were riveted to the floor-to-ceiling windows framing the enchanting view of the Pacific Ocean. "My god, Justin!" Nora said. "And we thought the Royal Hawaiian was impressive!"

"Thank you, Nora. That's quite a compliment. It's just a home, but we certainly feel blessed."

"Well, Justin. If you ever wanna sell, we get first dibs, right Nora?" Dave asked.

Nora rolled her eyes at her soon-to-be husband's wish.

"We'll certainly keep that in mind, Dave. Let me give you both a tour of the home. There are two wings for this property. This wing has the owner's suite, billiard room, office, and gymnasium. In the other wing, we have three guest suites, the library, kitchen, and dining area." White rattan furniture with ocean blue accent pillows filled the living area. Dave and Nora entered the sunken living room and walked out on the lanai.

Nora noticed the sliding glass doors were open. "What about flies or mosquitos? Aren't they a nuisance?"

"They've never been a problem here, dear. The wind off the water keeps them at bay." Mary Beth admitted neither of them had ever experienced a mosquito bite in Hawaii.

"And not a snake on the island, except the Honolulu Zoo. Mary Beth and I take gentle hikes in the Koolaus. It's nice to know you'll never run into one like we did in Ohio."

"I see why they call it paradise, Nora. And look at the size of that pool!"

They passed by a buffet table containing the catering. Following the ceremony, they'd enjoy BBQ spare ribs, shoyu chicken wings, prawn cocktail, spam musubi, and fresh-cut pineapple.

They felt the cushiony grass as they seemed to float across the plush yard leading to the water's edge. It was near sundown, and the enormous palm trees cast a comforting warm shadow over the multicolored orchid plants attached to the wooden pergola.

A portable sound system played a melody of slack key guitar and ukulele instrumentals. The photographer waited nearby with his camera, ready to capture the scenes.

A Rubenesque Hawaiian woman appeared beneath the pergola in a ruffled Pali orchard red muumuu. She wore a gold *illima* ribbon lei over a *Maile ti leaf.* The smile on Mindy's face was infectious as she made her way over. "Aloha and blessings to you both as you *omale*, get married." She greeted them with a hug. "Are we ready to begin?"

Justin picked up the conch shell and blew into the *pu* to announce the beginning of the 'ho'olaule'a', the celebration.

Dave and Nora assumed their spots in front of Mindy. Justin and Mary Beth stood at their respective sides.

Mindy began speaking Hawaiian with the *Oli Aloha*, a welcoming chant. "You will now exchange leis to show your love and *ho ohiki*, commitment, to one another."

Justin handed Dave his lei for Nora, a combination of tuberose, white ginger, and pink orchids. Mary Beth gave Nora a lush green *maile* leaf lei for Dave's neck.

"David and Nora, these leis reflect your love for one another and the commitment you are about to make." Mindy instructed them both to place the leis on one another. She began blessing the rings and laid both of their wedding rings in a koa wooden bowl she held. She dipped a ti leaf into a conch shell containing ocean water Dave held and sprinkled it over the rings to cleanse them.

Next, she tied the young couple's hands with another *maile* lei and chanted the *Aloha e nakinaki,* or "love that binds."

Dave and Nora exchanged rings. Dave spoke his vows first. "Nora, we balance one another, even when we fight. I mean disagree! Our relationship has a give and take, something like push and pull. And it all seems to fit together so perfectly. From the first day we met, I knew there was something about you I couldn't explain. I'll always be there for you. If you'll have me as your husband?"

Then it was Nora's turn. "David Meyers, I saw myself while reading your novel. You've convinced me how to trust, something I couldn't do until you came along. My world is so much better with you in it. You'll always be my hero. I promise I'll be by your side forever."

After they exchanged vows, the coupled completed the sand union. They each gathered sand from the beach and poured it into a bag to symbolize their unification.

Mindy congratulated them. *"Ho'omaika'i'ana!* I pronounce you man and wife!"

Nora and Dave exchanged a *honi,* or kiss.

Justin turned the speakers back up, and they could hear Don Ho singing the Hawaiian wedding song, *"Ke kali nei au."*

The friends gathered by the pool to indulge in pupus and cocktails and shared stories with one another. The newlyweds thanked everyone and returned to their suite, where they spent the night making tender young love.

9

 we will land in Cleveland soon. You can get up to stretch your legs or use the restroom. Thank you for flying the friendly skies, and we hope you enjoyed our service. It's a beautiful day in Cleveland, eighty-three degrees, with no rain in sight."

The captain's announcement startled Dave and Nora out of their deep slumber. Neither had slept on their first leg from Honolulu to Chicago, crammed into economy class.

Nora rubbed her eyes. "Hurry and get that second novel finished! I've become a first-class diva now that I have gotten to experience that level of luxury."

Dave stood to stretch his legs. "Well, don't get too used to it, Nora. It looks like we'll be flying economy for a while longer."

NORA'S PARENTS WERE waiting in Cleveland to pick them up. When she saw her father standing in the baggage claim area, she rushed over to kiss her parents. Driving back to Cooper's Cove, Nora told them everything she could fit into a one-hour drive. "Mom. Dad. It's such a magical place. We felt an incredible existence like nowhere else in the world."

"And, in Waikiki, we practically lived on the beach, but after getting married, we could only make it two more times."

"Hmm...busy with something else, were we?"

"Daddy, must you be so crass?" Nora sat there smiling at Dave. *If he only knew.*

THEY PASSED THE *Welcome to Cooper's Cove* sign inside the city limits. "Nora? Your father and I have been saving a surprise for you. We know you've wanted to buy a new home, so we are loaning you the down payment. Now remember, Nora, this isn't a gift but a loan. We expect you to pay it back after you've established yourselves."

"What a wonderful gift, Mom. Well, not a gift. Oh, you know what I mean."

"Honey, I do. And you already know we want to help you in any way we can."

Dave was excited as well. "Mr. and Mrs. Austin. Thank you so much! Is it okay if I call you Mom and Dad?"

Ben looked in his rear-view mirror. "Sure. Would you like me to call you son?"

Dave's eyes started welling up. "That'd be nice. And it's all right if I call you Mom?"

"You may, Dave, and welcome to our family." Grace knew the two young lovers belonged together.

Ben wheeled the Ford Crown Victoria onto a dirt lane with a sign, Benham's Cottages. He stopped in front of a nondescript small white bungalow. "I know it doesn't look like much on the outside, but it's furnished, and the rent is month to month. It's perfect for your situation."

Nora wasn't as sure as her father. "Daddy? It's nothing like I'd imagined. And you want us to live here until we find a home?"

"Awe, come on, Nora! It's not that bad," Dave insisted.

After the Austins drove away, he tried to pick her up in his arms. "Home sweet home! My dear! I'll carry you across the threshold."

"I'll take a pass, Dave. Maybe when we buy our new place."

Dave unlocked the rickety old door, and they went inside. It had a foul, musty beach odor.

"Eww! Dave! It stinks in here."

"What do you expect? Just a block from the lake? They turn the utilities off and board these places up in the winter. They're bound to smell like this. Some tourists even like that, you know?"

"That is so gross."

Glancing around the room, the couple observed a

threadbare sofa on a 1960s multicolored braided rug. Two avocado-green armchairs that looked like they'd seen better days sat on each side of the couch.

Nora peeked in the only bedroom and saw it contained an old bed with a sagging mattress. "Dave! You expect me to sleep in that after the one we slept on at the Royal Hawaiian?"

"It's just for a month or two, remember?"

Varnished knotty pine cabinets hung in the Pullman kitchen, and a midcentury red and yellow Formica dinette sat against one wall. Nora also noticed a minuscule bathroom off the kitchen. "Just one bath? Maybe we should have toured it before we rented it."

"It might not be The Royal Hawaiian, but I think it has character." Dave glanced around the room to see if there was a telephone.

"It's right there on the kitchen wall, honey. You promised your mom you would call her as soon as we got in."

Dave picked up the handset of the bright yellow wall phone and dialed his old number. "Mom! Aloha! We're home!"

"Hi, honey. It's so good to hear your voice, and I'm glad you're home safely. But I'm afraid I have some sad news to tell you."

Dave felt his heart drop and wondered what it could be.

"Joyce Panza called this morning. When she woke up, she found Rocco dead in their bed. She said he must have died during the night because his body was cold. The coroner believed it to be his heart. He was only sixty-seven! I'm sorry to have to tell you this."

"It's okay, Mom." Dave wasn't sure how he felt. He'd known Mario's father most of his life and he'd been like a second father. He'd cherish the memories, but the estrangement with Mario had left too broad a schism for him to want to reach out. He couldn't move beyond that. His best friend hated his wife.

"Dave, are you still there?" his mother asked.

"Yeah, I'm here, Mom. I'll call Mrs. Panza and Anthony and express my sympathy. I'm not calling Mario."

"You sure about that? You two go way back. You may regret not calling him."

"Mom, my only regret is not calling him a racist earlier than I did. He's always looked down on people of color. Sometimes, I feel complicit in his bad behavior. I could have called him out years ago when he thought he was being funny with his racist rants. I *don't* want to see him. It's good talking, and I love you, but I must go. A photographer took photos of the ceremony, and we'll be over later to show them to you." Dave hung up the phone.

Nora sat there looking sad. "I'm sorry, Dave; I wish there was something I could do."

He walked over and put his arms around his wife. "Just hold me, babe, just hold me."

***

ROCCO'S FUNERAL WAS three days later. Kathleen attended and offered her condolences to Joyce, Mario, and Anthony.

Mario asked nothing about Dave. But Joyce could tell the grief in Mario's eyes was not only for his father but for the death of a relationship he'd once held so near and dear to his heart.

QUENTIN TEWKESBURY WAS standing on his front porch in his pajama bottoms when Bertha, the meddling old codger who was close to seventy by now, came running over. The winter snow had melted away, exposing yellow daffodils and lavender crocuses. It was unseasonably mild for early spring in Ohio.

Quentin watched his nosey neighbor approach. "Bertha, why must you always be coming here to lecture me about my home and yard? I've lived here for over four years, and that baffling fat lady across the street in the old Roby mansion has been here since 1970! She hasn't done a damn thing to it and her house looks a hell of a lot worse than mine does. Why don't you go complain to her?"

"Wait a minute, buster. How the hell can you be sure she's overweight? No one's ever seen hide or hair of the woman since she moved in. What do you know I don't?"

"Oh, for Christ's sake, woman. Must you have your nose in everyone's business?" Quentin realized she would not let this go, and if he ever wanted any peace in his life, he'd better tell her what he knew. "If you need to know, I was looking out my kitchen window about a year ago." He scratched his bedhead hair. "No, come to think of it, it was a while later. Maybe the summer cause I can remember it was hot. I guess it doesn't matter. It was way early in the morning, say around six thirty. I noticed a couple of grocery sacks on her rear doorstep. Next thing you know, the door opened, and this humongous woman—"

"Watch it, buster; I'm sensitive to people calling women fat," she told him.

"Well, lose some weight then! Anyway, I saw her looking around so she could tell if anyone had seen her. Then she came out onto the stoop and grabbed her bags. She was one big lady! She hurried back inside and slammed the door shut. I've never seen her since."

Bertha was shaking. She couldn't restrain herself. "Tell me! What was she wearing? How about the color of her hair? How old do you think she was?"

"What, are you writing a fucking book? Go over there and ask her if you're that damn nosey. I've got better things to do with my time." He slammed the door in her face and sat on the sofa to light up a joint.

BERTHA WAS ECSTATIC! Now that she knew Charlotte was grossly overweight, what harm would she do if she slightly embellished Quentin's story? *Just to add some spice to it,* she thought.

The first person on her to-call list was Verna Schmudabeck. The two ladies had been running neck to neck on the gossip circuit for years, and now Bertha could finally scoop her! She picked up her phone and dialed. "Verna? It's Bertha. I have some reliable information to share with you about Charlotte Brookstone."

A sound came across the line like Verna had dropped a bathroom plunger and sat down on a toilet lid. "Do tell, honey. Whatchya got?"

"Well, I heard it from a very reliable source who asked to remain anonymous. She said she saw Charlotte outside in her driveway last summer, riding on one of those motorized scooters. You know, the same as the one I use at Riley's. That store is just too damn big for me to walk around the whole place and—"

"Yes! Yes! Yes! Bertha. I know. Now get back to your story!"

"My source told me Charlotte must weigh over three hundred pounds and that her fat ass was hanging over the sides of that poor scooter seat as it hauled her out to her garage. She told me Charlotte was wearing a chestnut brown wig. She said she knew it was a wig cause she saw gray hair sticking out the back of it. She said Charlotte had what looked like an expensive mink stole around her shoulders. Can you imagine? In hot weather? She told me it must have been eighty-five degrees the day she saw her! She was wearing one of those muumuus as they wear over there in Waikiki. My source told me the Robys sent it to her as a Christmas gift."

"Oh, Bertha, tell me more. You can't keep me hanging like this. Please, please! Tell me who told you all of this."

"Sorry Verna, that's about all I have for now. But, I

promise, I'll keep you informed if I get any more info." Bertha hung up the phone and wondered who she'd call next.

⁓

"HEIDI! ARE YOU all right?" Trish gently shook her lover's arm while she lay in their bed. Heidi had progressively gotten worse, no longer recognizing those around her. That sometimes included Trish. It was as if her mind had died, but the body was still around.

Heidi woke up. Slowly opening her eyes, she gazed into her companion's. "Trish. They are here." It was the first time Heidi had addressed her as Trish in over a year.

"Who's here, honey?"

"People. They're telling me to go to the light. Oh, Trish, it's so beautiful."

"Then go to the light, Heidi. I'll be okay."

"I love you, dear."

"I love you too, Mom." It was Trish's affectionate name for Heidi.

⁓

HEIDI CLOSED HER eyes and went to the light. In front of her, she saw a silver tunnel-like tube that seemed to pulsate around her. She stepped inside and noticed people passing by her. They seemed to talk to one another but not to her, as if they weren't aware of her presence. Heidi wondered if she was still back on the other side and not ready to come over. She thought, *But what about Trish? Will she be okay?*

A soothing female voice answered, "Don't worry about Trish, Heidi. I'll make sure she is."

Heidi felt entirely at peace and walked toward the light as the people had told her to. The intensity of its love propelled her closer to its source. As she moved farther, she felt nothing but bliss. She no longer had an attachment to anything on earth. It was as if she was free to do whatever she pleased.

She suddenly stopped and turned. She could see Trish sobbing over her dead body. But rather than feeling sad, Heidi felt indifferent. She knew Trish could go on without her. She was free to continue.

Heidi looked at everyone who'd played a part in her life. They seemed to change faces with one another, almost as if she was watching a movie about her life. One she needed to review before she crossed over.

A microphone on the stage of a large, heavenly auditorium suddenly appeared before her. She couldn't tell if anyone was in the audience, but absolute silence existed, and she could feel a heavenly glow above her head.

She heard the female voice again. "So, Heidi, have you learned anything? Did you make wise choices while you were there?"

Heidi moved closer to the microphone. She whistled into it before tapping it with her finger. "Hello? Is anyone there? Yes, I believe I did. I feel comfortable with the decisions I have made. Is this heaven? I may have been here before."

The voice answered. "Heaven is a state of mind. As is hell.

You created your heaven and hell when you were on Earth. Tell me, Heidi. Why did you choose to come to earth and be a teacher?"

Heidi thought about it for a few seconds. "I'm now aware they gave me a choice between teaching or life as a Hollywood movie star in the 1920s. I knew acting would have been good for my ego but probably not for my soul. So, I taught. I also believed I sometimes needed to be strict for all my children to learn."

The voice inquired, "Perhaps you may have been too strict? Such the day Davie Meyers pooped his pants? You may have ignored him and failed to call on him. Do you feel any remorse over that?"

"I didn't ignore him!" she pleaded. "The first day was difficult enough without screaming children interrupting me to get my attention. You must believe me! I was pre-occupied reading Dr. Seuss and never saw him waving his arm. If I had, I would have called on him."

"If you never saw him, how do you know he waved his arm?"

She heard a group of male voices whispering in the hall. Then a man's rich baritone voice bellowed, "Silence! This court has rendered judgment! You must return to earth and live the life of someone unable to focus and think properly. You will be born a gay boy with an attention deficit. Your birth year shall be 1907. You will experience the hurdles he must face daily. You may choose between life in Los Angeles or in Cleveland. Which do you prefer?"

"Cleveland. I don't like LA!""

"DAVE, WE'VE GOT to get out of this place! It's just too crowded for the both of us!" So began the couple's search for a new home. They'd viewed ten homes together, but none had met their search criteria. All were too small or too large, and Dave and Nora couldn't agree on a house, anyway. Dave wanted a home with a quiet place where he could write.

Not that any of that mattered—because Dave didn't wish to write. Dave hadn't written because there was nothing in his head to write about. Nothing arose to fill the void between his ears. He'd grown frustrated with himself, and disturbing messages that he wasn't good enough filtered back into his thoughts.

MEANWHILE, MARY BETH and Justin were playing bridge on their lanai in Honolulu with two Hawaiian friends they'd met at a Waikiki shell venue. "Justin, dear. I've heard nothing from my cousin Charlotte in over a year. She's returned none of my calls or answered any of my letters. She's one to stay out of the spotlight, so to say, but now I'm truly concerned."

"Calm down, Mary Beth. I'll telephone Dave after we've finished here and ask if he and Nora would check on her."

Justin telephoned that night. "Aloha, Dave! How are the newlyweds doing?"

"Aloha, Justin! It's great hearing your voice! Things are okay, but we're becoming discouraged from hunting for houses. We keep coming up empty-handed."

"Sorry to hear that. Mary Beth seems concerned about her cousin's welfare. Would you mind going and introducing yourselves? Please tell her we've tried reaching out to her."

"Sure, that'd be no problem, but are you sure she'll answer the door?"

"I'm uncertain, but at least you might try. I can call the police for a welfare check, but we thought that'd alarm her. Let us know what you find out. Good talking with you, Dave."

DAVE AND NORA rode to the old Roby mansion in the Mustang and parked in the circular red brick driveway. Dave sadly stared at the dismal setting before him. "Jeez, I can't believe she's ruined this place. It was such a beautiful home. And now look at it! She's weirder than everyone thought. How could she have stayed holed up inside all these years?"

"Only Charlotte knows, Dave! Let's see if she'll answer the door."

"I think we should go around to the back door, honey. That's where Buster told me they leave her groceries. He hasn't been here in over a year. He figured she likely orders now from that new Discount Food Mart. I guess Buster has had a difficult time competing with them."

They cut across the brick pathway leading to the kitchen

and noticed the door was slightly ajar as if someone had forgotten to close it completely. Dave rang the doorbell and waited. No response, so he pushed the door open and shouted, "Miss Brookstone! We're friends of Mary Beth and Justin! They asked if we'd come and see if you were okay!"

Still, no one answered.

"What do you think we should do, Nora? What if she's fallen and hurt herself? Let's call the police."

"I don't think we should wait, Dave. Let's go in."

They forced the door open as far as they could. Boxes of old magazines and newspapers blocked the entryway, and it did not appear as if anyone could get through the mess.

They carefully navigated down the hallway like Dave did so many times as a child, but without the clutter. The kitchen looked like a bomb had gone off. Dirty dishes sat in the sink, and the floors were filthy. Empty potato chip bags and Little Debbie boxes were strewn everywhere.

"One thing's certain, Nora. Charlotte's not been a perfect housekeeper."

They moved into the dining room, which fared no better than the kitchen. Charlotte had stuffed it full of worthless junk. Across the hall, she appeared to have used the living room as an indoor greenhouse. Dozens of withered potted house plants had ruined the once pristine white carpeting.

Dave called her name once again before they climbed the winding staircase. They could see five of the bedroom doors closed upstairs, but she'd left a sixth open. They crept toward it and peeked in. The room was dark, and they could see what appeared to be someone sleeping in bed. Dave called, "Charlotte! Wake up!"

She did not move, and Dave turned on the light switch.

Neither of them were prepared for the dreadful scene before them.

Charlotte had been dead for some time and looked mummified. Her face and lips had shriveled, and her eye sockets were empty. It appeared rats had enjoyed them for dinner and had also gnawed off her fingertips. She was wearing her nightclothes, and her once obese body had decomposed.

"I think I may throw up, Nora! This is terrible. She's been here for a while. I'll use the phone downstairs and call the police."

"Dave, this is unbelievable. I'm going with you! You're not leaving me alone up here!"

They returned to the kitchen, and Dave telephoned the police. They waited outside in the Mustang until the police and the county coroner arrived.

The coroner examined the body and told them it appeared she'd died of natural causes, but ordered an autopsy. Nick Foster was called to retrieve the corpse, or rather what remained of it, and transported the loathsome body to his mortuary.

The police chief asked, "You're friends with the Robys, am I correct? If you have their telephone number, may I have it?"

"You may, but it's in my address book at home. I'll call you with their number."

"That's fine. I'll telephone first, but considering you

know them personally, it'd be nice if you'd call as well. It may help to cushion their shock when I tell them what we have found."

After Dave and Nora returned to the cottage, she called the chief and gave him the Roby's number. The chief had telephoned and informed the Robys of their cousin's demise. Dave was preparing to call the Robys himself when he heard the phone ring.

"Dave. It's Justin. We just heard the devastating news. Mary Beth's quite beside herself. I've given her a sedative and she's gone to sleep. I'm sorry you both had to witness all that. I'll get busy with arrangements. Considering her body's condition, we'll have her cremated following the autopsy. There's no one else but us, so there'll be no service, as Charlotte requested. I'll also give the real estate agency a ring. We'll need to put the house on the market. From the sounds of things, I expect little for it."

Dave extended their sympathy and thanked him for calling. He hung up and realized their new home had materialized. "Nora! Let's buy Charlotte's house! Justin just told me he wouldn't get much for it, so I know we can afford it, and with the rest of your parents' down payment, we'll still have enough money left to rehabilitate the place."

NORA THOUGHT DAVE may have just gone loco. "But Dave! We don't need that much room. What would we do with a six-bedroom house?"

"Please! Let me finish. Remember that quaint bed-and-breakfast we walked past at Kailua Beach in Hawaii? It appeared to be the size of Charlotte's house. We could restore hers and turn it into a bed-and-breakfast for the summers! The money would come in handy. Think about it! The place will shine with a few coats of paint and some elbow grease."

"I don't know. Can't we continue to look for something else a bit more manageable?"

"I'm sure the structure is sound, and we can update its interior. We both know I'm just beginning as an author. There's no guarantee my luck will continue, and even though you've been doing well with your spot at the Brass Buckle, I'm afraid it won't be enough for us to live on. And I don't want to ask your parents for more money."

"Who is going to help me clean all those rooms? Not to mention six bathrooms! As well as make breakfast each morning? You'll be busy writing. Hopefully!"

"I have a solution for that. Remember my Aunt Billie in Florida I told you about? Mom said she's doing remarkably well at eighty and spry as a fox. I know she'd come up and help this summer! And I'll help as well. I promise!"

"It's still going to be a ton of work. You've seen it! That place is disgusting!"

"I know. But think about what it'll look like when we finish it. You'd understand if you could have seen the way it was when I was little. I know we can bring the mansion back to life. What do you say?"

Nora recalled Dave's mom telling her about his dad's idea to build the mobile home park, and she wanted to give

Dave a chance. "David Meyers, what can I say, but I love you? And I may have a name for it."

"What's that?"

"Well, the first thing you notice about the house is that small tower attached to the front, right? How does this sound? The Turret House Bed and Breakfast."

"Nora, that sounds incredible, and I love you!"

Dave called the Robys back and told them of their plan to transform their cousin's old home into an inn. He made an offer to purchase it.

"Dave, we're so happy you want to buy the place. Considering everything, we'll happily let you have it for less than the market. Mary Beth will be grateful the house will receive the love and attention it deserves."

They set closing for the spring of 1978.

This time, Nora accepted Dave's offer to carry her across the threshold. The first thing she noticed when he put her down was an oil portrait of Charlotte hanging above the fireplace in the living room. Nora suspected someone may have painted it in the late twenties when Charlotte had been a young girl. The artist had captured her from her right side in a full-length black velvet skirt with a satin white long-sleeved blouse. She had a string of pearls with a diamond and sapphire clasped around her neck. Nora sensed Charlotte's eyes seem to follow her about the room. "Doesn't she make you feel the least bit creepy?"

"I don't see that, honey, and it's probably best to leave it. We may offend the Robys if we take it down. We'll tell our guests she was the family matriarch. In fact, why don't we name a room after her? We can call it Charlotte's Roost."

"Whatever, but you won't find me roosting up there!"

Dave finished showing Nora the rest of the home. Justin had removed all the clutter, and a professional had cleaned and sanitized the premises. Finally, they could see beyond Charlotte's hoarding obsession. "Let's begin here in the kitchen, honey. Amos told me those maple cabinets are original to the home. I think they should remain, and we can install new granite countertops. They're all the rave now." He glanced around the room. "I can still picture Amos making their dinners while I sat on that stool over there and watched him while writing in my journal." He showed her a small room with a half bath down the hall from the kitchen. "This was Amos's room."

They walked in the living room. "Charlotte's antique furnishings complement this. We can replace the carpeting and wallpaper."

"Charlotte's taste in art and antiques was impeccable," Nora said. "I've never seen a crystal chandelier as faceted as this. And that gold-leaf mirror dates from the late 1800s. And notice the oil on the opposite wall? It's one of the finest examples of still art I've ever seen."

Dave looked at it. "Really? Looks like a bowl of fruit to me."

"Well, that bowl of fruit, mirror, and chandelier combined is worth more than your Mustang!"

"Wow! Justin told me they were leaving a few things for us as a wedding gift, but I never expected to see all of this."

"At least the Duncan Phyfe dining room set is a newer reproduction. An original would be worth many thousands of dollars." She counted ten chairs at the table. "If we use one bedroom as our own, that leaves five rooms to rent. With possibly ten guests a night, if we are full, this works out perfectly."

Nora opened the lid to the piano bench in the front parlor and discovered several pieces of vintage Broadway sheet music inside before moving across the hall.

"And here's my favorite room, sweetie." Dave slid the mahogany pocket doors into the walls, revealing a beautiful library. "Some of the same books I knew as a child are still here. I want to use this as my writing room. I found a well-lit room in the basement with a sink. It would make the perfect spot for you to sculpt and paint."

Upstairs, each of the vintage 1920s baths bore the original cast iron clawfoot tub and separate art deco tiled showers. Nora saw the smaller bedroom in the front tower. "We can name this the Turret Room to tie it to the inn's theme. I love the angels in the hand-painted domed ceiling."

"Well, Nora, that leaves three more rooms for us to name. We'll use Justin's old room as ours. I don't think you want to sleep in Charlotte's, do you?"

"That's affirmative! Pity the guests who do. Do you think we must tell them what happened in there?"

"People die in old houses all the time. If anyone asks about Charlotte, we can tell them she died in her sleep. Which she did, of course! We will leave out the how. So, Nora, what do you think?"

"It will be a lot of work, even with you and Aunt Billie helping. But I love you and trust your judgment. Do you think we will have everything ready for the summer tourist season?"

"Sure we will!"

Nora wasn't as sure.

10

 ached for her partner. Heidi had become so much a part of her; she felt empty without her. In the weeks following her death, she sat and cried. She felt ashamed. When Heidi had no longer recognized her, Trish secretly wished Heidi was dead so her suffering could end.

But now that she was gone, Trish would have given anything to have her back. She longed to sit with her partner just one more time and hold her hand. She kept one of Heidi's sweaters from her closet near her face. She closed her eyes, and with Heidi's perfume acting as her guide, she imagined her partner still there.

Her grief grew so deep that she sometimes felt she couldn't go on and considered ending her life. As time passed, Trish realized grief did not have a timetable, and everyone arrived at their destination at different times.

Day by day, the darkness lifted, and she returned to work. She could talk about Heidi and not end up crying. She could smile again.

An employee took notice. "You look happier now, boss! It's good to have you back."

"Thanks. I appreciate that. After Heidi died, it felt like I couldn't go on. But somehow, I knew I could. Like a guardian angel was helping."

"Maybe they were Trish! Hey! Our women's aerobics class begins in twenty minutes. Why don't you join us today?"

"That sounds like a great idea. I'll see you in there." Trish changed into her leotard, and when she came out of her office, she noticed an attractive lady standing to the side in the exercise room. She appeared very shy, so Trish introduced herself to the lovely gal in the red velour jogging outfit. "Hi, I'm Trish. I own the gym. I haven't seen you in here before, have I?"

"Oh, my goodness, no," she freely admitted. "I'm Diane Gale. My friend Steven Conrad suggested I join. I've never worked out a day in my life! Steven said it would be good for my mind and my body."

"Well, I think he's correct. He and Christopher seem like great guys. They're members here." Trish noticed Diane wasn't wearing a wedding ring. "I'm surprised they haven't told me about you."

"Oh, I'm not gay! Steven and I go way back. We dated in high school. He's such a gentleman. I enjoy spending time with him."

"Well, I have two suggestions for you, Diane: Don't overdo it your first week, and take the class at your own pace."

"Can you make me look like Jane Fonda?" They laughed, and Diane said, "My goal is to stay fit at my age."

"I know this isn't polite, Diane, but how old are you?"

"I don't mind you asking. I'm sixty-six and proud of it!"

Trish thought, *She should be. She's in remarkable shape for a woman her age. And she's five years older than me, not as old as Heidi was, but now that I'm older, it seems like a good fit. This may work out.*

The class began with a series of stretches. Diane bent effortlessly and touched her toes. Trish stared at her. She thought Diane graceful and limber like a younger Heidi. And they both displayed the same mannerisms. Trish knew she may have had her wires crossed and needed to proceed with caution. She didn't wish to frighten Diane away before she got the chance to get to know her better.

After class, Trish congratulated Diane on her first visit. "You looked awesome! You knew the moves and made it look so easy. I assumed you'd been doing aerobics for years."

Diane blushed. "Thank you for that compliment. Coming from you, it has meaning. You seem so powerful!"

"Diane, would you like to join me for dinner this weekend? Nothing elaborate. Porterhouse steaks on the grill and tossed salad? I have some interesting aerobics tapes we can watch on my Betamax recorder."

"That sounds lovely. I don't get out much. Except with Steven."

Trish thought she seemed obsessed over the gay man. "Okay, I'll jot down my telephone number and address for you."

"Oh, that's unnecessary. I know where you live." Diane appeared to realize she must have sounded like a stalker. "I mean, I know of the house you both lived in. It's that white brick ranch over on Lincoln Street, correct?"

"Yes, that's the place."

They set the date for Saturday night. Trish went back to her office and wrote a reminder. *Buy wine for Saturday night.*

TRISH HEARD THE doorbell chime. She looked at herself in the mirror. She'd chosen Jordache designer jeans with a tight yellow T-shirt that emphasized her nipples. She took one more glance at herself before she opened the front door.

Diane stood there with a bottle of Panza merlot in her hands. Trish thought she looked stylish in her blue and white full-skirt dress with long raglan sleeves. "Diane! You look terrific in that. It fits you nicely."

"Oh, it's just something I had hanging in my closet. I hope it's still in style! I brought along a bottle of red wine."

"Someone as pretty as you will never go out of style!"

"You flatterer! You sound just like Steven. His eyes lit up when I told him I was coming for dinner."

Trish thanked her for the wine and opened the bottle.

She filled their glasses. "A toast! To a blossoming new friendship!" They clinked their wine glasses, entered the living room, and sat on the divan. "So, I'm curious. How did you and Steven meet? You said you dated in high school?"

"We were in the same class, and he asked me out several times. I always jumped at the chance to go out with him. All the girls thought he was the cat's meow." Diane took a big gulp of her wine. "We went out on a few dates, and he was always a complete gentleman. I never suspected he was a homosexual, I mean, gay, until he told me a couple of years later. We've been best friends ever since."

Trish picked up her wineglass. "And what about all the years in between? Have you dated many other men?"

Diane took another gulp. She appeared to be getting nervous. "Oh, no! I had difficulty getting over him when he left for college. Sometimes, I think I may still have feelings for him. But I'd never come between him and Christopher. He loves Christopher very much."

"You mean to tell me, after all these years, you've never gone out with another man?"

"No; I'm happy being single and always have been. But I must admit, I get lonely now and then. But I'd never con-sider meeting a gentleman now. I'm too settled in my ways."

Trish refilled their glasses. They went outside to the flagstone patio, where she grilled their steaks. At the dining table, Trish told Diane about the life she'd shared with Heidi. She left out little.

"She sounds like a lovely woman. I knew of her. She taught so many children here."

"She was one of a kind, and I miss her every day. Can I grab anything else for you? I didn't make any dessert."

"My heavens, no! I don't know where I'd put it. May I help you with the dinner dishes?"

"No thanks, I'll put them in the dishwasher later. Let's go down to the rumpus room. I have my Betamax there." Trish grabbed another bottle of wine, and they went downstairs.

Diane looked around at the mirrors and workout equipment. "This looks almost like your gym, Trish."

"Thanks. I've made exercise part of my life. Would you care for another glass of wine?"

"Oh, I don't think so. I've already had three." But she accepted it anyway. She seemed to struggle focus on Trish's biceps through inebriated eyes. Slurring her words a little, she told Trish, "Your muscles are so impressive. It must take discipline to maintain your lovely form." Diane sat on the orange Naugahyde leather sofa.

Trish put the aerobics tape into the Betamax and pressed play. She sat close to Diane, who didn't move away. They watched the workout tape and each other. Trish put her arm behind Diane's shoulder and kissed her on her lips.

"Trish! What are you thinking?"

Rather than answer her, Trish pulled her closer and passionately kissed her.

~

AFTER SAVORING THE moment, Diane told her, "This feels wonderful. So natural."

Trish kissed her again and took her by the hand. She led Diane back upstairs to her bedroom. Trish unzipped her jeans and stepped out before slowly pulling her T-shirt over her head and revealing her generous breasts and silver-dollar-sized nipples.

Diane couldn't stop staring at the intriguing naked woman who stood before her. Trish removed Diane's dress and took off her undergarments. She carefully lay her back on the bed and slowly explored Diane's body with her hands and mouth, kissing and nibbling on her breasts. Trish slowly kissed her way down to her privates and made love to her. Diane arched her body and screamed out in ecstasy. In her moment of self-realization, Diane admitted to Trish, "If only I'd known what I was missing!"

Diane helped clean up the kitchen, and they kissed goodnight. Before leaving, Diane held Trish's hand. "Thank you for indoctrinating me into a part of myself I never knew existed. Will I see you again?"

"Oh, no worry there. I think we'll be spending a lot more time together. And you're welcome!"

THE FOLLOWING DAY, Diane telephoned Steven. "I've something significant to share with you both, and I can't do it over the telephone. May I come over?"

"Sure! We're hanging out on the deck, enjoying a Bloody Mary and watching the seagulls. Come on over." He hung up the telephone and went back out onto their deck. "Diane just called. She said she's on her way over. Says she has something important to tell us."

Christopher squealed with delight. "See? Didn't I tell you so? Diane's a lesbian, and her pussy is tighter than a nun's cunt!"

"Christopher, knock it off! You can be so vulgar! You don't even know why she's coming, and I don't want you embarrassing her if that is what she will tell us. It's hard enough coming out of the closet. I know that firsthand."

When she arrived, Steven offered her an eye-opener. They sat on the deck, and Diane told them what had transpired with Trish, leaving out the intimate details.

Christopher probed. "What did she do to you, honey? Was she good?"

"Christopher!" Steven shouted. "Must you?"

"No, that's perfectly all right, Steven. Yes, Christopher, Trish knew what she was doing. I honestly never realized I'd harbored those feelings for another woman. I just did what they taught me to do as a young lady." She looked at Steven. "You were the perfect excuse for me to hide behind and not accept my true nature."

Steven took her hand. "I'm happy for you, Diane. I'm glad you've found love."

Finally relieved of her burden, Diane declared, "I feel like a natural woman! Now I know what Aretha Franklin has been singing about!"

"You just go, girl!" Christopher camped. "Darling, we

are so delighted. It's quite chic for a gay couple to have les-bians as friends. We'll have such fun hanging out. You have a lot to learn, girlfriend!"

RESTORATION WORK KEPT grinding along at The Tur-ret House, and Dave and Nora were busy around the clock. It showed on their faces. "Nora, I'm so sick of painting. And I've put up so many sheets of wallpaper that I think the wallpaper paste tastes good now."

Nora took care of the final touches, such as choosing linens for the bedrooms and bath towels. There was so much to learn. They attended a weekend seminar in Cleve-land for aspiring innkeepers like themselves. So far, they'd instituted a manual reservation system, developed check-in and check-out procedures, and ordered compli-mentary toiletries for the rooms.

They asked to be listed in the *Summer Lodging* brochure and were working on a breakfast menu that Aunt Billie would sign off on when she arrived. Dave had telephoned his great-aunt earlier and asked her to come.

She'd seemed overcome. "Oh, Davie. It's so nice of you to think of me. I'd love to help Nora. But I'm moving a little slower than I used to."

Dave knew it wasn't true. His mom had visited the oc-togenarian in Florida and said Billie still washed floors on her hands and knees.

A WEEK AND a half later, Dave finished wallpapering a room they'd named Angler's Perch, a rustic old fisher's theme. Nora called up to him, "Honey, I'm going over to my parents. Do you need anything while I'm out?"

"No, thanks. Let's eat at the diner when you get home."

Nora closed the door. She wasn't going to her parents. She went to Kathleen's, and they drove to the airport to meet Aunt Billie's flight. She'd brought along a "special parcel."

Billie's park manager's dog had given birth to six Labrador puppies. Dave hadn't been able to stop talking about Sandy to Nora. Nora and Kathleen both knew how much he wanted another dog. Kathleen had planned to have the pup shipped on Aunt Billie's flight, and Nora and Kathleen met her at the baggage claim.

"Aunt Billie, I'd like you to meet Dave's new wife, Nora."

"I'm so glad for you, Nora. Dave spoke so highly of you. He's a wonderful boy!"

Oh really? Try living with him! Nora thought. She heard a whimpering coming from the crate on the baggage carousel. She lifted it off and set it down. When she opened the door, an energetic eight-week-old Labrador puppy emerged and peed on the concrete floor.

The three laughed, and Kathleen grabbed a tissue from her purse to clean it up.

"That's how I felt when I finally got off that plane," Billie joked. "I hate using those filthy airplane restrooms!"

Nora picked up the black Lab, and the dog licked her face. "Oh my gosh, she's a doll, isn't she? Dave's going to flip! Does she have a name yet?"

"No, dear, she doesn't, but the manager's wife was calling her Haddie."

Nora looked into the puppy's copper-brown eyes. "Haddie, huh? You know, I think Dave's going to like that name."

They loaded up and drove back to Cooper's Cove with their little surprise.

They rang the house doorbell, hoping to catch Dave off guard.

DAVE OPENED THE door holding a paintbrush between his teeth and a can of Sherwin-Williams paint in his right hand. When he saw Nora holding Haddie, the paintbrush fell out of his mouth. "Oh, my god! What did you do?"

Nora handed him the puppy.

Dave cuddled her and turned her over to see if it was a boy or girl.

"She's a girl, Dave. Her name is Haddie."

Dave looked up and realized Aunt Billie and his mom were also standing there. He hadn't seen his great aunt since his father's funeral. It was all too much for him, and he cried. But they were happy tears. "Aunt Billie! What a surprise! And Mom? Nora knew about this all along?"

"She wanted to surprise you, Dave, and from the looks of it, she has."

"Well, all of you have." He wiped away his tears and hugged Nora, then Aunt Billie and his mom. He set the little dog down. Everyone watched as she ran and peed in the grass before returning to chew on Dave's shoelaces. "Everyone, come on in! The place is still a mess, but it's come a long way, hasn't it, Nora?"

"Indeed, it has. You wouldn't believe the condition it was in." Nora and Dave had chosen not to elaborate on the condition of Charlotte.

Aunt Billie raved. "Everything is so beautiful. It's all so pretty. I'm afraid to touch anything."

Dave went to the car to bring in her luggage. He showed her to her room and turned on the light.

Aunt Billie looked at the blue wallpaper with white seashells. She noticed the twin-size bed and small bureau with a lamp shaped like a lighthouse. "Davie, this is lovely. It'll do just fine. I also like that it's right next to the kitchen."

"This used to be Amos's room. The Roby's butler, remember him?"

"Of course I do! I still have his recipe for trout almondine."

Dave pointed to her bathroom. "Nora and I added a shower. It was just a half bath before."

"Well, haven't you two thought of everything?"

They gathered in the living room and sat and chatted. Aunt Billie marveled at the Victorian settee she was sitting on before she brought them all up to date on her whereabouts in St. Petersburg. "It's changed so much from when I moved there! I don't even recognize it anymore."

"Aunt Billie! You should see the changes in Cooper's Cove! You wouldn't recognize it here, either. We have a big health club and an antique store downtown! We even have a Wendy's now, and, you know what? I told Nora we'd go to the diner to eat, but a 'Dave's Single' sounds pretty good right about now, wouldn't you agree?"

Everyone agreed it did.

DAVE GLIMPSED HIS neighbor across the street in the morning, tending his spring asparagus harvest. He went to introduce himself. "Hi, I'm Dave Meyers. My wife Nora and I are redoing the old Roby mansion across the street. We've been meaning to come over and say hi."

"Quentin Tewksbury here, but most people just call me Tewksbury. You're the author, correct? I just finished reading your book. I enjoyed it. You're planning on writing another, I presume?"

"That's the plan, but I haven't found the inspiration. I hope it finds me soon, or my agent will kill me."

"I see your bio says you went to school at Oberlin. How did you like it there? I've heard good things."

"It's a college that teaches you to analyze things. I learned to be an independent thinker. And, I guess, a good writer as well. Where are you from, Tewksbury?"

"Well, I'll tell you all about that, but do you like to get high?"

"Does a bear shit in the woods?"

They went inside and lit up a joint. The inside of Tewksbury's house looked as shitty as the outside. They passed the joint back and forth while Quentin shared his story. "I grew up in Pittsburg back in the forties. My parents used to come to Cooper's Cove for our summer vacations; then my dad got transferred to California in 1955."

"That's the year I was born!" Dave told him.

"Well, I would have been fifteen then. I liked it out there. Great weather, nice people, and some of the best weed on the planet, as I found out at UCLA. I graduated in 1963. I had a degree in business management, but it didn't interest me, so I became a drifter, never really answering anyone or anything. Until 1964. Uncle Sam decided my official residence should be in Saigon.

"When I returned in sixty-six, I opened a record shop in Long Beach for a few years before I made my way up the coast to Oregon. Man, do they grow some good shit up there! I met a girl and lived with her in a commune for a while, but I started doing too much acid. I cleaned up my act and came back to Ohio in early 1973 and found this place. Been here ever since."

"Hey, Tewksbury? Do you have more of this stuff? It's nice. Maybe I could get a little from you?"

"Sure! I grow it in my basement, Dave."

THE COUPLE TARGETED June first as the opening day and invited family and friends for the affair. After almost three months of nonstop renovating, they were ready to open and had polished the final details. Dave even manicured the grounds and gardens to fine detail.

Nora's parents and Dave's mother were on their invitation list. But who else could they invite to experience a night of luxury at their inn? They'd become closer to Christopher and Steven since Nora began selling on commission in their shop. Christopher had been bending Nora's ear about getting together with the two gay couples.

Finally, Nora had given in and told Dave they should all go out together. The six met at the Cliff House for dinner and drinks. After getting to know one another outside the gym, Dave and Nora had merged perfectly with the other four, and they laughed at each other's jokes. They seemed to share a special bond that sometimes existed between those who differed from others.

Besides their new friends, they also mailed invitations to Mary Beth and Justin in Hawaii. They hoped they'd come and see what they'd done to their old home after Charlotte left her mark.

Nora's parents would stay in Anglers's Perch, which overlooked the harbor. Kathleen would sleep in the Dreamcatcher Room. The eclectic suite featured a Native American theme of dreamcatchers, wooden flutes, and other Indian artifacts mounted on the walls. One of Nora's favorite paintings hung opposite the bed. She'd painted a tranquil nighttime scene of the moonlit lake, and the reflection on the water's calm surface had a soothing, sedating effect that they hoped would lull the guests to sleep.

They assigned Steven and Christopher the Vagabond Room, designed with a travelers' motif. An antique world globe on a gold base sat in one corner, and an antique Steamer's Trunk sat next to the bed and held travel journals.

Trish and Diane received the Turret Room, and they determined Justin and Mary Beth should stay in Charlotte's Roost, which bore little resemblance to her former place of lodging.

After everyone's arrival, the guests all gathered in the front parlor to get acquainted. Aunt Billie had prepared a chilled Maine lobster tray as an appetizer. Haddie acted as the inn's mascot, running around trying to chew on everyone's shoes before Dave called her out.

Justin stood and offered a pledge to their new home. "Dave and Nora? You've done a magnificent job of restoring this endearing abode. It just shines! The same as it did when Mary Beth and I lived here. Here's to you both!"

The other seven guests reiterated his comments, and Justin asked his wife, "Mary Beth! Would you care to entertain us on the piano?"

"Oh, Justin! Please don't embarrass me! It's been so many years since I've played." But she consented to the request, sat before the forte piano, and serenaded them with Henry Mancini's "Moon River" to the rousing applause of all of them.

The dining room table looked superb, with a cherry-red tablecloth and white linen napkins folded into swans. Nora had chosen tasteful bone china dinnerware embossed with red roses. An exquisite bird-of-paradise flower, compliments of Justin and Mary Beth, had graced the center of the table, surrounded by *ti* leaves, red ginger, anthurium, and pink orchids.

After dining on Aunt Billie's roast pork and gravy with butter-whipped mashed potatoes and sage stuffing, they all moved to the living room, where they enjoyed her Crêpes Suzette with vanilla ice cream for dessert. The group mingled for an hour before settling in for the evening.

All of them expected a peaceful night's rest.

IN THE MORNING, Dave woke at five. Nora had been up since four thirty and was downstairs helping Aunt Billie set up the breakfast buffet.

The smell of extra crispy bacon and freshly baked blueberry muffins lingered in the kitchen. Aunt Billie had prepared her favorite Quiche Loraine recipe, and a newly chilled fruit compote would conclude the morning's menu.

Dave showered and went to the kitchen, where he kissed Nora and Aunt Billie. He grabbed a coffee mug and filled it with the inn's special morning brew, a Hawaiian Kona coffee they'd discovered on their honeymoon.

Justin and Mary Beth were first to file into the dining room. They, too, had retrieved a cup of coffee from the large urn. Dave asked how their evening was.

"I slept like a baby, but Mary Beth seemed restless."

"I dreamed about Charlotte last night. It was the strangest of dreams! She was trying to tell me something. Charlotte looked like I remember her when we were both very young. It all seemed vivid and like she'd been in the room with us. Isn't that ridiculous?"

Justin reassured her. "It was just a dream, dear."

Dave and Nora looked at each other, uneasy.

The women were the next to arise. Trish asked Dave for black coffee, and Diane preferred a cup of chamomile tea with honey and lemon.

"So tell me, Trish, how was your evening?"

"You need a queen-size bed in the Turret Room, Dave! That full-size mattress is too small for two people. And you'd better call a plumber! Something must be wrong with your sink faucet. The water turned on by itself in the middle of the night."

"Trish accused me of forgetting to turn the water off completely. I know I shut it off before I went out."

Dave made a note to check the plumbing in their room.

Kathleen and the Austins rose early and walked along the lakefront. Steven and Christopher were the last to come down. Christopher was wearing a pink hoodie with sunglasses on and looked hungover.

"You don't think it has anything to do with the extra bottle of wine you took to our room, do you?"

"Excuse me, Steven? If I recall correctly, it was you who suggested we take it up. Thank you very much!"

Aunt Billie came out of the kitchen. "Alrighty, everyone!

Please sit at the table and help yourself to our breakfast buffet."

Kathleen counted ten place settings. "Do you have enough seats for all of us, Dave?"

"The three of us nibbled in the kitchen earlier, Mom. We won't be joining you. Nora and I need to run to Riley's."

THE GUESTS LINED up and ladened their plates with Aunt Billie's finest before they sat to eat. Christopher gossiped with Mary Beth and shared the juicy town tidbits courtesy of Bertha.

"Oh, I remember her! Telephone. Telegraph. Tell it to Bertha!"

Separate conversations began around the table. All at once, the serving spoon in the fruit compote fell out of the bowl and onto the floor. Aunt Billie retrieved it and took it to the kitchen for cleaning. When she returned, she scooped it in the fruit to keep it from falling out again.

As she turned away, the silver spoon flew out of the bowl and landed back on the floor.

They all were unsure of what they had just witnessed. The conversations ceased.

Aunt Billie wiped her hands on her apron. "Doesn't that just take the cake?" She picked it up again.

Ben was the first to say something. "I don't know about the rest of you, but I watched her put it back in that bowl securely. That thing flew out of there by itself."

"Oh honey, you're being silly," Grace told him. Kathleen sat and said nothing.

Steven joked, "Hey, this place sounds like it might be the setting for a good horror flick!" But all he got were a few nervous chuckles.

WHEN DAVE AND Nora returned home, Aunt Billie told them about the incident. "Kids, I swear to God. That spoon flew out of there like someone had grabbed it and thrown it on the floor! I've seen nothing like it!"

"Okay, Dave! Now, I'm more than a little creeped out," Nora said. "There must be a connection! And that faucet in the Turret Room? It's brand new. There's no way it could have turned back on by itself."

"You may be right. What if there is a ghost inhabiting our house? It could end up harming our business. Wait! What was the name of that girl we met at that shop in Oberlin? Her name was Lilly or something like that?"

"Her name was Lauren, silly. Her store was next to Holly's cat rescue. Remember? She called it The Enlightened One in Progress."

"Oh yeah! I still have her business card in my Rolodex. I'll try calling her."

Dave's call was successful, and Lauren did indeed remember him. "So, Dave! Have you finished your book yet?"

"That's incredible how you knew that, Lauren. I'm still amazed. I have. I'm visualizing a second, but I'm not doing well in that category. But that's not why I called. It appears we have a presence inhabiting our home. It doesn't appear evil, more like someone trying to play pranks on us. Do you have any suggestions?"

"Possibly a seance? I've been doing intensive research on the subject. And from what I've discovered, a seance might rid your home of unwelcome guests. I've already done five others. And all five had favorable outcomes. Possibly you'd like to schedule?"

"We would, Lauren. I'll call you back when we know a day and time; thanks."

They set it for the following Sunday night, as no guests had booked, and the inn would be vacant. Aunt Billie had plans to visit a friend in Vermillion.

Lauren told Dave to invite a few nonjudgmental friends and create a welcoming atmosphere for the spirit. Their guest list would include Steven, Christopher, Trish, and Diane. Seven would have been in attendance, but when Diane told Bertha the boys were joining them at a seance, she'd been beside herself.

"This is better than *The Outer Limits*! I want to go, Diane, pretty please? I love a good ghost story." Bertha's favorite sci-fi reruns were *The Outer Limits* and *The Twilight Zone*.

THE GROUP GATHERED in the dining room that weekend. Dave had draped black crepe paper draperies on the walls. Dimly lit candles cast shadows over the special effects he'd created. Almost as if he'd been summoning the spirit.

Lauren brought a special incense, which she lit and placed in the center of the table. The eight joined hands, and Lauren prayed for a white veil of protection as she closed her eyes and leaned back in her chair. "I'm calling upon the soul of Charlotte Brookstone! Please, make yourself known to us."

The candles began flickering, and they could feel a gentle breeze in the room. Suddenly, a ghostly apparition appeared above them and soon came into focus. It appeared confused.

Bertha screamed out in horror. "Saints preserve us!"

Lauren silenced her. They all recognized the illusion from the living room painting hanging over the mantel.

The ghost looked at all of them and asked Lauren, "Why are all these people in my home? There's too many. I like my privacy!"

Lauren explained, "Charlotte, don't be afraid. You're safe now. It's all right to move on. This couple is caring for your beautiful home. It's now a bed-and-breakfast. Where guests come to stay, that is who you see before you now."

Charlotte turned up her nose at everyone.

"May I say something?" Nora asked.

Lauren nodded.

"Charlotte, I'm Nora, and this is my husband, Dave. We love your home. You're welcome to stay, but if you do, please stop scaring our guests."

The ghost locked eyes with Bertha. "You! You're the fat

Polish lady who's been spreading lies about me! Just stop! It's not nice!"

"Oh, please, Charlotte! I promise I'll never tell another lie again." (Bertha later told Diane she'd had her fingers crossed when she'd said it.)

Christopher asked Lauren if he could have a word with the specter. "Charlotte, darling? You look stunning in those natural pearls around your neck. Is there any chance you could leave those behind for me when you leave?"

The ghost gave Christopher a nasty sneer before she looked at everyone else with a smile and slowly faded away. They all felt a whooshing vacuum sound as the apparition disappeared and the candles flickered again.

Lauren asked Dave to turn up the lights.

The participants tried to comprehend what they had just seen. Bertha was still shaking, and Diane had run out of tissues. Trish was already up from the table, walking around the room, looking for props. "You guys have a projector hidden somewhere, right? It's all theatrics!"

Steven spoke up. "Well, there's no doubt about it this time. This one's going to make a terrific movie. Imagine a small inn inhabited by a ghost who doesn't want to leave! I'm calling my old agent."

"Maybe so," Lauren told him, "but I don't believe she'll bother anyone again. She seemed at peace when she left."

Dave and Nora felt more at ease.

Nothing unusual occurred in the following weeks; none of their guests saw anything suspicious.

A few weeks later, the owners sat before the fireplace

one night, enjoying a glass of Panza Cabernet. Nora looked up at Charlotte's portrait. "She is beautiful, isn't she, Dave? I hope she keeps gentle watch over our home."

"Yeah, and let's hope that's all she does!"

DAVE PUT HADDIE in her puppy training harness and took her for a walk in Veterans' Park. A rainy Nor'easter had come through the previous evening, and everyone was enjoying the brisk, cool air it left behind after a week of sweltering humidity. He looked at the playground and noticed a young man sitting on one end of a teeter-totter. As he grew closer, he saw the man holding a little boy captive at the top.

Dave felt sick. It was Mario, and the little boy at the top was Dino Jamison. Dave turned to walk in the opposite direction.

"Hey, douchebag. What? You won't come and say hi?"

It had been four years, and the two still had not spoken. Dave had grown immune to the absence of his onetime bestie and given little thought to Mario's bizarre ménage à trois with the Jamisons and his odd devotion to their young son. "Hey kid," Dave yelled. "You better hold on tight. That dude is about to drop your butt to the ground!"

Dino giggled, and Dave froze! He recognized that laugh. He flashed back to the day on the teeter-totter when Mario dropped him. He'd never forget Mario's laugh.

It can't be! he thought. But when he looked up at the child's eyes, he knew Mario was the boy's father.

Dave felt like a fool. He'd heard the rumors but had brushed them off as idle town gossip. Now he knew it wasn't.

Mario introduced Dino to Dave. "You can call him Uncle Dave like you do me." He told Dave, "Dino has called me 'Uncle Mario' since he learned to talk."

Dave gave Haddie's leash to Dino and asked him to hold on to her while they talked. Dino led the puppy away on her leash.

Mario said, "She looks just like Sandy, except she's black."

"Like my wife?"

"Ouch. I deserved that." Mario paused. "Dave, I was wrong. After Dad died, Mom immediately told me I was being racist. Without my dad to egg me on, I realized what I had been saying was hurtful, and I needed to change. I guess that little guy over there had something to do with that."

"So, you're admitting it. He's your son?"

"Yes, he is." Mario told Dave the entire story. "We'd been so tight all those years, and then bam! Along comes Nora. I wanted to ask you to forgive me after I realized what a fool I'd been, but I figured you wouldn't be able to, so I let it go."

"Mario, I don't know if I can forgive you. You've hurt me deeply. And you've hurt Nora."

Mario cried. He finally no longer needed to carry on a charade with his best friend. He could be honest. It felt as if someone had lifted a ton of bricks from his chest. The two men hugged and sat back to watch Dino and Haddie play.

Mario said, "Boy, that brings back some nice memories, huh?"

Dave had a warm, fuzzy feeling. "I can see it now. He's your little twin. So, tell me, what do Christy and Kevin have to say about all of this?"

"What can they say? Kevin knows Dino is not his, and if it weren't for me, they wouldn't be able to put food on the table. Dude! Kevin's still washing dishes! Christy and I have a business arrangement, I guess is what you'd call it. And I love Dino more than his dad does. I mean, Kevin."

"This is a lot to take in, Mario. I'll need time to process all of it. But I promise I'll call you. I may have just found the other chance I've been looking for." Dave got up, retrieved Haddie and started walking away.

"Hey! Wait, douchebag! I hear you're a big-time fancy writer now. Rolling in the dough, I bet."

Dave stopped and turned around. He wanted to say, *No, Mario. I'm not. I'm running out of money and can't write another book. Oh. And another thing, I'm a fucked-up loser who will probably go broke.*

Instead, he said, "Hey, thanks, Mario. Yeah, it's going well for me. I'll probably have my second book out sooner than I thought. Things are great, man!"

As Dave continued walking away, thoughts that he wasn't good enough swelled further in his head. He couldn't help but think, *Maybe I am like my dad.*

11

 not spoken to his disgraced daughter since she'd returned. Molly disliked the man and avoided him at all costs. She had, however, made amends with her mother, Eleanor. Unbeknownst to the reverend, the two had been meeting secretly in other locations so Eleanor could be with her grandson, Alex.

The church Reverend Kingston commanded had lost most of its membership. Except for his wife and a few older members, attendance had dwindled.

Bertha was a Catholic and did not wish to drive forty miles to her usual church one Sunday, so she assumed the good Lord would give her a pass if she attended there instead.

The Reverend always seemed to deliver the same fire-and-brimstone sermon. On this Sunday, he appeared pissed! Leaning against his pulpit, he looked out over the few and asked, "Brothers and sisters? Are you aware sinners have held a seance in our town?"

Bertha looked down in shame.

"Thou shalt burn in hell for eternity!" he shouted. He slammed his fist into the ambo, and before he could slam and scream again, he looked at his audience and dropped dead.

Eleanor was sitting in the front row with Bertha. They tried reviving him. It was in vain. He'd suffered a massive coronary and been dead before hitting the ground.

Everyone watching knew their minister was dead. They could see him on his side with lifeless eyes staring into theirs as if he'd known their deepest and darkest secrets. They knew this would most likely serve as the death knell of his congregation.

A FEW WEEKS later, Eleanor and the remaining members voted to dissolve the church and sell its assets. Around the same time, a New Age church known as The Home was searching for a domicile in northern Ohio.

Thirty-four-year-old minister Patrick O'Brian heard about the now-vacant church. Desiring to move to Cooper's Cove, he requested a transfer from his church in Chicago, and they approved a new congregation.

The Home bore little resemblance to its former self.

They removed the bell tower and leaded glass windows. They also removed all the pews to make way for a more Zen-like atmosphere where members sat on modular seating and traded stories of love, inspiration, and sometimes their pain.

Some said The Home didn't feel the same as the church had. They felt the casual setting was less rigid than the previous church and its more structured environment.

Patrick spoke only of two themes: forgiveness and unconditional love. The Home appeared to differ from the doctrines of Reverend Kingston and others like him. Patrick taught, "We come to the planet without sin but with purpose. It's up to us to decide how we use it." He told his followers, "The journey appears lighter when we know we're already perfect in the eyes of a loving and forgiving God. Go out and behave like Jesus would. Give of yourselves and help others. Offer what you can to that homeless person on the street corner. Who are we to judge?"

Patrick asked all his faithful to feel good about themselves and change their way of thinking. He listened as parishioners shared their stories of wholeness and prosperity consciousness. His philosophy was simple. He told them, "Contentment is there for the taking. If you believe you deserve happiness, it will manifest in your life."

Many members savored their new church's philosophy, but some considered it blasphemy and said it went against their beliefs. They remained steadfast and cared not to take part. Some even picketed the services with signs that read *Repent and save your souls before it's too late!*

Not one to shy away from controversy, Patrick confronted the upset protestors at one of their gatherings. "Tell me, are we not all from the same Creator? Why would any of us wish to take away the rights of others to worship in their own way?"

"Most of you take comfort in knowing Jesus. Many of us may as well. God doesn't differentiate between our personal beliefs and concepts of *God* and the *source* eternal. Are we not all striving for the same purpose? Oneness with God? Your savior? Forever we are. Forever we shall be. Why allow our individual beliefs to divide us and keep us from our attainment?"

The disgruntled crowd dispersed but vowed to return. Patrick had not dissuaded them that day.

Ed and Pete were drinking at Smitty's and heard about the ways of The Home. "Shit, Pete! First, the Austins move in. Then, the queers and dykes. Now we have that New Age church, or whatever they call it."

"Yeah, Ed, I hear you, but times just ain't the same as they were forty years ago. I think we may need to change with them."

Ed hunched his shoulders, grabbed his mug, and chugged the rest of his Pabst.

Patrick continued with his message. He knew the secret.

WINTERS SEEMED TO drag in Cooper's Cove. But everyone knew the snow-covered empty streets, boarded-up businesses, and marina void of boats would soon give way to the rays of summer.

Nora kept busy conceiving clay into works of art to sell at the Brass Buckle. The previous year, she'd made almost as much as the inn had. Today, she sat in her art studio and listened to Dionne Warwick singing "Déjà vu."

Dave had a day of incompetent writing and went to the basement to join his wife as she worked. He sat and admired her while she cast a twenty-pound clay block into a largemouth Lake Erie bass. "Honey, you're unreal at this. It's a good thing you are. I hope we'll make enough money to stay open through the summer."

Nora threw down her sculpting tool. She brushed a piece of wet clay from her Afro. "You know what, Dave? It's good that I enjoy my work because this is getting old! Why can't you just put pen to paper and develop an idea? Begin somewhere! Maybe you've been smoking a little too much pot. You seem to be over at Tewksbury's every day."

"Nora, you're one to talk! I know it's not just the guests enjoying our wine. I've seen empty wine bottles on trash day with no guests!"

Nora was first to pull the plug in their arguing this time. "Dave. I'm sorry. I understand you use marijuana for creativity. Maybe that's the reason I drink wine for my spark. And I shouldn't be pressuring you about your book. I know how difficult it can be when I'm trying to create, and nothing's there. You'll find your inspiration soon."

"It's coming, Nora. I can feel it."

HOPEFUL PROFITS WERE on both their minds as the innkeepers began their second season. At least they knew what was in store for them, having already been through it. Aunt Billie arrived, suitcase in hand, waiting to unpack and get busy with chores in the kitchen. Haddie, a year old now, was pushing Nora over the edge with her boundless energy.

Nora couldn't understand why. "Dave? What's up with Haddie? If she isn't chewing one of our shoes, she's chewing something else, someplace else!"

"Oops. I forgot to tell you that part. Labs can be rambunctious for a little while."

"Why didn't you say something before convincing me you wanted another Labrador? She's incorrigible!"

"Relax already! She'll settle down soon. Once they turn two, labs become more docile and stop acting out."

"You mean I still have another year of this? Oh, Dave, I don't know if I can hold on that long!"

Dave knew she would. Haddie had chosen her as her primary master. Haddie loved Dave, but her devotion was to Nora.

Nora never admitted it though.

DAVE'S CONSCIENCE WEIGHED heavily on him. He hadn't shared his encounter with Mario at Veterans' Park with Nora. He wasn't sure he wanted to reopen a painful part of his past. But he also knew he needed to say something to his wife. They were honest in their relationship.

Nora was savoring a cup of their Kona coffee during a break in spring cleaning. "By the way, Dave, I saw Mario with Dino at Riley's yesterday. He's growing fast."

Dave stopped chewing his fried bologna and cheese sandwich. "Yeah, about that. There's something I've been meaning to tell you." He swallowed the bite and took a deep breath. "Mario is Dino's father." He waited for his wife's response.

"Dave. I've known that for a couple of years now."

"What? I thought we didn't keep secrets!"

"I can explain that. It was our junior year of college when you couldn't understand why Mario was taking the boy everywhere and how strange you thought all that was."

"Yes. How could I forget?"

"Well, one day, I looked hard at Dino. The kid has the same eyes as Mario. And the same hair and complexion. And the same smile! It wasn't hard for me to figure it all out. Notice how Mario treats Dino as if the boy is his son? I don't know how Mario and Christy ended up like this, but something happened. By the way, Dave. How do you know Dino is his son? You've known of this all along and haven't told me?"

"I didn't know, Nora. Not until I saw the two together at Veterans' Park a while back. How could I not have seen this? He's my best friend. Or was."

"That's probably why, honey. You couldn't see past the

irresponsible goof-off he was. I don't think you ever imagined him as a father, did you?"

"No. That's the last thing I could have ever pictured. But he's surprised me. I'm amazed at what a good dad he is. You can see how much they love one another."

Nora breathed a sigh of relief. "I'm glad it's finally out in the open. Considering how you two ended things, I wanted to say something but didn't think it was my place."

"Well, I wish you would have. It may have saved me a lot of frustration. I don't know what to do. I want to be friends with him again, but now that he's told me this, I think I need to stay clear of him. He's got way too much baggage!"

"Play it cool. People can't keep secrets like this hidden forever. Especially in a small town. It'll probably all play out. It's Mario's baggage. Not yours. He may need a best friend when all this is over."

THE FIRST TURRET House guests of that season were fantastic. But, as Aunt Billie pointed out, "There's always one bad apple to spoil the bunch."

She was referring to a wealthy couple visiting from New Zealand. Mr. and Mrs. Roland Smith III of Auckland had arrived late the previous evening after a grueling twenty-hour flight from New Zealand. Mr. Smith was a well-known financier and world traveler. His wife, Elizabeth, had grown up in Cooper's Cove. She came from a poorer family with six children to feed. When she turned eighteen in 1926, she ran off to Chicago, where she met her wealthy future husband during one of his business trips there. She'd been working as a cigarette girl at the Furry Kitty Cat, a cheesy burlesque club downtown.

After a whirlwind romance and honeymoon, the couple settled back in New Zealand, where Elizabeth liked a snobbish, wealthy society. She hadn't wished to remember her roots in Cooper's Cove, but Roland decided he would like to see where his now-pretentious wife had her humble beginnings.

The Smiths were eating breakfast when Dave and Nora came into the dining room to introduce themselves. Elizabeth immediately began complaining. "Dear, you really must do something about your rather impersonal welcome. No one was here to greet us last night, and lugging those heavy suitcases up those stairs was debilitating."

Dave and Nora had waited until midnight for the couple, then left a note on the front door with instructions on how to find their room.

Mrs. Smith reminded Nora of a guest the previous summer who complained because her bed ruffle was touching the floor. The guest had also insisted a painting hung crooked.

"I'm very sorry about that and apologize. Have you found everything else to be to your liking?"

"I don't know about Elizabeth, but I found the Vagabond Room charming! Reminds me of our weary travels!"

"Well, if you ask me, young man, your breakfast buffet leaves something to be desired. I found your coffee weak, and those scrambled eggs were rubbery and bland!"

Aunt Billie glared at her, waiting to refill her cup.

Dave thought his great-aunt seemed ready to pour the hot coffee into Elizabeth's lap. "Oh shit! Aunt Billie? Don't do it!" he whispered. He grabbed her arm when he noticed she was about to pour it into Elizabeth's lap.

"Again, we're very sorry about everything." Nora asked the couple if there was anything else they could do to make it right.

"May you offer us some suggestions for our first day in town? I'm originally from here but haven't been back in years, and we'd like to explore the town as well. We will have lunch with one of my childhood friends later."

Dave told them, "Whatever you do, don't miss the winery. My friend's dad used to own it before his death. His sons run it now, and it's still popular."

Roland and Elizabeth moseyed out onto the inn's veranda to read. Instead, they spent the rest of the morning people-watching on Shoreline Avenue. Sightseeing would have to wait.

They later noticed the clock and realized it was almost time to meet her friend for lunch. "My goodness, Roland! Where does the time go?"

"More than likely, it passes through us, Elizabeth. It's there. We don't seem to notice it as we get older."

Elizabeth held his hand as they strolled, and she bragged

about the family she'd known growing up there. "Roland, I want you to know my parents were very well off here. We lived in a wonderful home on the lake, but it's no longer here. I was an only child, and after I turned eighteen, I rebelled against my parents for being overly strict. I intended to attend college, but being young and foolish, I chose the position at the Furry Kitty Kat instead. Do you understand? To blow off some pent-up teenage steam, you might say."

They stopped out front of the diner, and she gave Roland the once over, straightening his tie before she said to him, "Dear, I need to tell you something. When you meet my friend, you may consider her somewhat below our social standing, and she can be crude. We were so close as children; I wished to see her again."

When they walked inside, her old school chum saw the well-dressed couple and waved them to her table. "Youhoo! Howdy do, Liz! When I saw that expensive highfalutin dress, I knew it had to be you! It's wonderful to see you again, you old scoundrel. So, this is the rich guy you roped in Chicago?"

Elizabeth looked at Roland uncomfortably. Then she smiled. "Oh, Bertha! You haven't changed a bit, have you? You're still the jokingly funny girl you were back then. I was telling Roland how utterly charming you are. May we sit down?"

"Be my guest, honey. I bet all your ritzy-ditsy friends down under make fun of us peons here in Cooper's Cove. I remember your family was so poor some of those six kids had holes in their shoes!"

Elizabeth appeared horrified. "You see Roland? I told you she'd pull your leg when you met her. Bertha's just so witty."

"Witty? You know damn well your mom and dad could hardly afford to put food on the table for all eight of you."

"Why, Bertha! You have such a vivid imagination and are quite the jokester. Don't you remember we lived in that sprawling lakefront home?" Her eyes pleaded with Bertha to play along.

"Jokester! Who the fuck are you calling a jokester? If you hadn't met your rich husband, you wouldn't have a pot to piss in!"

Roland couldn't restrain himself any longer and started laughing. "Elizabeth, my dear! Do you mean to say you weren't wealthy? And that you had five brothers and sisters?"

Elizabeth knew she had blown her cover.

Roland reassured her. "Elizabeth, my company's attorney had your family thoroughly vetted before I married you. The Furry Kitty Cat? Cigarette girl? Come now, dear. I loved you regardless and always will."

Elizabeth's demeanor changed completely when she heard that. "Oh, Roland. Now you can understand why I wanted to see this wonderful gal again. She used to make me laugh so hard I peed my pants!"

The two classmates spent the next hour catching up on the last fifty years as Roland sat and smoked his pipe. As he listened to the two long-lost friends, he smiled and nodded to his wife's newfound sense of self.

AFTER NINETY-EIGHT YEARS on the planet, Cora Jensen discovered it was her time to leave. The curmudgeonly senior spinster still lived in the same home as when she was born.

Everyone could still see Cora driving her 1939 Nash, chugging along Shoreline Avenue, until the day before she died. The town had finished the new freeway, and Cora thought the new shortcut to Riley's made sense since she made fewer turns. Unfortunately, the higher speed drivers didn't like it when they approached her car traveling below the minimum speed of forty-five miles per hour. Cora was proud she had edged her speed up to thirty-five.

Bertha worried about her senior friend's driving habits and attempted unsuccessfully to talk her out of driving. Cora always passed the required eye exam and received a new license, much to the dismay of many motorists.

Bertha had always been there for her. She checked in on her twice a week to see if she needed anything. Cora never did but enjoyed Bertha's company all the same. She considered Bertha her best friend. On Cora's July Fourth birthday, Bertha always remembered to bake her a star-spangled-banner chocolate birthday cake.

Cora knew she could be a gossip, but that didn't matter— quite the contrary, as Bertha kept her abreast of who was doing who in town.

During one of her evenings, Cora had just left her cat

out before retiring. She was proud of Bootsy, who did not require a litter box. Like an excellent kitty, she did her duty in Cora's begonia flower beds outside her front door and returned promptly when finished.

Cora went to bed with the cat on her lap. She opened her hardback copy of Stephen King's *The Dead Zone* and began reading. King was Cora's favorite author. She'd read all his books and admired the author's macabre imagination. She was hooked on Johnny Smith's clairvoyant visions.

Suddenly Cora stopped reading and put the novel down. Something told her to open her daily devotions to the day's reading. *God sees when the footsteps all falter. When the pathway has grown too steep. When He touches the weary eyelids and gives His dear one sleep.*

Cora closed the book, along with her eyelids, and fell into eternal rest.

She followed the people before her as they walked along the silver tube to the bright light. The closer she got, the swifter she walked. She felt someone touch her arm and guide her through a door to the auditorium. Cora knew the place. She had been there many times before.

The familiar microphone on the stage appeared before her. She tapped it as Heidi had. It reverberated throughout the hall, and Cora knew the mic was live. "Hellooooo! Anyone home?"

"Welcome back, Cora! My, that certainly was a long life. So, tell me? What did you think? Was it everything you thought it would be when you chose your assignment?"

Cora remembered the soothing voice. "Oh, Sue Ellen, it was!" Cora had been here so many times, she knew her guide by first name. "I'm grateful for every experience I had. It was gratifying, although my time during the Great Depression was trying."

"Well, Cora, I'm pleased to tell you! You have earned the right to choose your existence for the next life. Is there someplace special you'd like to incarnate or anyone you'd like to be?"

Cora contemplated. "Yes, I believe there is, Sue Ellen. May I choose the period of the High French Renaissance, say 1514? I want to be born an architect and design something such as the Château de Chenonceau. And make me wealthy. I've learned to appreciate wealth."

"Very well, Cora. Enjoy your time on earth, and I'll await your return!"

BERTHA DISCOVERED CORA dead the following morning. Cora hadn't answered her phone, so Bertha checked on her in person. Cora had a peaceful expression; Bertha thought she looked like she was sleeping.

All of Cora's heirs were dead, so after her last survivor had died, Cora had rewritten her will, leaving all her assets to Bertha. She'd wished to be cremated and left specific instructions to Bertha: *Whatever you do, don't let Nick put me in that damn bank teller's window!*

She wished her ashes to be scattered from her Nash

LaFayette at Rocky Point, where she had enjoyed watching the sunsets.

⁓

CORA'S ATTORNEY CONTACTED Bertha a few days after she'd died. "Bertha, Cora made you the heir to her estate. We'll meet in my office later, but may I review a few details with you now if you have time?"

Bertha was hoping for the Nash. She knew the classic 1939 automobile with its 15,000-mile odometer reading was worth money. It'd sure come in handy. Up to now, she had survived on her social security pension alone. "Now's as good as any time. Did she leave me the car?"

"Bertha, you'll be happy to hear she did. Her estate is quite valuable as well. I think you'll be happy with the number I will give you."

Bertha knew Cora's small, older cottage wasn't worth much. What else did she have to leave her? The tight skinflint wouldn't even buy new clothes.

"Bertha, your friend Cora has been buying shares of Coca-Cola stock since the thirties, and her portfolio is worth almost one million dollars today."

Bertha about dropped the phone. "You've got to be kidding me. Praise Jesus! I knew Cora enjoyed drinking her Coca-Cola, but holy shit; I never knew she liked it that much!"

A day later, Nick called and told her Cora's ashes were ready to be picked up. Bertha grabbed the keys to the Nash and drove down Shoreline Avenue, honking the car's horn, just as Cora had done so many times. When she rounded the curve at Rocky Point, she rolled down her window and dumped the ashes out of Cora's urn, singing, "I'd like to buy the world a Coke!"

Bertha couldn't help but smile all the way to her bank!

12

IT WAS ANOTHER damp and rainy spring day that northern Ohioans know all too well.

Dave was tinkering in his garage, most likely the last time he'd be able to before the inn opened. Once they got busy, *if* they got busy, he knew he'd have to help like he'd promised.

But then again, he'd made other promises, too. He'd promised a book and promised Nora the business would be successful. And now he couldn't guarantee either. Too many what-ifs lived in his mind. *What if I can't even write the new book? What if the inn doesn't make enough money? And what if we lose this place because of me? What then?*

Aunt Billie entered the garage and startled him out of his pity party.

He looked up from his worktable. "Oh, sorry! I didn't see you there. What's up?"

"Nora asked me to come and ask what you have planned guest-wise for the season. And I think I better tell you this, Dave. I overheard her speaking on the telephone the other morning. She was talking with her mother, and Grace asked Nora to begin the repayment plan."

Dave thought, *Shit. Just what I need right now!* "Tell her the bookings are running higher than last season."

It was partly true. Reservations were up, but they'd charge less for rooms this year. Two new budget hotels had opened on Vacationland Highway.

Dave hoped his luck would turn around soon.

DINO JAMISON TURNED five. Christy and Kevin had worked out a custody agreement between Mario and his son. Dino would spend Saturdays hanging out with his Uncle Mario and a few holidays in between.

Attention to the strange throuple had faded. Besides the Jamisons and now the Meyers, no one knew for sure who his father was. No one seemed to care, except those already involved.

DAVE'S RELATIONSHIP WITH Mario stood stagnant; he and Nora met him for drinks, but Dave noticed Nora seemed uncomfortable around him.

Before the couple went to bed, she confided in Dave, "I think he's still hiding something from you. What it is, I'm not sure. But I don't think he's been completely upfront."

"Nora? I'm exhausted, honey. I'd rather go to sleep than talk about Mario."

THE WEATHER THE following week took a turn for the better. One of Aunt Billie's favorite sayings was *Don't like the weather in northern Ohio? Stick around. It'll change!*

That may have been true, and as the temperature hit seventy-five degrees this long-awaited day, Dave washed and waxed his Mustang and pulled the classic back into the first bay.

The mansion's garage held three parking stalls; they also housed Nora's run-around car, a black 1979 Dodge Colt Turbo. He saw the tarp covering the machine in the third bay. It hadn't been off since he'd towed it from his mom's garage.

He walked over and pulled the tarp off. The yellow Doodlebug sat there in all its glory, and memories of the peach orchard returned.

The 1932 Ford looked the same, except it hadn't started it in years. Knowing the battery would be dead, he bought a new one. He tried again, hoping it would fire up. But the old motor wouldn't turn over. It seemed like the engine had frozen up.

Dave recalled some of what he had learned in the high school auto shop, but nothing like what was required to give the Doodlebug's engine new life. Then he remembered his shop partner from high school. Warren Holtzman had been a mechanical genius and could tell him what the truck needed.

Warren had just begun law school the last he'd heard. The two had not kept in touch since. He dialed Warren's number and heard an automated voice say it was no longer in service.

Dave still had the telephone number for his parents. The couple had spent winters in Fort Lauderdale and summers in Cooper's Cove.

"Hello? Mrs. Holtzman? This is Dave Meyers."

"Hi there, Dave! My gosh, it's been a while. Warren asked about you the last time I spoke with him."

"Well, I tried his number in Boston, but the recording says it's no longer in service."

"Warren no longer lives in Cambridge, Dave. He dropped out of law school after his father passed away while we were in Florida."

"Oh! I'm sorry to hear about that, Mrs. Holtzman. I didn't know."

"His dad had kidney disease, which had progressively worsened, and he'd been on dialysis for three years. He'd wished to keep it all quiet."

"Well, how is Warren handling it? Where is he now?"

"Dave, he's not living that far. When he gave up law school, he moved to Akron, where he bought a mechanic's auto repair garage. He's doing well. He plans on opening his second shop in Canton next month. He's happy."

"Wow! I never expected that."

"I didn't either, Dave. I'm just glad he is."

"That makes two of us! Could I have his new number, please?"

He thanked her, offered condolences, and then dialed Warren's number.

"Holtzman's Garage. Warren speaking. How may I be of service today?"

"Boy, don't you sound like a well-educated grease monkey!"

"Dave! Long time no see. I guess Mom and Dad's rather noteworthy investment in my future has now turned into this. I couldn't do it anymore. I was so depressed and read more copies of *Car and Driver* than I ever did of any lawbook."

"What made you leave Harvard?"

"After dad died, I came clean to Mom. She understood. Dad never would have. I don't have any regrets."

"Warren, I'm proud of you. Few would have done what you did. I can't wait to tell Nora! I'm calling because I tried starting the Doodlebug. I even put in a new battery, but nothing. Any suggestions?"

"I'm sure the cylinders froze. I'm driving over to see Mom on Sunday. I'll stop by afterward and look."

"Thanks. I'd appreciate it. And should I add? Congratulations!"

WARREN'S SUPPOSITION PROVED correct. The number two-cylinder head was stuck. The pair spent two separate days working on the old Ford. Like the pro he was, Warren had the antique auto up and running.

Dave went inside to get Nora and Aunt Billie. Haddie came running out with them. The two women were ecstatic when they saw the idling Doodlebug, and Haddie barked her approval.

"Hey Warren, what do you say we put a couple of lawn chairs on the back and take the old girl out for a spin?"

"Hey, watch that, mister!" Aunt Billie snapped.

"Oh, I'm sorry! I meant the Doodlebug."

"I know you did, Davie. I was toying with ya!"

Dave got behind the wheel, and Warren sat opposite, with Haddie riding in the middle. Nora and Aunt Billie sat perched on the folding chairs on the truck's rear bed. Dave pulled out of the inn onto Shoreline Avenue and honked the ahooga horn. The tourists all turned and waved. Aunt Billie told Nora, "We must look like Granny and Elly Mae Clampett up here!"

Dave stopped before the Main Street Diner, where Molly and Alex Kingston had just eaten lunch with Russ. All three stood outside, and everyone waved except Nora, who couldn't stop staring at Alex as he stared back. Who did she know inside the seven-year-old's eyes?

Dave pulled away. Nora couldn't stop thinking about Alex. It was as if she was experiencing a moment of déjà vu.

THE TWO SECRET lovers were in his office. They'd just finished putting together the Labor Day edition of the *Courier*. All the employees had gone home except for the editor and his secretary. They'd had to hide what they were doing for a few years now.

"Kathleen, you know I love you." Wilson was putting his pants back on.

Kathleen had just gotten into her bra and was pulling on her pantyhose. "I love you too, Wilson, but we can't have what you want. This town is still too small. I can hear Bertha now. 'You know, don't you? Those two have been doing it for years!' And if I were to get married again, I'm certain Dave would disapprove of it."

"You needn't concern yourself with what Bertha or Dave think. Dave's a young adult now and married to an African American girl. Don't you think someone of his intellect would want the best for his mother? I think he'd be happy for you, not condemn you."

"There's still Frank. I miss him. I sometimes see his face when you and I make love. It frightens me. It is as if I've been cheating on him."

"Kathleen, have you ever stopped to think perhaps Frank wants you to be happy? He's there not to upset you but to tell you how much he loved you. Maybe he's chosen me for you? Please! Let's get married. I treasure you. Always have. I remember the day you applied for the job, like yesterday."

"But Wilson! I must ask. The rumors about your wife. Are any of them true?"

"Some were. Some weren't. We did indeed argue. But it was about her cheating, not mine. I was always faithful to her. She wanted out. And I let her go. I agreed to all her demands."

"I'm pleased to hear that, but how do I explain to Dave that we've been lovers since his father died? It's as if I've been living a lie right in front of him."

Wilson hugged her. "I don't think you'll have to. He's more astute than you've given him credit for."

KATHLEEN MET NORA for coffee at the new expresso shop downtown. "Nora, how does one choose from all those fancy coffees and cappuccinos they have on that board? My god. You can't even get a cup of black coffee, except maybe the diner."

Nora chuckled. "Mom, they also sell regular coffee here if that's what you'd like. They call it the 'Nothing Added.'"

"Yes. Except for another quarter! Fancy pants coffee bar! Who would have thought?"

They sat at one of the black cast iron bistro sets. "Mom, everything changes, I guess. What did you need to talk to me about?"

Kathleen began. "Where do I begin, Nora? Truth is... Wilson and I have been more than just employer and employee. I may have fallen for him the week after he hired me. But I'd still been married. We did nothing until after

Frank died. I felt ashamed. I thought I was betraying my dead husband. Wilson and I hid it from Dave.

"Then, after Dave began working at the *Courier*, we kept our relationship strictly professional in his presence. I'm sure he hasn't romantically linked us yet."

Nora took her left hand. "I'm so happy for you! You have someone to spend the rest of your life with. Frank would have wanted that. And as far as Dave goes, you needn't be concerned. He loves Wilson as much as you. He's the one who boosted Dave's writing career. Why don't you come over for dinner Saturday night and speak to Dave?"

Kathleen accepted Nora's invitation.

NORA BAKED HER mother's lasagna recipe, and Dave made the salad. It was his version of a Caesar salad minus the anchovies, which he hated. Nora tried reasoning that it wasn't a Caesar salad but was to him. To keep the peace, she'd learned to agree.

Dave was watching *Hart to Hart* on ABC in his library when he heard the telephone ring.

"Dave? It's for you."

"Who is it, Nora?"

"I don't know! He wouldn't say. I'm trying to check on my lasagna!"

He turned down the volume on the television before answering the extension. "Hello."

"Dave? This is Maurice Donovan. I'm worried because I haven't heard from you in a while. The publisher is asking for an update, and I don't know what to tell them. How's it coming with the book?"

"Hi, Maurice. Sorry I haven't gotten back to you. I'm running behind with the project. Can't seem to get myself organized."

"God damn it, Dave! I'm not shitting around! Either you come up with what you promised them, or you'll owe them more money than you ever could hope to make! And you'll effectively block yourself as an author for the rest of your career!" The agent hung up.

Dave tried to compose his thoughts. *This is great! Not only is my writing stuck, but now I must work with the threat of a lawsuit hanging over my head. This is not good.*

He heard the doorbell ring and realized it was probably his mom.

She opened the door and let herself in. "Dave? Nora? Anyone home?"

"I'm in the library, Mom."

Kathleen went to the library and kissed her son's cheek. "What's the matter, honey? You look pretty glum."

"Well, let's just say I've seen better days. I just got off the phone with Maurice, and he told me the publisher is threatening to sue me if I don't have the book ready soon."

"I'm sorry to hear that, Dave. Weren't you supposed to have another ready by this time?"

"I was. I'm at a loss for words. Literally! I can't get it

together as I did for *Above the Rainbow.* I keep drawing blanks. And now Maurice threatens me with this."

They sat on the overstuffed maroon leather couch, and his mother told him, "Dave, stop worrying about something you have little control over other than your thoughts and desires. I have faith in you. I know you'll find the inspiration soon, and this book will be even better than *Above the Rainbow.*"

"Hope you're right, Mom! Nora said you wanted to talk with me about something?"

"Yes. I do. Don't hate me for this, but Wilson and I are in love. We've seen each for a while. But we did nothing with each other while your father was alive. I loved your dad."

Dave dipped a carrot stick into a tub of Lawson's French Onion Dip and grabbed a Triscuit cracker from Nora's vegetable and cheese platter. "I had a hunch you two were. Wilson's always treated you wonderfully. We both know how Dad could be. I'm glad you found each other. I watched the embrace he gave you at Dad's funeral. I saw some of your grief lighten then, and I secretly hoped something like this would happen. You deserve it. I've respected your privacy and never pried. Nora shared with me what you two talked about."

"That's a relief, honey. I'm glad you feel the way you do about Wilson. And none of those rumors you may have heard about him are true."

"I think Wilson will make a terrific stepdad! When's the big day?"

"We're planning a small ceremony like you and Nora had. Christmas Eve. We'd like to have it at The Turret House and ask Reverend Patrick if he'll officiate."

"It sounds like a plan, Mom!"

THE CEREMONY WAS simple. A freshly fallen snow blanketed the grounds, and candle luminarias lined the brick sidewalk leading to the inn. Dave and Nora decked the inn out in its Christmas splendor. A ten-foot-tall Norfolk pine reached toward the living room ceiling, its shimmering blue Christmas lights mirroring the gold ornaments and silver tinsel. Nora's handcrafted ceramic angel sat atop the tree. It seemed to watch over the couple as they took each other's hand in marriage before Reverend Patrick. Dave, Nora, and her parents were the only guests at the intimate gathering.

That evening, Dave and Nora made love, grateful for their love and the beautiful gifts the universe had given them.

The newlyweds spent their honeymoon on a Caribbean cruise. When they returned to Cooper's Cove, Kathleen sold her home on Jefferson Street, and they began matrimony in a newly built luxury condominium at the country club.

BERTHA WENT HOG wild that winter over her newfound wealth. Thus far, she'd lived a simple life, and her house was modest by Cooper's Cove standards, but she'd been happy.

After Cora died and left her the fortune, Bertha behaved like a kid in a candy store, spending her prosperity. She spared no expense in remodeling her home. She wished her kitchen to resemble Julia Child's on her PBS cooking show *The French Chef.*

The town's handyperson was a gifted carpenter whose work was always quality, and Bertha hired him to do the renovation. The worker had extravagant taste, even if he had little money. He'd been born with a silver spoon in his mouth but had lost it gambling and now worked odd jobs for those who would hire him.

More probably would have, but he had his nose high in the air. He reveled in spending money as long as it was someone else's. And Bertha's new budget had no end.

He liked to boast, "Nothing but the finest, Mrs. Murkowski. I've read everything there is to know in *Architectural Digest,* and I promise, when I'm finished, you'll possess a home your friends will truly envy! You must understand not everyone can be like us. If you have it, don't be afraid to flaunt it!"

Bertha had no problem taking the man's advice to heart. She threw out all her old clothes to make way for the latest fashions in 1980. Her friends thought the sixty-nine-year-old portly woman looked ridiculous in her shoulder-padded dresses and puffed-up hairdos more befitting a woman half her age.

However, Bertha thought her new look complemented

her unique personality. No longer was she Bertha the happy cook; she became Bertha the pretentious, much as her friend Elizabeth Smith had become in New Zealand.

That did not go over well in a town where practically everyone knew her. Her now former friends weren't the least bit envious of the nouveau riche woman's inheritance, and she was losing friends fast.

VERNA SCHMUDABECK STOOD in line with Evie Crandall at the checkout counter of Riley's. "Evie, I just don't get it. Bertha and I've been friends through thick and thin, and now she thinks she's better than me! She has her head stuffed so far up her fat ass; she doesn't see what a snob she's become."

"I know what you mean. We had lunch last week at the diner, and she asked Russ if he offered beef chateaubriand! Russ just laughed at her, and she threw her menu on the floor. She told him, 'Never mind! Just bring me one of your shitty hamburgers!' I felt so embarrassed for her."

"Well, I don't know what's gotten into her. She's tighter than Cora ever was! You'd think with a million in the bank, she'd want to share some of it with her friends. I guess she's forgotten where she came from. Money will do that, you know."

Bertha may have had more wealth than she ever dreamed possible, but she soon discovered it didn't buy happiness. She missed the old Bertha. She decided to call Elizabeth. "Operator? This is Bertha Murkowski. I want to place a person-to-person call to Mrs. Roland Smith the III, in Auckland, New Zealand. What's that? Yes, I'll hold."

The international operator had her on hold for one minute.

"Hello?"

"Elizabeth darling. This is Bertha. I'm calling to let you know I'm wealthy! Cora Jensen left me a fortune in Coca-Cola stock."

"Bertha, you don't sound like yourself. Are you okay? You've never called me darling."

"I'm fine, Elizabeth. I thought it would impress you to hear I've joined the ranks of the well to do."

"I am happy for you, Bertha, but did you not learn anything from our conversation with Roland at the diner that day? Please! Stop with the attitude. No one likes a pompous snob who thinks they are superior to everyone else. We're all equal in God's eyes. It took me many years to learn that."

The conversation with her old friend brought Bertha back to reality. She called all her girlfriends and apologized.

Evie told her, "Bertha, we're all glad you're finally off your high horse! Do you think you'll come back to the Ladies Bowling League soon? We all miss you!"

Bertha was back at the lanes the following Wednesday in her JCPenney slacks and a T-shirt that said *Vegas, Baby!* She had a surprise in store for all the women. "I'm grateful you've all forgiven me. I let my ego get in my way. I forgot who my friends are. I want to make it all up to you, so I'm giving you all a three-day weekend at Caesars Palace!"

Bertha chartered a United Airlines DC-8 and flew 250 townspeople, those she felt had been a meaningful part of her life. She reserved all fourteen opulent suites for her girlfriends and provided free rooms to the other 236 guests, along with $500 each in gambling money.

The old Bertha was back.

ALEX KINGSTON TURNED eight years old and began asking his mother about his dad. So far, he'd been told his father had gone away when he was just a baby and that she'd raised him alone. Alex's curious little mind wanted to know more.

Molly thought about it all. She'd held the secret for so long because she felt the child was too young to understand. She remembered the night. It was her junior year in 1972. He asked her on a date, and she accepted, thinking she'd have a good time with the popular boy. They drove out to Rocky Point, and he brought two bottles of wine.

They sat and watched the stars and got very drunk, and he took advantage of her. She tried fending him off, but she was unable to. The muscular youth ripped off her panties and forced himself on her in the back seat. He thought he was playing it safe and pulled out before he came. But he had impregnated her. She hated him, and instead of spending the rest of her life with someone who'd taken advantage of her, she swore she'd never tell him about the boy.

Molly wondered if this was how Christy Jamison felt when she'd learned she was pregnant. Christy didn't love him either. She remembered the day Christy brought Dino into the daycare center. Molly had stopped dead in her tracks when she saw the eyes of the child. *That bastard*, she thought. Not about the child, but about the father, who she realized was Mario. The bastard had also gotten Christy pregnant, forcing her to live a lie, much like Molly had been doing all these years.

Molly wondered, *What would Mario Panza say if I told him he has another son?*

"NORA, LOOK AT that little brat screaming over there." Dave and Nora were shopping at the new mall on the outskirts of town. They were browsing Macy's when they heard a commotion in the toy section. A boy was screaming at his mother because she would not buy him an expensive Atari video game. Nora and Dave walked over and saw it was Alex Kingston and Molly. The boy, embarrassed, looked up at Nora.

Nora realized what it was about the boy plaguing her. She hadn't known him in a previous life; she knew who he was now. He had Mario's same eyes and expression.

Dave held Nora's hand, and they walked away after acknowledging them both. "You know, Nora, that kid's a real brat. You'd think Molly would have done a better job raising him."

Nora dreaded her feelings. *Oh, god! Do I tell Dave my suspicions or keep my mouth shut? Is he ready to know this latest revelation about his friend?*

She wanted to tell Dave. But she'd keep it to herself until she had definite proof. *Dave will understand,* she thought.

IT WAS VALENTINE'S Day in the quiet town, and Dave and Nora settled on a calm evening at the inn. The winter had been mild in Cooper's Cove. The temperature reached a balmy fifty degrees, and Dave grilled barbecued chicken on the patio. He whipped up his signature Caesar salad, and Nora baked a low-carb cauliflower cheese casserole. After they finished, they sat in front of the fireplace. Nora had bought fresh strawberries, and they dipped them into a chocolate fondue pot. Dave opened one of the wines Mario had given them as a Valentine's Day gift.

While sipping the excellent merlot, which Nora had declined, and savoring the delicious, sweet California strawberries, Dave gave Nora her Valentine's card. She opened the envelope and saw a black Labrador puppy on the cover. "Oh! She's so cute!" She showed the card to the Lab. "Look

Haddie! Here's a picture of you. Have you been moonlighting on us?"

Dave carefully opened his card and slid it out of the envelope. The yellow lab on the front resembled Sandy. Nora had scrawled a message on it: *Thank you for being the wonderful husband you've been. I have a gift for you, but it won't be ready until August. Happy Valentine's Day! Love, Nora and Haddie.*

Dave coated another strawberry with chocolate and put it in his mouth. "I thought we said no gifts, honey. I have nothing for you."

"Oh, but you've already given me mine. You're going to be a father."

He stopped eating. "What? Nora! You're not kidding, are you?"

"I saw the doctor for a checkup this morning. It seems the queasy tummies I've been having are morning sickness. He thinks I'm about seven weeks pregnant."

"I can't believe it!" He hugged his pregnant wife. "I'm so happy. I feel like I did when you gave me Haddie. When's the baby due?"

"Most likely in August. I may have gotten pregnant on Christmas Eve."

"Now I know how Mario feels about Dino! I'm so grateful. I'm blessed. I didn't think loving you more than I already do was possible. I love you beyond the Milky Way."

"Oh yeah? I love you beyond the universe, Dave. I win!"

Dave was about to do her one better before he realized

their precarious financial situation. The inn hadn't made enough money last summer to enable them to repay Nora's parents. They seemed to be just skimming by. Now they were going to have a baby.

She looked at his face. "What's wrong, babe?"

"I'm scared, Nora. Where's the money coming from if things don't work out like we planned?"

"Come here," she said.

He laid his head on her lap.

She looked into his sparkling blue eyes and saw his fears. "Don't think about that right now. This is a time to celebrate. Everything seems to work out in life. You're always telling me that."

"You know what? You're right!"

They spent the rest of the evening lounging around and making plans for the baby's arrival. "Boy or girl?" Dave asked. "Which are you hoping for?"

"Either, Dave, as long as it's healthy."

"Same here."

Nora thought it might be a good time to tell him her suspicions about Alex. "Dave? Do you remember when we were shopping at the mall and saw Alex Kingston throwing that fit?"

"How could I forget?" he asked.

Nora sat up on the sofa. "I think Mario is Alex's dad, too."

"What the fuck, Nora!" Dave's face turned red, and he felt his pulse rising. "What are you talking about? What makes you think he's Alex's father as well?"

"I had my suspicions, Dave. When I saw Alex screaming at Molly that day, I finally realized it. Alex may not have Mario's coloring, but I'd know those eyes anywhere. He's going to swoon over all the girls like his father has. And he has his dad's charming character."

"What the fuck were you thinking? I already knew about Dino! You could have told me!"

Nora couldn't believe Dave was swearing at her. She'd never realized he would be this upset with her. This was a side of him she'd rarely witnessed. "My god! Dave! What if I'd been wrong? With all that was going on between the two of you, I didn't wish to complicate things if my suspicions weren't true. I thought you'd understand."

"Well, you thought wrong!"

Nora felt like crying. She showed the sadness on her face. She'd never meant to upset Dave. "I'm so sorry, Dave. I guess I shouldn't have kept this from you. I was only trying to protect you from any more hurt if I was wrong."

Dave's mood changed when he saw the hurt in his wife's eyes. "Honey, I'm sorry I swore at you. It shocked me; that's all. It wasn't right of me to take my anger out on you like that."

"It's okay. I know you didn't mean to."

The mood in the room brightened. "Well, the plot thickens! What do you think happened, Nora? You think Mario knows he's the father?"

"I'm still not positive, but I'd say no if I were a gambler. Molly doesn't even like Mario and probably doesn't want him to know."

"Shit, Nora, this is unreal!"

She laughed. "Honey, are you surprised to learn any of this? We're talking about Mario, remember?"

"Yeah, you're right. I wonder how many other kids he has out there?"

"I'm not sure of that, either. I hope no more. But I can tell you one thing. Whenever you see a baby out there, see if you can see Mario!"

13

 his couch, thinking about what he'd left out of his story. He wished he could have been honest with Dave from the very beginning. He'd omitted something essential but didn't wish to spend the rest of his life in prison.

Dave called him and asked if he could come over and get high. "I need another quarter of bud as well."

"I got plenty, Dave. I just took in a new harvest, and this shit is fantastic. Come on over."

Dave told Nora, "I'm visiting Mary Jane at Tewksbury's house."

"Tell her I said hi." Nora kissed her husband goodbye. Her baby bump had grown, and Dave thought his wife looked more radiant than ever.

He walked down the front steps of the veranda and faced the dreaded eyesore. Quentin's asparagus patch seemed to be waving at him. It was harvesting season for the enticing crop of green stalks. Dave knew what the garden would look like once the last cutting was done: gnarly green wisps blowing in the wind for all the inn's guests to enjoy. Dave had already asked Quentin if he would prune it once the plant stopped producing.

"No can do, Dave. The stalks must remain over the winter for the next growing season. I want my new crop to be nice and healthy."

Wonder if the old stoner would notice if I chopped it all down tonight? he thought.

He knocked, and the aging hippie opened the door to let him in. Dave smelled the skanky odor and saw the overflowing ashtrays on the coffee table. He saw the dirty bongs lining the fireplace mantle and thought, *Quentin must have had a busy winter!*

They sat on the floor, and Tewksbury lit up. "Try this, Dave. It's heavy sativa, gives me a nice mellow buzz, and helps me focus."

Dave took a puff and held it for a few seconds before he let it out. He rarely coughed anymore. "Very nice, Tewksbury. Very nice." He handed it back.

Quentin took a long hit and inhaled what appeared to be almost half of it. He finally exhaled a humongous plume of smoke. "There's something I need to tell you, Dave. I wasn't honest with you when I told you how I got here. I want you to keep what I'm about to tell you in confidence, right?"

Dave sat there stoned and nodded.

Tewksbury had told him an abridged version of what

had happened. Now, he'd say it in its entirety. "It was 1973, or around that time when I arrived. I was pretty fucked up and had been staying at a boarding house over on Green Street. I went up to Cleveland to this seedy little bar on the west side that caters to men who like to dress in women's clothing.

"Dave, my sexuality vacillates on the Kinsey Scale, and every once in a while, I need to venture out, if you know what I mean?"

Dave didn't, but he nodded anyway.

"I saw this attractive gal at the bar. She was short and a little chunky, just the way I like my ladies. I thought she slightly resembled an overweight Jayne Mansfield. She smiled at me and nodded to the empty bar stool beside her, so I sat and introduced myself. She told me her name was Felicia, and I asked if I could buy her a drink.

"She had an intense voice and told the bartender she wanted another one of her gin fizzes. Felicia was singing the song on the jukebox. If I remember correctly, the verse went, 'Brandy, you're a fine girl...' Ah, I can't remember all the words, but I dig that group Looking Glass, don't you?"

Dave admitted, "Can't say I know who they are, Quentin."

"Well, anyway, Felicia took a sip of her gin fizz and asked, 'You new around here?' I gave her a synopsis of my life and asked if she had a place we could go. She told me, 'Oddly enough, I do. It's also in Cooper's Cove.' Then she added, 'Small world, isn't it?'

"I agreed it was and told her, 'Baby, I'm very discreet. How about I follow you back to your place?'

"We left in separate cars, and when we got to her house, she took me upstairs and removed my shirt. Then she asked, 'So, do you like to be topped, handsome?'

"I pushed her hand away. 'Whoa, whoa, whoa!' I said. 'Ain't nothing going up my ass!'

"I'd thought by the way she looked, she enjoyed getting screwed, so I started walking toward the door. The old drag queen pulled off his wig and showed me his bald head. He screamed, 'Thanks for wasting my time, fucker!' He picked up a glass vase and threw it at me. I ducked, and it shattered against the wall behind me."

"He kept shouting, 'Get out, get out of my house!' and the cross-dresser charged at me. I stepped aside, and he slipped on his stilettos and tumbled headfirst down the stairs. I rushed down to see if he was okay. And there he was! That funeral home director, Donald Woesten, lay there dead! He must have broken his neck.

"I freaked, Dave. My initial reaction was to pick up the phone and call the police, but who'd believe me when I told them a drag queen had thrown a vase at me and accidentally fallen down his stairs? Especially in this town?"

"I carefully retraced my steps and wiped down everything I had touched. I was in a hurry and left the pile of shattered glass from that vase. Usinga hand towel, I carefully picked up the phone and called the police. I disguised my voice. I said, 'Check out 1455 Shoreline Avenue. Someone there needs help,' and I discreetly left and returned to the boarding house.

"A few months later, I noticed the sheriff's auction at

Donald's house. I was the high bidder and have lived here ever since, keeping a low profile except for our fucking next-door neighbor Bertha! She's worse than Gladys Kravitz on *Bewitched*. If I were going to kill anyone, it'd be someone like her!

"So, there you have it, Dave. Hell of a thing to carry on my conscience."

Dave reassured him, "Quentin, relax, dude, and stop beating yourself up over this. Donald did himself in. Not you."

"Yeah, I guess you're right. It's good to tell someone. Takes the power out of it. This stays between us, right?"

"Right, Tewksbury! Light up another one, dude! This is too kinky for me!"

AUNT BILLIE TREATED the expectant mother as if she had a disability. The worrisome aunt asked Nora to take a break as they were washing windows, getting ready for another season.

"Please, Aunt Billie! I can do more than you think. The baby isn't due till August, and the doctor said it's perfectly okay for me to work like I've always done."

"Well, he may be right, dear. But, if you get tired, you stop and sit down! I can take care of everything by myself."

Dave thought the eighty-two-year-old had more energy than the two of them combined. They kicked off with breakfast at the diner and a shopping trip to stock up on everything the inn needed. On their way home, they honked at Mario's car as he pulled into the parking lot at Rocky Point.

~

MARIO WAS RETRIEVING Dino's beach ball from his car's trunk when he noticed a mother and her young son playing with their ball in shallow water. Mario set down their beach gear, and the two waded in.

The young woman turned to him. "Well, if it isn't Mario Panza and his little friend Dino. I think it's great you two get to spend so much time together. The Jamisons must appreciate what you have done for their son."

Molly told the boys to play on the beach. "What's with all the sarcasm, Molly? Can't a neighbor take a little kid swimming while his mom and dad must work?"

"Oh, is that what you're calling it? Just helping. Right? Cut the shit, Mario. You're a jerk, and you've always been. I know Dino is yours. You may have been able to fool everyone else in this town, but you can't fool me. Where'd you knock her up? Was it here, like you did me?"

Mario gaped. He turned and saw Alex playing with Dino. He noticed Alex resembled his mother, except for his eyes, which were a dead ringer for his own. The older boy was teasing Dino, holding the ball out of his reach, and Dino was crying.

"See Mario? Alex can be a brat, just like his father. That's the part of him I don't like."

Mario took a moment to absorb it all. Looking at another

biological son, he told Molly, "I don't understand. I know I was drunk, but I pulled out before I came, or so I thought."

"In case you don't know by now, Einstein, it doesn't take much to get a girl pregnant. He's yours. No question about it. But he's also a kind, thoughtful little boy."

"Why did you wait all these years to let me know? Had you told me, I would have married you. I know it doesn't mean much now, but I am truly sorry."

"Mario, I hated you! You raped me! And part of me still does. But I need to consider Alex now. He's been asking who his father is, and he has a right to know. I haven't figured out yet how I will tell him." She looked to make sure the boys couldn't hear. "I guess I could say, 'Your father raped me, and I hated him, so I decided not to marry him.'"

"Molly! I feel terrible. I know it doesn't mean much now, but I hope you forgive me." Mario looked at his two beautiful boys. He had given life to them both but knew only one. The other was a stranger. "I've missed a lot of birthdays with him, haven't I? Where do we go from here?"

"I'm not sure, Mario. We'll have to figure that out. But I'll tell you one thing. You will not smother him like you did with Christy's! It will take a while for Alex to adjust to all this. We don't know how he will react to you once he knows the truth."

"I'll do whatever you want. Please, just let me be a part of your lives."

Molly caught it when he said part of their lives, not just Alex's. "Before I tell Alex anything, I want you to tell Christy what you did to me. She needs to know. You and I can talk about Alex later. But I won't tell Alex anything until you've talked to her. She mustn't find out any other way. The girl has enough on her plate as it is."

THE FOLLOWING DAY, Mario sat at his kitchen table, trying to figure out what he would say to Christy and Kevin. How could he look her in the eyes and admit what he'd done to Molly? He figured she'd hate him as well. He went outside and walked through his neighbors' side gate.

Dino was swinging on his swing set. "Hi, Uncle Mario. Mommy and Daddy are inside."

"Yeah, thanks, buddy. I'll talk to you in a little while." Mario opened their front door like he had done many times and walked in. "Hey, you guys."

Christy shouted, "We're in here, Mario."

He went into their living room and saw them watching *Good Morning America*. The show's host, David Hartman, was interviewing Stephen King. Mario sat in a chair. He was nervous.

"What's up with you?" Christy asked. "You look like you've seen a ghost."

"I might as well have. There's no easy way to tell you this, so I'll come right out and say it. I have another illegitimate son."

"You're not kidding, are you, Mario?"

"No; I wish I was, Christy. Molly Kingston told me Alex is mine. I ran into them at Rocky Point yesterday, and she told me I got her pregnant when she was a junior. She claims I raped her. We were both drunk. I know that's not an excuse."

"Oh Jesus, Mario! Can't you keep it in your pants? Why's she telling you this now? It's a little late, isn't it?"

"She told me Alex wants to know more about his dad. Molly said she wanted to tell him the truth but won't until I've told you what I did. She said she wouldn't allow me to have a relationship with him unless I do. I know she feels sorry for you both, but she said she doesn't want me to make the same mistake with her son that I've forced you to do. She wishes it all out in the open."

"You mean she's gonna tell the whole town about us?"

"Kevin. I've screwed things up. We can't hide this any longer. I'm going to see if I can make it right."

Christy looked livid. "Yes, you've fucked things up, haven't you, Mario? It's bad enough you've messed up our lives, but now we find you've screwed with someone else's. I hope whatever you and Molly do is better than what the three of us have! Good luck! You're going to need it."

Mario went home, not stopping to say hi to Dino. He lay on his bed and sobbed. "What have I done? What the fuck have I done?"

CHRISTY AND KEVIN thought the same thing. "Kevin, I'm going to call Molly. I want to hear what she thinks about all this. I don't care what people may think anymore."

"What's the big deal, Christy?"

"The big deal is, you idiot, I care what Dino thinks. Our son's only six. How do you think he'll react when we tell him Mario is his real father and he has a half-brother?"

Kevin didn't have the answer to that one.

MOLLY WAS AT home, hoping to hear from Mario. She wondered if he'd dared tell Christy when she heard the phone ring. Thinking it was him, she picked up the receiver. "Mario?"

A woman's voice answered. "No, it's Christy, Molly."

"Oh. I'm sorry. Hi Christy. Has Mario been there?"

"He left about half an hour ago. He blew me away. I never expected this and wish I'd never told him about Dino. He's ruined so many people's lives."

"Christy, why did you tell Mario about Dino? You could have said nothing, and no one would have been wiser."

"It's complicated. In the beginning, I hadn't intended to. But then I realized forcing Mario to go through life never knowing he had a son would be cruel. I couldn't do that to another person. I wanted nothing from him other than to clear my conscience, I guess?"

"So, what *are* your plans, Christy? I'm telling Alex everything I know. I'm sorry if I'm letting the cat out of the bag, so to speak, but enough of these kinds of secrets. They're bad for one's soul."

"I guess I have some catching up to do. Better late than never, right? It'll be good to be honest with my parents, especially, and with Joyce as well. They've done a convincing part playing along all these years and never wished to embarrass me by asking further questions."

"What about Kevin? How is he handling all of this?"

"He's too busy playing Pac-Man to worry about anything!"

MOLLY SAT ALEX down and opened up about his birth father. Without getting into detail, she told him she did not like Mario when she found out she would have a baby and hadn't wanted to marry him.

Rather than being upset, Alex seemed happy. "I like Mario! He acts goofy, like me. If Dad ever returned, I hoped he'd be someone like Mario. Thank you for telling me, Mom."

"Alex, there's something else you need to know, honey. Dino Jamison is what we call your half-brother. Mario is Dino's real daddy. Sometimes, people make mistakes and don't tell the truth. That happened here, and everyone's being honest about it now, including me."

"I think that's cool, Mom. I have a dad and a brother!"

DINO'S PARENTS WERE trying to figure out how to tell a six-year-old he had a different father than the one he'd always known and that his older friend Alex was his half-brother.

Kevin had an idea. "Hey, Christy! Why don't we tell him

he has two dads? Dad number one and Dad number two. Dino already looks at Mario that way, anyway."

"Kevin, that might work for now. He's too young to understand any of this. We'll tell him about Alex when he gets a little older."

Both boys knew the truth when everything was over and done.

Kevin and Christy sat with Dino and told him there was something he needed to know about Uncle Mario. But before she could explain, he told them, "I know all about the birds and the bees. I know who Uncle Mario is. I heard you talking to Daddy about me and Mario and Alex."

Christy's mind eased. Maybe now everyone involved could move on with their lives.

It wasn't long before the local busybodies caught wind of the news, and word spread quickly throughout the town. Christy spent her days holding her head high, even though she knew they were talking about her behind her back. She no longer cared. They'd lifted a burden from her shoulders.

The windbags already knew not to mess with Molly!

A MYSTERIOUS CALIFORNIA couple booked a room under a fictitious name. When they'd mailed their reservation, they had requested the Dreamcatcher room for the July 4th holiday—no other information.

Dave and Nora were preparing for a busy weekend when they heard tapping on the front door's stained-glass window.

"I'll get it," Dave yelled, but Nora beat him to the punch. They opened the door together and saw Matt and Veronica standing before them.

"What a surprise, you guys! Dave and I thought of you a few months ago and wondered what happened to you both."

Veronica offered her left hand and showed Nora a wedding ring with a rather generous diamond setting. Nora was so happy for them both and hugged her old roommate.

"My god, girl! I guess we're not the only ones with a surprise. It looks like you're going to be a mother!" Veronica said.

"And I'm going to be a father!" Dave cut in before he grabbed Matt's hand and about shook it off. "Nora and I never expected this! We thought you two ended the relationship back at Oberlin. When did all this happen?"

Matt told them the story. "After graduation, the distance proved too great for us. We were both in love and knew it after we went home. We called each other daily, the opposite of what either of us planned to do."

"He's right. I was doing well in New York and made a few trips to San Francisco to visit him in grad school. Little did he know, on one of those, I interviewed for a job as a curator for an art gallery. We moved in together a year ago and got a place in Marin County."

"I told Veronica, let's return to Ohio for our honeymoon. We haven't been back since we graduated. We were looking for a place to stay and found your inn in the national B&B guide. When we saw the owner's name, we knew it had to be you. We thought we would surprise you. Hence, the fictitious names on our reservation request!"

Dave and Nora invited their guests in and showed them to the Dreamcatcher room. After allowing the two to unpack, Dave and Nora gave a tour of the house and explained its history and that of the town. Matt and Veronica met Aunt Billie, who whipped up a nice lunch for everyone of salmon patties with fresh broccoli and iceberg wedge salads served with her homemade celery seed dressing. She'd also squeezed a jug of ice-cold lemonade.

Afterward, they all went out on the veranda to talk. "So, Dave," Matt said. "We've been waiting. When's your next book coming out?"

"I thought it would have by now. My creative juices haven't flowed this time as well. Besides, we've been busy here at the inn." He looked uncomfortably at Nora. "I'm more than a little bummed out by all of it. I hate this pressure, but the baby has helped ease a little of that."

Veronica wanted to know all about the baby and when it was due.

"The baby is coming next month, and it can't be too soon! I feel as big as a house, and I'm tired of being unable to lie down or stand up alone. Dave and Aunt Billie have been a terrific help, though."

"Well, you're glowing! You both seem so happy together. I told Matt opposites seem to attract, and you two prove it. From our college days, you both can be stubborn. How do you make it work?"

"That's simple, Veronica. I let him think he's right. Saves us a lot of arguments."

"Hey Matt, good buddy! What do you say we go over to

my neighbor's and smoke? The guy's a little strange but has an incredible bud."

"That sounds like a mighty fine idea, mi amigo." Matt followed Dave down the steps while the girls discussed Veronica's curator position at the gallery.

After introductions, the men fired up Tewksbury's bong. Tewksbury and Matt seemed to hit it off well.

Quentin told him he had spent two months living in Haight-Ashbury in 1966 and knew Marin County well. "Guess I forgot to include that as part of my story, Dave. I told you I was pretty fucked up! When I had my bookshop in Long Beach in sixty-six, my buddy asked me to come spend a few weeks with him. Man, that part of the city was wild! I remember there was this head shop that sold marijuana and LSD. I took a hit of acid while sitting in a bar on Haight Street, talking with another hippie. As the acid took effect, the dude's face started melting and came off onto the floor. I about crapped my pants and ran out of the place. Phew! That was one bad trip."

Matt laughed at Tewksbury's story. "The Bay Area is incredible, and Veronica wanted to live there. The days are warm and arid in Marin, and the nights have a mild evening chill, which is great for sleeping. And the hiking there is incredible!"

Tewksbury agreed. "My buddy took me to a nude beach under the Golden Gate Bridge. We about froze our asses off, and it was daytime!"

"Yeah, you must head farther north to experience the real Marin."

Dave interrupted them. "Hey, we must get going. The parade starts in a little while. Matt, would you and Veronica like to join us? I've entered the Doodlebug, and Nora even painted signs promoting The Turret House. And Aunt Billie has decorated the truck with red, white, and blue streamers."

They said goodbye to Tewksbury and went to the garage to get the truck. Matt and Haddie rode in the front with Dave. Aunt Billie held court in the back. The couple had christened their great aunt "the guiding light of The Turret House." She sat proudly upon her makeshift throne adorned in a bright red coronation robe with a diamond tiara in her hair. Her pink sash said *Queen for the day.*

Nora and Veronica were in the car behind them, Dave's Mustang. Warren Holtzman had asked his mom to ride with him his 1963 LeMans advertising Holtzman Auto Repair. Trish and Diane borrowed Steven's Thunderbird convertible to promote the Dynamic Health Club, and behind them, Bertha Murkowski brought up the tail end in Cora's classic Nash LaFayette.

The procession started with the high school band marching to Olivia Newton-John's current hit "Magic."

Dave noticed how the town's parade had grown over the years and felt the excitement it had created in him as a child. This year proved no different as he watched those on the sidewalks whistle and cheer as the Doodlebug passed by. The kids shouted, "Blow the ahooga horn!" Aunt Billie tossed pieces of saltwater taffy at them as they scrambled to pick them up.

Later that evening, the friends gathered on blankets at Veterans' Park to watch the fireworks display, except for Nora and Aunt Billie, who saw the pyrotechnics from their lawn chairs. A spectacular show ensued. People *oohed* and *ahhed*. When it ended, Dave scooted over to Nora and put his ear to his wife's belly. He whispered, "What d'ya think of all that, little one?"

"What are you doing, Dave?"

"Talking to the baby. They can hear in there, you know?"

What Nora knew was that Dave would be the most incredible father for their child.

Matt and Veronica left on Monday afternoon to fly back to California after promising the couple they'd return.

"Or," Dave told them, "maybe Nora, the baby, and I can come out and see you both someday!"

Regardless, they all knew good friends could be hard to find and intended to stay in touch this time.

⁓

"DAVE! I THINK my water just broke." It was August fifteenth, and they'd closed the inn for a few days.

They were still in bed. Dave looked at the alarm clock and saw it was five a.m. He jumped up and put on his pants, rushing around to his wife's bedside to help her. Nora was trying to maneuver, and Dave yelled, "Come on, honey, hurry! The baby's coming!"

"Dave, please! Relax! I know it is. We'll have plenty of time to make it to the hospital."

He picked up the small bag she had packed and helped her downstairs.

Aunt Billie was already up enjoying a cup of tea. "Oh my, it looks like it's time. Don't worry; I'll take care of every-thing here and call Nora's parents and Kathleen to let them know the baby is coming. You two better get going!"

Dave backed Nora's car out of the garage and put his wife into the passenger seat. He almost forgot to put her over-night bag in the rear hatch. He gunned the car's engine and sped down the driveway.

"Dave, please. Slow down! I want to get there in one piece!"

They arrived at the hospital's maternity ward and checked Nora in. Her contractions were getting closer, and the doctor told her it would be soon.

They'd taken a Lamaze class together, and Dave thought he was ready, but most everything he'd learned in the class left his head. He acted like a nervous wreck before Nora finally told him, "Baby, calm down. Breathe, remember?"

"Nora, you're telling me what I'm supposed to be telling you!"

After twelve more hours of grueling labor, the baby cried.

"Congratulations, Mr. and Mrs. Meyers. You have a beau-tiful baby girl." The nurse handed the child to Nora for her to hold.

Dave had tears in his eyes as he saw his wife cradling his newborn daughter. She had delicate caramel skin and blonde hair. "My god, Nora, she's beautiful, isn't she? She looks like both of us. I love you so much!"

Nora smiled at her husband and told him she loved him more.

Dave gazed down upon the beautiful creation in his wife's arms. "Welcome to the world, Destiny Kathleen Meyers!" He kissed his daughter on the top of her head.

The couple had chosen Destiny if it were to be a girl and had been undecided about a boy's name. When selecting a middle name, they both loved Kathleen, and Dave liked how those two sounded together.

Grace, Ben, Kathleen, and Wilson joined them at the hospital later, and everyone gushed over the new arrival. They took baby Destiny home the following day.

IT TOOK A while for everyone to get acclimated to having a baby in the inn. Some guests complained about the baby crying in the middle of the night, and Dave suggested to Nora, "That place in Hawaii had separate owners' quarters. Maybe we should remodel the attic."

"Well then, Dave, finish the book! Then we'll talk about it. Thank God Aunt Billie is still here. I'm glad we'll be closed by the time she leaves. I couldn't handle all this without her."

The telephone rang; it was Mario asking to come over and see the baby. Nora told him, "Go ahead, Dave, tell him he's welcome to."

When Mario arrived, he came through the kitchen's screen door and yelled, "Hey, Nora! Where's my cup of coffee?"

Nora came around the corner with the baby and joked, "It's down at the diner, Mario." She kissed him on the cheek.

"Dave, she's got your hair, dude." He saw the baby's skin color and said to Nora, "She's beautiful. I'm sorry for all the hurtful things I've said about you. I hope you can forgive me."

"Already done! And we'll tell Destiny to call you Uncle Mario, and it'll be okay this time."

14

 at The Home Sunday morning. Over 300 people stood in line to hear Reverend Patrick O'Brian's lecture. The crowd had spilled out onto the patio, where they could listen to his message over the outdoor speakers.

It was hot and humid at the lake that morning, but Dave and Nora still thought Destiny should be there. They both felt that even though she could not speak, she could hear and maybe hear about love and, in time, perhaps find her calling in life. The couple had been attending The Home on and off for a few months, and like everyone, they always liked what Patrick had to say. They'd also been seeing Patrick for counseling, and he'd been their guiding force to give life to Destiny.

The minister saw the family from his office and went out to congratulate the new parents and meet their great aunt. "I've heard so much about you. I feel as if I know you, Aunt Billie."

"Well, thank you, Reverend. Dave and Nora have said such good things about you and your ministry."

Patrick smiled at the parents and their new daughter. "You must be so proud! You've brought another bright ray of consciousness into our world."

The family sat, and Nora's parents and Kathleen and Wilson located seats near them, along with Mario's mother, Joyce, and his brother, Anthony.

As the other congregants continued to stream in, Bertha took her place in the front along with Verna, Evie, Gertie, and the other women from the Perfectly Quaffed. Bertha looked around and told Evie, "My gosh! It looks like the whole town is here today. Oh, lookie! There's Ed and Louise. They must be speaking to each other this week!"

"Well, I'll tell you one thing, Bertha! I'm not speaking to Dale again if he doesn't tell me he's sorry!"

"What he'd do, honey?"

"He told me he doesn't love me anymore and wants a divorce." She started crying.

"There, there, sweetie, it'll be all right. You'll see." Bertha and turned to Verna and whispered, "If that woman tells me again how much Dale doesn't love her, I'm going to throw up! They love to fight as much as Ed and Louise do! Makes them happy, I guess."

Bertha saw Pete York and his wife beside Buster Riley and Russ. Then she noticed Trish and Diane with Steven and Christopher. A few rows back, she could see the Jamisons with Mario. Kevin was holding onto Dino's hand, and Bertha tried getting the other gal's attention by pointing at Mario and nodding her head toward the Jamisons. Too many people were watching her, so she turned around and gave up.

Molly and Alex Kingston soon joined the Jamisons, along with Molly's mother, Eleanor.

Even Tewksbury showed up. He smiled at Bertha, then wedged himself in. Bertha gave him an annoyed look as she tried moving her girth to accommodate her neighbor.

The eclectic service began with music. Patrick had selected The Youngblood's song "Everybody Get Together." When it finished, he came out on stage. "I hope you've all brought love with you today. The world certainly could use more of it. Would any of you agree with me when I say we all want to be loved? From the first moment we arrive on the planet until the day we leave, love could be what we all strive to focus on and talk about. Many of the world's ills may disappear. People may become more merciful about the feelings of others and not hurt one another."

"We're all guilty of things we may have done and said that have caused us pain in our hearts and those of others. I offer a solution for that. It's called forgiveness, and it's so easily given if we've chosen to do so.

"Holding grudges serves no purpose other than continuing to eat away at our souls. For those of you here who may have experienced that, today's a good day to forgive.

But the person we may need to forgive first is ourselves. Our world could be a better place because of it."

Everyone's thoughts silently echoed the young minister's spoken words.

Dave and Nora glanced at Mario. Nora could tell by the look in his eyes how sorry he was for everything.

Dave smiled at his best friend and accepted Mario's benignity.

Molly reached over and took Mario's hand, and Christy and Kevin did the same with theirs.

Steven turned to Christopher, who looked down in disgrace at his unfaithfulness. Steven, undeterred, hugged his partner, and they both cried.

Diane smiled at the act of forgiveness and reached out to take Trish's hand.

Ed put his arm around Louise. Pete looked over at him and winked. Evie turned and saw Dale smiling at her. She thought of the hurtful things she'd been saying to him.

Quentin's contemplative face revealed what he may have been thinking. Even Bertha took another good look at herself, recalling the scolding she'd received from Charlotte's ghost.

Many decided their lives were not working, and reparations had to be made. There seemed to be a sense of espousal in the air. They all seemed to know a gentler universe was possible, and they gave thanks for all it had given them.

Residents who hadn't spoken to one another in years exchanged hugs at a coffee social held in the gardens. There were many apologies that day, and they hoped more would follow. Love had been in The Home.

At least for a day.

⁓

LATER THAT EVENING, Aunt Billie prepared her Sunday supper: a beef roast, garlic mashed potatoes, and honey-glazed carrots and peas. She also baked an angel food cake to celebrate Destiny's arrival.

The baby settled on her formula instead.

Dave and Aunt Billie did the dinner dishes while Nora went to lie down. After they finished, the two went into the parlor and played Chopsticks, the only song they both knew.

"Aunt Billie, I love you! You mean so much to us. I'm so grateful you've played an important role in my life. I'll never forget our time at the orchard and drive-in."

Aunt Billie's eyes teared up. "Davie, it's been a delight. I love you and Nora and the baby as well. I'm blessed. You've always been a good boy, and your dad loved you. He may not have been able to show it the way you wished he could have, but I know he did."

Dave locked the front door before kissing his aunt goodnight and climbing the steps. Destiny was sleeping soundly in her bassinet, and he was careful not to disturb her before he lay down beside his mate. He kissed Nora on the nape, and she gave a slight grunt of approval.

Exhausted by the day's heat and events, he fell asleep.

HE WOKE IN the morning and gazed at the ceiling tiles above his head. He seemed to have drifted back from them and was now in bed. He looked over at the clock—six thirty a.m.

He realized it was August eighteenth, 1980. He knew the date because he'd gone to bed the previous evening, the seventeenth, exhausted by all the excitement.

Then it came over him: he'd been dreaming. The last thing he remembered was being unable to sleep and going down to the veranda to smoke a joint.

It seemed like he had been gone for the last twenty-four years, but had dreamed his entire life in one evening, up to the present.

Dave felt extreme gratitude for everything in his life: his new daughter, his loving wife, and everyone else whose beingness who had touched his own.

It seemed so natural, and now he knew it was. He sat up and rubbed his eyes. A lingering realization came over him. He was not like his father! Life was not a shit sandwich!

The realization brought new opportunities each day to experience growth to its fullest.

Finally, Dave understood what he'd been searching for all along. He could see it in others but had not seen it himself.

He was good enough and worthy of love. He felt whole and complete. He became aware he possessed a talent he'd been ignoring.

He was a writer! So much time he'd spent struggling, and the secret had been there before him all along. He'd been too blind to see it until now. It was the power of love! The change was possible both for himself and the world around him.

He pulled on a pair of jeans and went downstairs, where he heard Nora and Destiny with Aunt Billie in the kitchen. "Nora, it's here!" he said.

"What are you talking about, Dave?"

Aunt Billie looked around the kitchen as if trying to find what Dave was referring to.

"No; the secret, you guys! It's been here all along. Now I understand!" He hugged and kissed all three like he never had before. Or maybe he had.

"What's come over you, Dave? You okay?"

The author smiled at his wife and walked down the hallway to his library, where he drew the pocket doors closed and sat before his Royal Aristocrat, as he had so many times before. He grabbed the typing paper from the tray and rolled it into the carriage. He looked out his window at Tewksbury's asparagus patch and nodded his approval.

His thoughts and words flowed as he typed the first line of his new novel: *It was one of those hot and sticky summer nights in Ohio...*